THE ELITE

ALSO BY KIERA CASS

The Selection
The Prince (available as an ebook only)

THE ELITE

KIERA CASS

HARPER TEEN

An Imprint of HarperCollinsPublishers

HarperTeen is an imprint of HarperCollins Publishers.

The Elite
Copyright © 2013 by Kiera Cass
www.epicreads.com

Library of Congress Cataloging-in-Publication Data
Cass, Kiera.
    The Elite / Kiera Cass. — 1st ed.
        p. cm.
    Summary: "Sixteen-year-old America Singer is one of only six girls
still competing in the Selection—but before she can fight to win
Prince Maxon and the Illean crown, she must decide where her own
heart truly lies"— Provided by publisher.
    ISBN 978-0-06-205996-3 (trade)
    ISBN 978-0-06-226285-1 (int'l ed.)
    [1. Marriage—Fiction. 2. Contests—Fiction. 3. Social classes—
Fiction. 4. Princes—Fiction. 5. Love—Fiction.
6. Revolutionaries—Fiction.] I. Title.
PZ7.C2685133Eli 2013   2012038124
[Fic]—dc23   CIP
                                                                AC

Typography by Sarah Hoy
16 17   CG/RRDH   20
❖
First Edition

Call out the servants! The queen is awake!

(For Mom)

CHAPTER 1

THE ANGELES AIR WAS QUIET, and for a while I lay still, listening to the sound of Maxon's breathing. It was getting harder and harder to catch him in a truly calm and happy moment, and I soaked up the time, grateful that he seemed to be at his best when he and I were alone.

Ever since the Selection had been narrowed down to six girls, he'd been more anxious than he was when the thirty-five of us arrived in the first place. I guessed he thought he'd have more time to make his choices. And though it made me feel guilty to admit it, I knew I was the reason why he wished he did.

Prince Maxon, heir to the Illéa throne, liked me. He'd told me a week ago that if I could simply say that I cared for him the way he did for me, without anything holding me back, this whole competition would be over. And sometimes

I played with the idea, wondering how it would feel to be Maxon's alone.

But the thing was, Maxon wasn't really mine to begin with. There were five other girls here—girls he took on dates and whispered things to—and I didn't know what to make of that. And then there was the fact that if I accepted Maxon, it meant I had to accept a crown, a thought I tended to ignore if only because I wasn't sure what it would mean for me.

And, of course, there was Aspen.

He wasn't technically my boyfriend anymore—he'd broken up with me before my name was even drawn for the Selection—but when he showed up at the palace as one of the guards, all the feelings I'd been trying to let go of flooded my heart. Aspen was my first love; when I looked at him . . . I was his.

Maxon didn't know that Aspen was in the palace, but he did know that there was someone at home that I was trying to get over, and he was graciously giving me time to move on while attempting to find someone else he'd be happy with in the event I couldn't ever love him.

As he moved his head, inhaling just above my hairline, I considered it. What would it be like to simply love Maxon?

"Do you know when the last time was that I really looked at the stars?" he asked.

I settled closer to him on our blanket, trying to keep warm in the cool Angeles night. "No idea."

"A tutor had me studying astronomy a few years ago. If

you look closely, you can tell that the stars are actually different colors."

"Wait, the last time you looked at the stars was to *study* them? What about for fun?"

He chuckled. "Fun. I'll have to pencil in some between the budget consultations and infrastructure committee meetings. Oh, and war strategizing, which, by the way, I am terrible at."

"What else are you terrible at?" I asked, running my hand across his starched shirt. Encouraged by the touch, Maxon drew circles on my shoulder with the hand he had wrapped behind my back.

"Why would you want to know that?" he asked in mock irritation.

"Because I still know so little about you. And you seem perfect all the time. It's nice to have proof you're not."

He propped himself up on an elbow, focusing on my face. "You *know* I'm not."

"Pretty close," I countered. Little flickers of touch ran between us. Knees, arms, fingers.

He shook his head, a small smile on his face. "Okay, then. I can't plan wars. I'm rotten at it. And I'm guessing I'd be a terrible cook. I've never tried, so—"

"Never?"

"You might have noticed the teams of people keeping you up to your neck in pastries? They happen to feed me as well."

I giggled. I helped cook practically every meal at home. "More," I demanded. "What else are you bad at?"

He held me close, his brown eyes bright with a secret. "Recently I've discovered this one thing. . . ."

"Tell."

"It turns out I'm absolutely terrible at staying away from you. It's a very serious problem."

I smiled. "Have you really tried?"

He pretended to think about it. "Well, no. And don't expect me to start."

We laughed quietly, holding on to each other. In these moments, it was so easy to picture this being the rest of my life.

The rustle of leaves and grass announced that someone was coming. Even though our date was completely acceptable, I felt a little embarrassed and sat up quickly. Maxon followed suit as a guard made his way around the hedge to us.

"Your Majesty," he said with a bow. "Sorry to intrude, sir, but it's really unwise to stay out this late for so long. The rebels could—"

"Understood," Maxon said with a sigh. "We'll be right in."

The guard left us alone, and Maxon turned back to me. "Another fault of mine: I'm losing patience with the rebels. I'm tired of dealing with them."

He stood and offered me his hand. I took it, watching the sad frustration in his eyes. We'd been attacked twice by the rebels since the start of the Selection—once by the simply disruptive Northerners and once by the deadly Southerners—and even with my brief experience, I could understand his exhaustion.

Maxon was picking up the blanket and shaking it out, clearly not happy that our night had been cut short.

"Hey," I said, urging him to face me. "I had fun."

He nodded.

"No, really," I said, walking over to him. He moved the blanket to one hand to wrap his free arm around me. "We should do it again sometime. You can tell me which stars are which colors, because I seriously can't tell."

Maxon gave me a sad smile. "I wish things were easier sometimes, normal."

I moved so I could wrap my arms around him, and as I did so, Maxon dropped the blanket to return the gesture. "I hate to break it to you, Your Majesty, but even without the guards, you're far from normal."

His expression lightened a bit but was still serious. "You'd like me more if I was."

"I know you find it hard to believe, but I really do like you the way you are. I just need more—"

"Time. I know. And I'm prepared to give you that. I only wish I knew that you'd actually want to be with me when that time was over."

I looked away. That wasn't something I could promise. I weighed Maxon and Aspen in my heart over and over, and neither of them ever had a true edge. Except, maybe, when I was alone with one of them. Because, at that moment, I was tempted to promise Maxon that I would be there for him in the end.

But I couldn't.

"Maxon," I whispered, seeing how dejected he looked at my lack of an answer. "I can't tell you that. But what I can tell you is that I *want* to be here. I *want* to know if there's a possibility for . . . for . . ." I stammered, not sure how to put it.

"Us?" Maxon guessed.

I smiled, happy at how easily he understood me. "Yes. I want to know if there's a possibility for us to be an us."

He moved a lock of hair behind my shoulder. "I think the odds are very high," he said matter-of-factly.

"I think so, too. Just . . . time, okay?"

He nodded, looking happier. This was how I wanted to end our night, with hope. Well, and maybe one more thing. I bit my lip and leaned into Maxon, asking with my eyes.

Without a second of hesitation, he bent to kiss me. It was warm and gentle, and it left me feeling adored and somehow aching for more. I could have stayed there for hours, just to see if I could get enough of that feeling; but too soon, Maxon backed away.

"Let's go," he said in a playful tone, pulling me toward the palace. "Better get inside before the guards come for us on horseback with spears drawn."

As Maxon left me at the stairs, the tiredness hit me like a wall. I was practically dragging myself up to the second floor and around the corner to my room when, suddenly, I was quite awake again.

"Oh!" Aspen said, surprised to see me, too. "I think it makes me the worst guard ever that I assumed you were in your room this whole time."

I giggled. The Elite were supposed to sleep with at least one of their maids on watch in the night. I really didn't like that, so Maxon insisted on stationing a guard by my room in case there was an emergency. The thing was, most of the time that guard was Aspen. It was a strange mix of exhilaration and terror knowing that nearly every night he was right outside my door.

The lightness of the moment faded quickly as Aspen grasped what it meant that I hadn't been safely tucked in my bed. He cleared his throat uncomfortably.

"Did you have a good time?"

"Aspen," I whispered, looking to make sure no one was around. "Don't be upset. I'm part of the Selection, and this is just how it is."

"How am I supposed to stand a chance, Mer? How can I compete when you only ever talk to one of us?" He made a good point, but what could I do?

"Please don't be mad at me, Aspen. I'm trying to figure all this out."

"No, Mer," he said, gentleness returning to his voice. "I'm not mad at you. I *miss* you." He didn't dare say the words aloud, but he mouthed them. *I love you.*

I melted.

"I know," I said, placing a hand on his chest, letting myself forget for a moment all that we were risking. "But that doesn't change where we are or that I'm an Elite now. I need time, Aspen."

He reached up to hold my hand in his and nodded. "I can give you that. Just . . . try to find some time for me, too."

I didn't want to bring up how complicated that would be, so I gave him a tiny smile before gently pulling my hand away. "I need to go."

He watched me as I walked into my room and shut the door behind me.

Time. I was asking for a lot of it these days. I hoped that if I had enough, everything would somehow fall into place.

CHAPTER 2

"NO, NO," QUEEN AMBERLY ANSWERED with a laugh. "I only had three bridesmaids, though Clarkson's mother suggested I have more. I just wanted my sisters and my best friend, who, coincidentally, I'd met during my Selection."

I peeked over at Marlee and was happy to find she was looking at me, too. Before I arrived at the palace, I had assumed that with this being such a high-stakes competition, there'd be no way any of the girls would be friendly. Marlee had embraced me the first time we met, and we'd been there for each other from that moment on. With a single almost-exception, we'd never even had an argument.

A few weeks ago, Marlee had mentioned that she didn't think she wanted to be with Maxon. When I'd pushed her to explain, she clammed up. She wasn't mad at me, I knew that, but those days of silence before we'd let it go were lonely.

"I want seven bridesmaids," Kriss said. "I mean, if Maxon chooses me and I get to have a big wedding."

"Well, I won't have bridesmaids," Celeste said, countering Kriss. "They're just distracting. And since it would be televised, I want all eyes on me."

I fumed. It was rare that we all got to sit and talk with Queen Amberly, and here Celeste was, being a brat and ruining it.

"I'd want to incorporate some of my culture's traditions into my wedding," Elise added quietly. "Girls back in New Asia use a lot of red in their ceremonies, and the groom has to bring gifts to the bride's friends to reward them for letting her marry him."

Kriss piped up. "Remind me to be in your wedding party. I love presents!"

"Me, too!" Marlee exclaimed.

"Lady America, you've been awfully quiet," Queen Amberly said. "What do you want at your wedding?"

I blushed because I was completely unprepared to comment.

There was only one wedding I'd ever imagined, and it was going to take place at the Province of Carolina Services Office after an exhausting amount of paperwork.

"Well, the one thing I've thought about is having my dad give me away. You know when he takes your hand and puts it in the hand of the person you marry? That's the only part

I've ever really wanted." Embarrassingly enough, it was true.

"But everyone does that," Celeste complained. "That's not even original."

I should have been mad that she called me out, but I merely shrugged. "I want to know that my dad completely approves of my choice on the day it really matters."

"That's nice," Natalie said, sipping her tea and looking out the window.

Queen Amberly laughed lightly. "I certainly hope he approves. No matter who it is." She added the last words quickly, catching herself in the middle of implying that Maxon would be my choice.

I wondered if she thought that, if Maxon had told her about us.

Shortly after, the wedding talk died down, and the queen left to go work in her room. Celeste parked herself in front of the large television embedded in the wall, and the others started a card game.

"That was fun," Marlee said as we settled in at a table together. "I'm not sure I've ever heard the queen talk so much."

"She's getting excited, I think." I hadn't mentioned to anyone what Maxon's aunt had told me about how Queen Amberly tried many times for another child and failed. Adele had predicted that her sister would warm up to us once the group was smaller, and she was right.

"Okay, you have to tell me: Do you honestly not have any other plans for your wedding or did you just not want to share?"

"I really don't," I promised. "I have a hard time picturing a big wedding, you know? I'm a Five."

Marlee shook her head. "You *were* a Five. You're a Three now."

"Right," I said, remembering my new label.

I was born into a family of Fives—artists and musicians who were generally poorly paid—and though I hated the caste system in general, I liked what I did for a living. It was strange to think of myself as a Three, to consider embracing teaching or writing as a profession.

"Stop stressing," Marlee said, reading my face. "You don't have anything to worry about yet."

I was about to protest but was interrupted by a cry from Celeste.

"Come on!" she yelled, slamming the remote against the couch before pointing it at the television again. "Ugh!"

"Is it just me or is she getting worse?" I whispered to Marlee. We watched as Celeste hit the remote over and over before giving up and going to change the channel manually. I guessed if I had grown up as a Two, that would be something worth getting worked up over.

"It's the stress, I think," Marlee commented. "Have you noticed that Natalie's getting, I don't know . . . more aloof?"

I nodded, and we both looked over to the trio of girls playing their card game. Kriss was smiling as she shuffled, but Natalie was examining the ends of her hair, occasionally pulling out a strand she didn't seem to like. Her expression was distracted.

"I think we're all starting to feel it," I confessed. "It's harder to sit back and enjoy the palace now that the group is so small."

Celeste grunted, and we peeked over at her but quickly averted our eyes when she caught us looking.

"Excuse me for a moment," Marlee said, shifting in her seat. "I think I'm going to go to the bathroom."

"I was just thinking the same thing. Do you want to go together?" I offered.

Smiling, she shook her head. "You go ahead. I'll finish my tea first."

"Okay. I'll be back."

I left the Women's Room, taking my time walking down the gorgeous hallway. I wasn't sure I would ever get over how spectacular it was here. I was so distracted that I ran smack into a guard as I turned the corner.

"Oh!" I said.

"Pardon me, miss. Hope I didn't startle you." He held me by my elbows, helping me regain my footing.

"No," I said, giggling. "It's fine. I should have been watching where I was going. Thanks for catching me. Officer . . ."

"Woodwork," he answered, giving me a quick bow.

"I'm America."

"I know."

I smiled and rolled my eyes. Of course he knew.

"Well, I hope the next time I run into you, it won't be quite so literal," I joked.

He chuckled. "Agreed. Have a nice day, miss."

"You, too."

I told Marlee about my embarrassing run-in with Officer Woodwork when I got back and warned her to watch her step. She laughed at me and shook her head.

We spent the rest of the afternoon sitting by the windows, chatting about home and the other girls as we drank in the sunshine.

It was sad to think about the future just then. Eventually the Selection would be over, and while I knew Marlee and I would still be close, I would miss talking to her every day. She was the first real friend I'd ever made, and I wished I could keep her beside me all the time.

As I tried to stay in the moment, Marlee gazed dreamily out the window. I wondered what she was thinking about; but everything was so peaceful, I didn't ask.

CHAPTER 3

THE WIDE DOORS OF MY balcony were open, as well as the one to the hallway, and my room was filled with the warm, sweet air blowing in from the gardens. I had hoped the soft breezes would be a consolation for the fact that I had so much work to do. Instead they distracted me, making me ache to be anywhere but stuck at my desk.

I sighed and reclined in my seat, letting my head drape over the back of the chair. "Anne," I called.

"Yes, miss?" my head maid answered from the corner where she was sewing. Without looking, I knew that Mary and Lucy, my other two maids, had perked up, waiting to see if they could serve me as well.

"I command you to figure out what this report means," I said, pointing a lazy arm at the detailed account on military statistics that sat in front of me. It was a task that all the Elite would be tested on, but I couldn't bring myself to focus on it.

My three maids laughed, probably from both the ridiculousness of my demand and the fact that I'd issued one at all. I wouldn't have called leadership one of my strong suits.

"I'm sorry, my lady, but I think that might be overstepping my boundaries," Anne answered. Even though my request was a joke and her answer was, too, I could hear the genuine apology in her voice for not being able to help me.

"Fine." I moaned, heaving myself into an upright position. "I'll simply have to do it myself. The whole lot of you are worthless. I'm getting new maids tomorrow. This time I mean it."

They all chuckled again, and I focused on the numbers one more time. I was getting the impression that this was a bad report, but I couldn't be sure. I reread paragraphs and charts, furrowing my brow and biting the back of my pen as I tried to concentrate.

I heard Lucy laugh quietly, and I looked up to see what she was so amused by, following her eyes to the door. There, leaning against the frame, was Maxon.

"You gave me away!" he complained to Lucy, who continued to snicker.

I pushed back my chair in a rush and ran into his arms. "You read my mind!"

"Did I?"

"Please tell me we can go outside. Just for a little while?"

He smiled. "I have twenty minutes before I have to be back."

I pulled him down the hall, the excited chatter of my maids fading behind us.

There was no denying the gardens had become *our* place. Almost every chance we got to be alone, we came out here. It was such a stark contrast to how I used to spend my time with Aspen: holed up in the tiny tree house in my backyard, the only place we could be together safely.

Suddenly I wondered if Aspen was around somewhere, indistinguishable from the numerous guards in the palace, watching as Maxon held my hand.

"What are these?" Maxon asked, brushing across the tips of my fingers as we walked.

"Calluses. They're from pressing down on violin strings four hours a day."

"I've never noticed them before."

"Do they bother you?" I was the lowest caste of the six girls left, and I doubted any of them had hands like mine.

Maxon stopped moving and lifted my fingers to his lips, kissing the tiny, worn tips.

"On the contrary. I find them rather beautiful." I felt myself blush. "I've seen the world—admittedly mostly through bulletproof glass or from the tower of some ancient castle—but I've seen it. And I have access to the answers of a thousand questions at my disposal. But this small hand here?" He looked deeply into my eyes. "This hand makes sounds incomparable to anything I've ever heard. Sometimes I think I only dreamed that I heard you play the violin, it was so beautiful. These calluses are proof that it was real."

At times the way he spoke to me was overwhelming, too romantic to believe. But though I cherished the words in my heart, I was never completely sure I could trust them. How did I know he wasn't saying such sweet things to the other girls? I had to change the subject.

"Do you really have the answers to a thousand questions?"

"Absolutely. Ask me anything; and if I don't know the answer, I know where we can find it."

"Anything?"

"Anything."

It was tough to come up with a question on the spot, much less one that would stump him, which was what I wanted. I took a moment to think of the things I'd been most curious about when I was growing up. How planes flew. What the United States used to be like. How the tiny music players that the upper castes had worked.

And then it hit me.

"What's Halloween?" I asked.

"Halloween?" Clearly, he'd never heard of it. I wasn't surprised. I'd only seen the word once myself in an old history book my parents had. Some parts of that book were tattered beyond recognition, with pages missing or mostly destroyed. Still, I was always fascinated by the mention of a holiday we knew nothing about.

"Not so certain now, Your Royal Smartness?" I teased.

He made a face at me though it was clear he was only playing at being annoyed. He checked his watch and sucked in a breath.

"Come with me. We have to hurry," he said, grabbing my hand and launching himself into a run.

I stumbled a bit in my little heels, but I kept up pretty well as he led me back to the palace with a huge grin on his face. I loved when Maxon's carefree side came through; too often he was so serious.

"Gentlemen," he said as we raced past the guards by the door.

I made it halfway down the hall before my shoes got the better of me. "Maxon, stop!" I gasped. "I can't keep up!"

"Come on, come on, you're going to love this," he complained, tugging my arm as I slowed. He finally eased back to my pace but was obviously itching to move faster.

We headed toward the north corridor, near the area where the *Reports* were filmed, but ducked into a stairwell before we got that far. We went up and up, and I couldn't contain my curiosity.

"Where are we going exactly?"

He turned and faced me, immediately serious. "You have to swear never to reveal this little chamber. Only a few members of the family and a handful of the guards even know it exists."

I was beyond intrigued. "Absolutely."

We reached the top of the stairs, and Maxon held open the door for me. He took my hand again and pulled me down the hallway, finally stopping in front of a wall that was mostly covered by a magnificent painting. Maxon looked behind us to make sure no one was there, then reached behind the frame on the far side. I heard a faint click, and the painting swung toward us.

I gasped. Maxon grinned.

Behind the painting was a door that didn't go all the way to the ground and had a small keypad on it, like the kind on a telephone. Maxon punched in a few numbers and then a tiny beep sounded. He turned the handle as he looked back to me.

"Let me help you. It's quite a high step." He gave me his hand and gestured for me to walk in first.

I was shocked.

The windowless room was covered with shelves full of what appeared to be ancient books. Two of the shelves contained books that had curious red slashes on the bindings, and I saw a massive atlas against one wall, opened to a page that held the shape of some country I couldn't name. In the middle was a table with a handful of books on it, looking as if they'd been handled recently and left out for quick recovery. And finally, embedded in one wall was a wide screen that looked like a TV.

"What do the red slashes mean?" I asked in wonder.

"Those are banned books. As far as we know, they may be the only copies that still exist in all of Illéa."

I turned to him, asking with my eyes what I didn't dare say out loud.

"Yes, you can look at them," he said in a manner that implied I was putting him out but with an expression that said he had been hoping I'd ask.

I lifted one of the books carefully, terrified that I might accidentally destroy a one-of-a-kind treasure. I flipped through the pages but ended up setting it back down almost immediately. I was simply too awestruck.

I turned around to find Maxon typing on something that looked like a flat typewriter attached to the TV screen.

"What's that?" I asked.

"A computer. Have you never seen one?" I shook my head, and Maxon didn't seem too surprised. "Not many people have them anymore. This one is specifically for the information held in this room. If anything about your Halloween exists, this will tell us where it is."

I wasn't fully sure of what he was saying, but I didn't ask him to clarify. In a few seconds his hunt produced a three-bullet list on the screen.

"Oh, excellent!" he exclaimed. "Wait right there."

I stood by the table as Maxon found the three books that would reveal what Halloween was. I hoped it wasn't something stupid and that I hadn't made him go through all this effort for nothing.

The first book defined Halloween as a Celtic festival that marked the end of summer. Not wanting to slow us, I didn't bother mentioning I had no idea what a Celtic was. It said they believed that spirits passed in and out of the world on Halloween, and people would put on masks to ward off the evil ones. Later, it evolved into a secular holiday, mainly for children. They dressed up in costumes and went around their towns singing songs and were rewarded with candy, creating the saying "trick or treat," as they did a trick to get a treat.

The second book defined it as something similar, only it mentioned pumpkins and Christianity.

"This will be the interesting one," Maxon claimed, flipping through a book that was much thinner than the others and handwritten.

"How so?" I asked, coming around to get a better look.

"This, Lady America, is one of the volumes of Gregory Illéa's personal diaries."

"What?" I exclaimed. "Can I touch it?"

"Let me find the page we're searching for first. Look, it even has a picture!"

And there, like an apparition, an image from an unknown past showed Gregory Illéa with a tight expression on his face, his suit crisp and his stance tall. It was bizarre how much of the king and Maxon I could see in the way he stood. Beside him, a woman was giving the camera a halfhearted smile. There was something to her face that hinted she was once very lovely, but the luster had gone out of her eyes. She seemed tired.

Surrounding the couple were three figures. The first was a teenage girl, beautiful and vibrant, grinning widely and wearing a crown and a frilly gown. How funny! She was dressed as a princess. And then there were two boys, one slightly taller than the other and both dressed as characters I didn't recognize. They looked like they were on the verge of mischief. Below the image was an entry, amazingly enough, in Gregory Illéa's own hand.

THE CHILDREN CELEBRATED HALLOWEEN THIS YEAR WITH A PARTY. I SUPPOSE IT'S ONE WAY TO FORGET WHAT'S GOING ON AROUND THEM, BUT TO ME IT FEELS FRIVOLOUS. WE'RE ONE OF THE FEW FAMILIES REMAINING WHO HAVE ENOUGH MONEY TO DO SOMETHING FESTIVE, BUT THIS CHILD'S PLAY SEEMS WASTEFUL.

"Do you think that's why we don't celebrate anymore? Because it's wasteful?" I asked.

"Could be. If the date's any indication, this was right after the American State of China started fighting back, just before the Fourth World War. At that point, most people had nothing—picture an entire nation of Sevens with a handful of Twos."

"Wow." I tried to imagine the landscape of our country like that, blown apart by war, then fighting to pull itself back together. It was amazing.

"How many of these diaries are there?" I asked.

Maxon pointed to a shelf with a row of journals similar to the one we held. "About a dozen or so."

I couldn't believe it! All this history right in one room.

"Thank you," I said. "This is something I would never even have dreamed of seeing. I can't believe all this exists."

He was beaming. "Would you like to read the rest of

it?" He motioned to the diary.

"Yes, of course!" I practically shouted before my duties came back to me. "But I can't stay; I have to finish studying that terrible report. And you have to get back to work."

"True. Well, how about this? You can take the book and keep it for a few days."

"Am I allowed to do that?" I asked in awe.

"No." He smiled.

I hesitated, afraid of what I held. What if I lost it? What if I ruined it? Surely he had to be thinking the same thing. But I would never have an opportunity like this again. I could be careful enough for the sake of this gift.

"Okay. Just a night or two and then I'll give it straight back."

"Hide it well."

And I did. This was more than a book; it was Maxon's trust. I tucked it inside my piano stool under a pile of sheet music—a place my maids never cleaned. The only hands that would touch it would be mine.

CHAPTER 4

"I'M HOPELESS!" MARLEE COMPLAINED.

"No, no, you're doing great," I lied.

I'd been giving Marlee piano lessons nearly every day for more than a week, and it genuinely sounded like she was getting worse. For goodness' sake, we were still working on scales. She hit another sour note, and I couldn't help but wince.

"Oh, look at your face!" she exclaimed. "I'm terrible. I might as well be playing with my elbows."

"We should try that. Maybe your elbows are more accurate."

She sighed. "I give up. Sorry, America, you've been so patient, but I hate hearing myself play. It sounds like the piano is sick."

"More like it's dying, actually."

Marlee collapsed into laughter, and I joined her. Little did I know that when she'd asked for piano lessons, my ears would be in for such painful—but hilarious—torture.

"Maybe you'd be better at the violin? Violins make very beautiful music," I offered.

"I don't think so. With my luck, I'd destroy it." Marlee rose and went over to my little table, where the papers we were supposed to be reading were pushed to one side and my sweet maids had left tea and cookies for us.

"Oh, well, that's fine. The one here belongs to the palace anyway. You could throw it at Celeste's head if you wanted."

"Don't tempt me," she said, pouring us both some tea. "I'm so going to miss you, America. I don't know what I'll do when we don't get to see each other every day."

"Well, Maxon's very indecisive, so you don't have to worry about that just yet."

"I don't know," she said, turning serious. "He hasn't come right out and said it, but I know that I'm here because the public likes me. With the majority of the girls gone, it won't be long before their opinions change and they have a new favorite, and then he'll let me go."

I was careful with my words, hoping she'd explain the reason for the distance she'd put between the two of them but not wanting her to shut down on me again. "Are you okay with that? With not getting Maxon, I mean?"

She gave a small shrug. "He's just not the one. I'm fine with being out of the competition, but I really don't want to leave," she clarified. "Besides, I wouldn't want to end up with a man who's in love with someone else."

I sat bolt upright. "Who is he—"

The look in Marlee's eyes was triumphant, and the smile hiding behind her cup of tea said *Gotcha!*

She had.

In a split second, I realized that the thought of Maxon being in love with someone else made me so jealous I couldn't stand it. And the moment after that—the understanding that she meant me—was infinitely reassuring.

I'd put up wall after wall, making jokes at Maxon's expense and talking up the merits of the other girls; but in a single sentence, she found her way behind all that.

"Why haven't you ended this, America?" she asked sweetly. "You know he loves you."

"He never said that," I promised, and that was true.

"Of course he hasn't," she said, as if this would be obvious. "He's trying so hard to catch you, and every time he gets close you push him away. Why do you do that?"

Could I tell her? Could I confess that while my feelings for Maxon went deep—deeper than I knew, apparently— there was someone else I couldn't let go of?

"I'm just . . . not sure, I guess." I trusted Marlee; I really did. But it was safer for us both if she didn't know.

She nodded. It looked like she could tell there was more to it than that, but she didn't press me. It was almost comforting, this mutual acceptance of our secrets.

"Find a way to be sure. Soon. Just because he's not the one

for me doesn't mean Maxon's not a great guy. I'd hate for you to lose him because you were afraid."

She was right again. I was afraid. Afraid that Maxon's feelings weren't as genuine as they seemed, afraid of what being a princess might mean for me, afraid of losing Aspen.

"On a lighter note," she said, setting down her cup of tea, "all that talk about weddings yesterday made me think of something."

"Yes?"

"Would you want to, you know, be my maid of honor? If I get married someday?"

"Oh, Marlee, of course I would! Would you be mine?" I reached to grab her hands, and she took them happily.

"But you have sisters; won't they mind?"

"They'll understand. Please?"

"Absolutely! I wouldn't miss *your* wedding for the world." Her tone implied that my wedding would be the event of the century.

"Promise me that even if I get married to a nobody Eight in an alley somewhere, you'll be there."

She gave me a disbelieving look, positive that no such thing could ever happen. "Even if that's the case. I promise."

She didn't ask me to make a similar vow for her, which made me wonder as I had in the past if there was another Four back home who she had her heart set on. I wouldn't press her though. It was clear we both had secrets; but Marlee was my best friend, and I would do anything for her.

★ ★ ★

That night I was hoping to spend some time with Maxon. Marlee had me questioning a lot of my actions. And thoughts. And feelings.

After dinner, as we all stood to leave the Dining Room, I caught Maxon's eye and tugged my ear. It was our secret sign to ask for time together, and it was rare to pass up an invitation. But tonight Maxon's expression was disappointed as he mouthed the word "work" to me. I gave him a mock pout and a tiny wave before leaving for the night.

Perhaps it was for the best anyway. I really needed to think on some things where Maxon was concerned.

When I rounded the corner to my room, Aspen was there again, standing guard. He looked me up and down, taking in the snug green dress that did amazing things for the few curves I had. Without a word, I walked past him. Before I could turn the handle on my door, he gently grazed the skin on my arm.

It was slow but brief, and in those few seconds I felt that need, that sense of longing, that Aspen tended to inspire in me. One look at his emerald eyes, hungry and deep, and I felt my knees start to go shaky.

I moved into my room as quickly as I could, tortured by our connection. Thank goodness I barely had time to think about what Aspen made me feel, because the moment the door shut, my maids swarmed around me, preparing me for bed. As they chatted away and brushed my hair, I tried to let myself forget about everything for a moment.

It was impossible. I had to choose. Aspen or Maxon.

But how was I supposed to decide between two good possibilities? How could I make a choice that would leave some part of me devastated either way? I comforted myself with the thought that I still had time. I still had time.

CHAPTER 5

"So, Lady Celeste, you're saying that the quantities aren't sufficient, and you feel the number of men taken in the next draft should be raised?" Gavril Fadaye, the moderator of discussions on the *Illéa Capital Report* and the only person who ever interviewed the royals, asked.

Our debates on the *Report* were tests, and we knew it. Even though Maxon didn't have a timeline, the public was aching for the field to narrow; and I sensed the king, queen, and their advisers were, too. If we wanted to stay, we had to perform, whenever and wherever they said. I was glad I'd made it through that awful report about the soldiers. I remembered some of the statistics, so I stood a decent chance of making a good impression tonight.

"Exactly, Gavril. The war in New Asia has been going on

for years. I think one or two rounds of inflated drafts would give us the numbers we need to end it."

I really couldn't stand Celeste. She'd gotten one girl kicked out, ruined Kriss's birthday party last month, and literally tried to rip a dress off my back. Her status as a Two made her consider herself a cut above the rest of us. To be honest, I didn't have an opinion about the number of soldiers Illéa had, but now that I knew Celeste's, I was unwaveringly opposed.

"I disagree," I said in as ladylike a tone as I could manage. Celeste turned my way, her dark hair whipping over her shoulder in the process. With her back to the camera, she felt perfectly comfortable blatantly glaring at me.

"Ah, Lady America, you think increasing the numbers is a bad idea?" Gavril asked.

I felt the heat of a blush on my cheeks. "Twos can afford to pay their way out of the draft, so I'm sure Lady Celeste has never seen what it does when families lose their only sons. Taking more would be devastating, particularly for the lowest castes, who tend to have larger families and need every member to work in order to survive."

Marlee, beside me, gave me a friendly nudge.

Celeste took over. "Well, then what should we do? Certainly you aren't suggesting that we sit back and let these wars drag on?"

"No, no. Of course I want Illéa to be done with the war." I paused to gather my thoughts and looked across at Maxon for some sort of support. Next to him, the king looked peeved.

I needed to switch directions, so I blurted out the first thing that came to mind. "What if it was voluntary?"

"Voluntary?" Gavril asked.

Celeste and Natalie chuckled, which made it worse. But then I thought about it. Was it such a terrible idea?

"Yes. I'm sure there would need to be certain requirements, but perhaps we'd get more out of an army of men who wanted to be soldiers as opposed to boys who were only doing what it took to stay alive and get back to the life they left behind."

A hush of consideration fell on the studio. Apparently, I'd made a point.

"That's a good idea," Elise chimed in. "Then we'd also be sending out new soldiers every month or two as people sign up. It might be invigorating to the men who've been serving awhile."

"I agree," Marlee added, which was usually the extent of her comments. She clearly wasn't comfortable in debate situations.

"Well, I know this might sound a little modern, but what if it was open to women?" Kriss commented.

Celeste laughed aloud. "Who do you think would sign up? Would you be heading into the battlefield?" Her voice dripped with an insulting disbelief.

Kriss kept her head together. "No, I'm not soldier material.

But," she continued, to Gavril, "if there's one thing I've learned from being in the Selection, it's that some girls have a frightening killer instinct. Don't let the ball gowns fool you," she finished with a smile.

Back in my room, I allowed my maids to stay a little later than usual to help me get the pile of pins out of my hair.

"I liked your idea of the army being voluntary," Mary said, her nimble fingers hard at work.

"Me, too," Lucy added. "I remember watching my neighbors struggle when their oldest sons were taken. It was almost unbearable when so many didn't come home." I could see a dozen memories flash before her eyes. I had some of my own.

Miriam Carrier was widowed young; but she and her son, Aiden, managed all right, just the two of them. When the soldiers had shown up at her door with a letter and a flag and their meaningless condolences, she'd caved in on herself. She couldn't make it on her own. Even if she had the ability, she didn't have the heart.

Sometimes I saw her begging as an Eight in the same square where I had said my good-byes to Carolina. But it wasn't as if I had anything to give her.

"I know," I said to Lucy's reflection.

"I thought Kriss went a bit too far," Anne commented. "Women in battle sounds like a terrible idea."

I smiled at her prim face as she focused intently on my

hair. "According to my dad, women used to—"

A short burst of knocks came at the door, startling all of us.

"I had a thought," Maxon announced, walking in without waiting for an answer. It appeared we had a standing date Friday nights after the *Report*.

"Your Majesty," they said together, Mary dropping pins as she sank into her curtsy.

"Let me help you," Maxon offered, coming to Mary's aid.

"It's all right," she insisted, blushing fiercely and backing out of the room. Far less subtly than I'm sure she intended, she made wide eyes at Lucy and Anne, begging them to leave with her.

"Oh, um, goodnight, miss," Lucy said, tugging on the hem of Anne's uniform to get her to follow.

Once they were gone, Maxon and I both broke down into laughter. I turned to the mirror and continued to work the pins out of my hair.

"They're a funny lot," Maxon commented.

"It's just that they admire you so much."

Modestly, he waved the compliment away. "Sorry I interrupted," he said to my reflection.

"It's fine," I answered, tugging out the last pin. I ran my fingers through my hair and draped it over my shoulder. "Do I look okay?"

Maxon nodded, staring a little longer than necessary. He came to his senses and spoke. "Anyway, this idea . . ."

"Do tell."

"You remember that Halloween thing?"

"Yes. Oh, I still haven't read the diary. It's well hidden though," I promised.

"It's fine. No one's looking for it. Anyway, I was thinking. All those books said it fell in October, right?"

"Yes."

"It's October now. Why don't we have a Halloween party?"

I spun around. "Really? Oh, Maxon, could we?"

"Would you like that?"

"I would love it!"

"I figure all the Selected girls could have costumes made. The off-duty guards could be spare dance partners since there's only one of me and it would be unfair to make everyone stand around waiting for a turn. And we could do dancing lessons over the next week or two. You did say there wasn't much to do during the days sometimes. And candy! We'll have the best candies made and imported. You, my dear, will be stuffed by the end of the night. We'll have to roll you off the floor."

I was mesmerized.

"And we'll make an announcement, tell the entire country to celebrate. Let the children dress up and go door-to-door doing tricks, like they used to. Your sister will love that, yes?"

"Of course she will! *Everyone* will!"

He deliberated a moment, pursing his lips. "How do you think she would like celebrating here, at the palace?"

I was stunned. "What?"

"At some point in the competition, I'm supposed to meet the parents of the Elite. Might as well have siblings come and do this around a festive time as opposed to waiting—"

His words were cut off by me barreling into his arms. I was so elated by the possibility of seeing May and my parents, I couldn't contain my enthusiasm. He wrapped his arms around my waist and stared into my eyes, his own glittering with delight. How did this person—someone I'd imagined would be my polar opposite—always seem to find the things that would make me the happiest?

"Do you mean it? Can they really come?"

"Of course," he answered. "I've been longing to meet them, and it's part of the competition. Anyway, I think it would do all of you good to see your families."

Once I was sure I wouldn't cry, I whispered back, "Thank you."

"You're quite welcome. . . . I know you love them."

"I do."

He chuckled. "And it's clear you'd do practically anything for them. After all, you stayed in the Selection for them."

I jerked back, putting space between us so I could see his eyes. There was no judgment there, only shock at my abrupt movement. I couldn't let this pass though. I had to be absolutely clear.

"Maxon, they were part of the reason I stayed in the beginning, but they're not why I'm here now. You know that, right? I'm here because . . ."

"Because?"

I looked at Maxon, his adoring face so hopeful. *Say it, America. Just tell him.*

"Because?" he asked again, this time with an impish smile coming to his lips, which made me soften even more.

I thought about my conversation with Marlee and the way I'd felt the other day when we talked about the Selection. It was hard to think of Maxon as my boyfriend when there were other girls dating him, but he wasn't just my friend. That hopeful feeling hit me again, the wonder that we might be something special. Maxon was more to me than I'd let myself believe.

I gave him a flirtatious smile and started walking toward the door.

"America Singer, you get back here." He ran in front of me, wrapping an arm around my waist as we stood, chest to chest. "Tell me," he whispered.

I pinched my lips together.

"Fine, then I shall have to rely on other means of communication."

Without any warning, he kissed me. I felt myself dip backward a bit, completely supported by his arms. I placed my hands on his neck, wanting to hold him to me . . . and something shifted in my head.

Usually when we were alone together, I could block out the other girls. But tonight I thought about the possibility of someone else in my place. Just imagining it: someone else in Maxon's arms, making him laugh, *marrying* him . . . It broke my heart. I couldn't help it; I started to cry.

"Darling, what's wrong?"

Darling? The word, so tender and personal, enveloped me. In that moment, any desire I had to fight my feelings for Maxon disappeared. I wanted to be his dear, his darling. I wanted to be Maxon's alone.

It might mean welcoming a future I never thought I would and saying good-bye to things I never intended to, but the thought of leaving him now wasn't something I could handle.

It was true that I wasn't the best candidate for the crown, but I didn't deserve to be in the running at all if I couldn't at least be brave enough to confess how I felt.

I sighed, trying to keep my voice steady. "I don't want to leave all this."

"If I remember correctly, the first time we met, you said it was like a cage." He smiled. "It does grow on you, though, doesn't it?"

I gave my head a small shake. "Sometimes you can be so stupid." A weak laugh pushed through my choked-up throat.

Maxon let me pull away just enough so I could look into his brown eyes.

"Not the palace, Maxon. I could care less about the clothes or my bed or, believe it or not, the food."

Maxon laughed. It was no secret how excited I had been about the extravagant meals here.

"It's you," I said. "I don't want to leave you."

"Me?"

I nodded.

"You want me?"

I giggled at his bewildered expression. "That's what I'm saying."

He paused a moment. "How— But— What did I do?"

"I don't know," I said with a shrug. "I just think that we'd be a good us."

He smiled slowly. "We'd be a wonderful us."

Maxon pulled me in, roughly by his standards, and kissed me again.

"Are you sure?" he asked, holding me at arm's length, staring intently at me. "Are you absolutely positive?"

"If you're sure, I'm sure."

For a flicker of a second, something changed in his expression. But it passed so quickly, I wondered if it—whatever it was—was even real.

In the very next moment, he led me over to the bed, and we perched on the edge together, holding hands as my head rested on his shoulder. I was expecting him to say something. After all, wasn't this what he had been waiting for? But there were no words. Every once in a while he'd let out a long sigh, and in that sound alone I could hear how happy he was. That helped me not to feel so anxious.

After a while—perhaps because neither of us knew what to say—Maxon sat up straighter. "I should probably go. If we're going to add all the families to the celebration, I need to make extra plans."

I pulled back and smiled, still giddy that I was going to get to hug my mom, dad, and May soon. "Thank you again."

We stood together, walking toward the door. I held on to his hand tightly. For some reason, I dreaded letting it go. It felt like this whole moment was fragile somehow, and if it shifted too much it might break.

"I'll see you tomorrow," he promised in a whisper, his nose millimeters away from mine. He looked upon me with such adoration that I felt silly for worrying. "You're astonishing."

Once he was gone, I closed my eyes and pulled in everything from our short time together: the way he stared at me, the playful smiles, the sweet kisses. I thought about them over and over as I got ready for bed, wondering if Maxon was doing the same thing.

CHAPTER 6

"LOVELY, MISS. KEEP POINTING AT the sketches, and the rest of you, try not to look at me," the photographer asked.

It was Saturday, and all the Elite had been excused from our obligatory day of sitting in the Women's Room. At breakfast, Maxon made his announcement about the Halloween party; and by the afternoon, our maids had started working on costume designs, and photographers had shown up to document the whole process.

Now I was attempting to look natural as I went over Anne's drawings while my maids stood behind the table with pieces of fabric, containers of sequins, and an absurd amount of feathers.

The camera snapped and flashed as we tried to give several options. Just as I was about to pose with some gold fabric held up to my face, we had a visitor.

"Good morning, ladies," Maxon said, strolling through the open doorway.

I couldn't help but stand a little straighter, and it felt like my smile was taking over my face. The photographer caught that moment before addressing Maxon.

"Your Majesty, always an honor. Would you mind posing with the young lady?"

"It would be my pleasure."

My maids stepped back, and Maxon picked up a few sketches and stood right behind me, the papers in front of us in one hand and his other settled low on my waist. That touch conveyed so much to me. *See,* it said, *soon I'll get to touch you like this in front of the world. You don't have to worry about anything.*

A few pictures were taken, and the photographer left for the next girl on his list. I realized my maids had inconspicuously dismissed themselves at some point as well.

"Your maids are quite talented," Maxon said. "These are wonderful concepts."

I tried to act like I always did with Maxon, but things felt different now, better and worse at the same time. "I know. I couldn't be in better hands."

"Have you settled on one yet?" he asked, fanning out the papers on my desk.

"We're all fond of the bird idea. I think it's meant to be a reference to my necklace," I said, touching the thin string of silver. My songbird necklace was a gift from my dad, and I preferred it over the heavy jewelry the palace provided for us.

"I hate to say this, but I think Celeste has picked something avian as well. She seemed awfully determined," he said.

"That's all right," I replied with a shrug. "I'm not crazy about feathers anyway." My smile faltered. "Wait. You were with Celeste?"

He nodded. "Just a quick visit to chat. I'm afraid I can't stay long here, either. Father's not thrilled about all this, but with the Selection still going on, he understood that it would be nice to have some more festivities. And he agreed it would be a much better way to meet the families, all things considered."

"Like what?"

"He's eager for an elimination, and I'm supposed to do one after I meet with everyone's parents. The sooner they come, the better in his eyes."

I hadn't realized sending someone home was part of the Halloween plan. I thought it was just a big party. It made me nervous, though I told myself there was no reason I should be. Not after our conversation last night. Of all the moments I'd shared with Maxon, nothing seemed quite so real as that one.

Still scanning the designs, he spoke absentmindedly. "I suppose I ought to finish my rounds."

"You're leaving already?"

"Not to worry, darling. I'll see you at dinner."

Yes, I thought, *but you'll see all of us at dinner.*

"Is everything all right?" I asked.

"Of course," he answered, offering me a quick kiss. On the cheek. "I have to run. We'll talk again soon."

And, just as suddenly as he appeared, he was gone.

As of Sunday, the Halloween party was eight days away, which meant the palace was a hurricane of activity.

On Monday the Elite spent the morning with Queen Amberly taste testing and approving a menu for the party. It was easily the best task we'd been given so far. That afternoon, however, Celeste was missing from the Women's Room for a few hours. When she returned around four, she announced to us all, "Maxon sends his love."

Tuesday afternoon we greeted extended members of the royal family who were coming to town for the festivities. But that morning we all watched out the window as Maxon gave Kriss an archery lesson in the gardens.

Meals were full of guests who had come to stay early, but Maxon was often missing, as well as Marlee and Natalie.

I felt more and more embarrassed. I'd made a mistake by confessing my feelings to Maxon. For all his talk, he couldn't really be interested in me if his first instinct was to spend time with everyone else.

I'd all but lost hope by Friday when I found myself sitting at the piano in my room after the *Report*, wishing that Maxon would come.

He didn't.

I tried to put it out of my mind on Saturday, as the Elite were obligated to entertain the influx of ladies at the palace in the Women's Room in the morning and have yet another dance rehearsal in the afternoon.

Thank goodness our family chose to focus on music and art as Fives, because I was a terrible dancer. The only person in the room worse than me was Natalie. Obnoxiously enough, Celeste was the epitome of gracefulness. More than once the instructors asked her to help others in the room, the result of which was Natalie nearly twisting her ankle because of Celeste's intentionally poor guidance.

Smooth as a snake, Celeste faulted Natalie's two left feet for her problems. The teachers believed her, and Natalie laughed it all off. I admired Natalie for not letting Celeste get to her.

Aspen had been there for all the lessons. The first few times I avoided him, not really sure I wanted to interact with him. I heard rumors that the guards were switching schedules so fast it was dizzying. Some wanted to go to the party desperately while others had girls back home and would be in huge trouble if they were seen dancing with someone else, especially since five of us would be eligible again soon and in very high demand.

But seeing as this was our last formal rehearsal, when Aspen was near enough to offer me a dance, I didn't turn him down.

"Are you all right?" he asked. "You've seemed down the last few times I've seen you."

"Just tired," I lied. I couldn't talk with him about boy problems.

"Really?" he asked doubtfully. "I was sure that it meant bad news was coming."

"What do you mean?" Did he know something I didn't?

He sighed. "If you're preparing to tell me that I need to stop fighting for you, that's not a conversation I want to have."

In truth, I hadn't even thought about Aspen in the last week or so. I was so consumed by my mistimed words and mistaken guesses, I couldn't consider anything else. And here, while I'd been worried about Maxon letting me go, Aspen had been worrying about me doing the same to him.

"That's not what it is," I answered vaguely, feeling guilty.

He nodded, satisfied with that response for now. "Ouch!"

"Oops!" I said. I genuinely hadn't meant to step on him. I worked to focus a little more on the dancing.

"I'm sorry, Mer, but you're terrible." He was chuckling even though the heel of my shoe had to have hurt him.

"I know, I know," I said breathlessly. "I'm trying, I swear!"

I pranced around the room like a blind moose, but what I lacked in grace I made up for in effort. Aspen, kindly, did his best to make me look good, attempting to be a little less on the beat to be in time with me. That was so typical of him, always trying to be my hero.

By the end of that last lesson, I at least knew all the steps. I couldn't promise I wouldn't accidentally take out a visiting diplomat with an energetic kick of my leg, but I'd do my best. As I considered that image, I realized it was no wonder Maxon was having second thoughts. I'd be an embarrassment to take to another country let alone receive anyone here. I just didn't have that princess air about me.

I sighed and went to get a cup of water. Aspen followed me while the rest of the girls left.

"So," he started. I did a sweep of the room to make sure no one was watching. "I have to assume that if you're not worried about me, you're worried about him."

I lowered my eyes and blushed. How well he knew me.

"Not that I'm cheering for him or anything, but if he can't see how amazing you are, he's an idiot."

I smiled, continuing to study the floor.

"And if you don't get to be princess then, so what? That doesn't make you any less incredible. And you know . . . you know . . ." He couldn't get out what he wanted to say, and I risked looking at his face.

In Aspen's eyes I saw a thousand different endings to that sentence, all of them connecting him to me. That he was still waiting for me. That he knew me better than anyone. That we were the same. That a few months at the palace couldn't erase two years. No matter what, Aspen would always be there for me.

"I know, Aspen. I do."

CHAPTER 7

I STOOD IN LINE WITH the other girls in the massive foyer of the palace, bouncing on the balls of my feet.

"Lady America," Silvia whispered, and that was all it took to know I was behaving in an unacceptable way. As our main tutor for the Selection, she took our actions quite personally.

I tried to still myself. I envied Silvia and the staff and the handful of guards who were moving around the space if only for the fact that they were allowed to walk. If I could do the same, I knew I'd feel much calmer.

Maybe if Maxon was here already it wouldn't be so bad. Then again, maybe it would make me more anxious. I still couldn't figure out why, after everything, he hadn't made any time for me lately.

"They're here!" I heard through the palace doors. I wasn't the only one who made sounds of delight.

"All right, ladies!" Silvia called. "Best behavior! Butlers and maids against the wall, please."

We tried to be the lovely, regal young women Silvia wanted us to, but the second Kriss's and Marlee's parents made it through the doorway, it all fell apart. I knew that both girls were only children, and it was obvious their parents missed them too much to bother with decorum. They ran in screaming, and Marlee dashed out of the line without so much as a pause.

Celeste's parents were more put together, though they clearly were thrilled to see their daughter. She broke rank as well, but in a much more civilized way than Marlee. I didn't even register Natalie's or Elise's parents, because a short figure with wild red hair blazed around the open door, her eyes searching.

"May!"

She heard my call and saw my waving arm and rushed to me, Mom and Dad following her lead. I knelt on the floor, embracing her.

"Ames! I can't believe it!" she crooned, admiration and jealousy in her voice. "You look so, so beautiful!"

I couldn't speak. I could barely even see her, I was crying so much.

A moment later, I felt the steady arms of my father taking us both in. Then Mom, abandoning her usual propriety, joined us, and we all held one another in a heap on the palace floor.

I heard a sigh that I knew was Silvia's, but I really didn't care at the moment.

Once I could breathe again, I spoke. "I'm so happy you guys are here."

"We are, too, kitten," Dad said. "Can't even tell you how much we missed you." I felt his kiss on the back of my head.

I twisted so I could hug him better. I didn't know until this very moment how badly I had needed to see them.

I reached for Mom last. I was shocked that she was so quiet. I couldn't believe she hadn't already demanded a detailed report of my progress with Maxon. But when I pulled back, I noticed the tears in her eyes.

"You're so beautiful, sweetheart. You look like a princess."

I smiled. It was nice not to have her question or instruct me for once. She was just happy in the moment, and that meant the world to me. Because I was, too.

I noticed May's eyes focus on something over my shoulder.

"That's him," she breathed.

"Hmm?" I asked, looking down at her. I turned to see Maxon watching us from behind the grand stairwell. His smile was amused as he made his way to where we were huddled on the floor. My father stood immediately.

"Your Highness," he said, his voice full of admiration.

Maxon walked up to him, hand outstretched. "Mr. Singer, it's an honor. I've heard so much about you. And you, too,

Mrs. Singer." He moved to my mother, who had also risen and straightened her hair.

"Your Majesty," she squeaked, a little starstruck. "Sorry about all that." She motioned to the floor as May and I stood, still holding each other tightly.

Maxon chuckled. "Not at all. I'd expect no less enthusiasm from anyone related to Lady America." I was sure Mom would want an explanation for that later. "And you must be May."

May blushed as she extended her hand, expecting a shake but getting a kiss. "I never did get to thank you for not crying."

"What?" she asked, blushing even more in her confusion.

"No one told you?" Maxon said brightly. "You won me my first date with your lovely sister here. I'll be forever in your debt."

May giggled back. "Well, you're welcome, I guess."

Maxon put his hands behind his back, his education coming back to him. "I'm afraid I must meet the others, but please stay here for a moment. I'll be making a short announcement to the group. And I'm hoping to get to speak with you more very soon. So glad you could come."

"He's even cuter in person!" May whispered loudly, and I could tell by the slight shake of his head that Maxon had heard.

He went off to Elise's family, who were easily the most refined of the group. Her older brothers looked as rigid as the guards, and her parents bowed to Maxon as he approached. I wondered if Elise had told them to do that or if that was just who they were. They all looked so polished, with matching heads of jet-black hair topping their small, smartly dressed frames.

Beside them, Natalie and her very pretty younger sister were whispering to Kriss as their parents shook hands. The whole space was full of warm energy.

"What does he mean, he expected enthusiasm from us?" Mom demanded in a low whisper. "Is this because you yelled at him when you met? You haven't been doing that again, have you?"

I sighed. "Actually, Mom, we argue pretty regularly."

"What?" She gaped at me. "Well, stop it!"

"Oh, and I kneed him in the groin once."

There was a split second of silence before May barked a laugh. She covered her mouth and tried to stop, but it kept coming out in awkward, squeaky sounds. Dad's lips were pressed together, but I could tell he was on the verge of losing it himself.

Mom was paler than snow.

"America, tell me you're joking. Tell me you didn't assault the prince."

I didn't know why, but the word *assault* pushed us all over the edge; and May, Dad, and I bent over laughing as Mom stared at us.

"Sorry, Mom," I managed.

"Oh, good lord." She suddenly seemed very excited to meet Marlee's parents, and I didn't stop her from going.

"So he enjoys a girl who stands up to him," Dad said once we all calmed down. "I like him more already."

Dad looked around the room, taking in the palace, and I stood there trying to absorb his words. How many times in the years Aspen and I had been dating in secret had he and my father been in the same room? A dozen at least. Maybe more. And I'd never really worried about him approving of Aspen. I knew getting him to consent to me marrying down a caste would be hard, but I had always assumed I'd get his permission in the end.

For some reason, this felt a thousand times more stressful. Even with Maxon being a One, with him being able to provide for the lot of us, I was suddenly aware that there was a chance my dad might not like him.

Dad wasn't a rebel, out burning houses or anything. But I knew he was unhappy with the way things were run. What if his issues with the government extended to Maxon? What if he said I shouldn't be with him?

Before I could go too far down that path of thought, Maxon bounded up a few of the steps so he could see all of us.

"I want to thank you again for coming. We're so pleased to have you at the palace, not only to celebrate the first Halloween in Illéa in decades, but so that we can get to know all of you. I'm sorry my parents weren't able to greet you as well. You will meet them very soon.

"The mothers, sisters, and Elite are invited to have tea with my mother this afternoon in the Women's Room. Your daughters will be able to escort you there. And the gentlemen will be having cigars with my father and myself. We'll have a butler come for you, so no worries about getting lost.

"Your maids will escort you to the rooms you'll use for the duration of your stay, and they will get you properly suited for your visit, as well as for the celebration tomorrow night."

He gave us all a quick wave and went on his way. Almost immediately, a maid was at our side.

"Mr. and Mrs. Singer? I'm here to escort you and your daughter to your quarters."

"But I want to stay with America!" May protested.

"Sweetie, I'm sure the king gave us a room every bit as nice as America's. Don't you want to see it?" my mother encouraged.

May turned to me. "I want to live exactly how you live. Just for a little while. Can't I stay with you?"

I sighed. So I'd have to forgo some privacy for a few days, so what? There was no way I could say no to that face.

"Fine. Maybe with two of us, my maids will actually have something to do."

She hugged me so tightly, it was instantly worth it.

"What else have you learned?" Dad asked. I looped my arm through his, still getting used to him in a suit. If I hadn't seen Dad a thousand times in his dirty paint clothes, I could have sworn he was born to be a One. He looked so young and smart in the formal outfit. He even seemed taller.

"I think I told you everything we were taught about our history, how President Wallis was the last leader of what was the United States, and then he led the American State of China. I didn't know about him at all, did you?"

Dad nodded. "Your grandpa told me about him. I heard he was a decent guy, but there wasn't much he could do when things got as bad as they did."

I'd only learned the solid truth of the history of Illéa since I'd been at the palace. For some reason, the story of our country's origin was mostly passed on orally. I'd heard several different things, and none of them was as complete as the education I'd received in the last few months.

The United States was invaded at the beginning of the Third World War after they couldn't repay their crippling debt to China. Instead of getting money, which the United States didn't have, the Chinese set up a government here, creating the American State of China and using the Americans as labor. Eventually the United States rebelled—not only against China, but also against the Russians, who were trying to steal the labor force set up by the Chinese—joining with Canada, Mexico, and several other Latin countries to form one country. That was the Fourth World War, and—while we survived it, became a new country because of it—it was pretty economically devastating.

"Maxon told me that right before the Fourth World War people hardly had anything."

"He's right. It's part of why the caste system is so unfair. No one had much to offer in the way of help in the first place, which is why so many people ended up in the lower castes."

I didn't really want to go down this path with Dad, because I knew he could get really worked up. He wasn't wrong—the castes weren't fair—but this was a happy visit, and I didn't want to waste it talking about things we couldn't change.

"Besides the little history, it's mostly etiquette lessons. We're getting a bit more into diplomacy now. I think we might have to do something with that soon, they're pushing it so hard. The girls who stay will have to anyway."

"Who stay?"

"It turns out one girl will be going home with her family. Maxon's supposed to make an elimination after meeting you all."

"You sound unhappy. Do you think he'll send you home?"

I shrugged.

"Come on now. You must know if he likes you or not by this point. If he does, you have nothing to worry about. If he doesn't, why would you even want to stay?"

"I guess you're right."

He stopped walking. "So which is it?"

This was kind of embarrassing to talk about with my dad, but I wouldn't have talked about it with Mom either. And May would be worse at interpreting Maxon than I was.

"I think he likes me. He says he does."

Dad laughed. "Then I'm sure you're doing fine."

"But he's been a little . . . distant this last week."

"America, honey, he's the prince. He's probably been busy passing legislation or something like that."

I didn't know how to explain that Maxon seemed to be making time for everyone else. It was too humiliating. "I guess."

"Speaking of legislation, have you all learned anything about that yet? About how to write up proposals?"

I wasn't any more excited about this topic, but at least it was boy-free. "Not yet. We've been reading a lot of them though. They're hard to understand sometimes; but Silvia, the woman from downstairs, she's sort of a guide or tutor or whatever. She tries to explain things. And Maxon is helpful if I ask him questions."

"Is he?" Dad seemed happy about this.

"Oh, yes. I think it's important to him that we all feel like we could be successful, you know? So he's really great about explaining things. He even . . ." I deliberated. I wasn't supposed to mention the book room. But this was my dad. "Listen, you have to promise not to say anything about this."

He chuckled. "The only person I ever talk to is your mother, and we all know she can't be trusted with a secret, so I promise I won't tell her."

I giggled. Trying to imagine Mom keeping anything to herself was impossible.

"You can trust me, kitten," he said, giving me a little side hug.

"There's a room, a secret room, and it's full of books,

Dad!" I confessed quietly, double-checking to make sure no one was around. "There are books that are banned and these maps of the world, old ones with all the countries like they used to look. Dad, I didn't know there used to be that many! And there's a computer in there. Have you ever seen one in real life?"

He shook his head, stunned.

"It's amazing. You type what you're looking for, and it searches through all the books in the room and finds it."

"How?"

"I don't know, but that's how Maxon found out what Halloween was. He even . . ." I looked up and down the hall again. I decided there was no way Dad would tell about the library, but if I told him I had one of those secret books in my room, it might be too much.

"He even?"

"He let me borrow one once, just to see."

"Oh, that's very interesting! What did you read? Can you tell me?"

I bit my lip. "It was one of Gregory Illéa's personal diaries."

Dad's mouth dropped open before he composed himself. "America, that's incredible. What did it say?"

"Oh, I haven't finished. Mostly, it was to figure out what Halloween was."

He considered my words for a moment and shook his head. "Why are you worried, America? Clearly, Maxon trusts you."

I sighed, feeling foolish. "I guess you're right."

"Amazing," he breathed. "So there's a hidden room around here somewhere?" He looked at the walls in a whole new way.

"Dad, this place is crazy. There are doors and panels everywhere. For all I know, if I tipped this vase, we might fall through a trapdoor."

"Hmm," he said, amused. "I'll be very careful making my way back to my room then."

"Which you should probably do soon. I need to get May ready for tea with the queen."

"Ah, yes, you and your teas with the queen," he joked. "All right, kitten. I'll see you tonight for dinner. Now . . . how best not to fall into a secret hatch?" he wondered aloud, spreading his arms out like a protective shield as he walked.

Once he got to the stairwell, he tentatively put his hand on the rail. "Just so you know, this is safe."

"Thanks, Dad." I shook my head and made my way back to my room.

It was difficult not to skip down the halls. I was so happy my family was here, I could hardly stand it. If Maxon didn't send me home, it was going to be harder than ever to be separated from them.

I rounded the corner to my room and saw that the door was open.

"What did he look like?" I heard May ask as I approached.

"Handsome. To me anyway. His hair was kind of wavy, and it never stayed down." May giggled, and so did Lucy as she spoke. "A few times, I actually got to run my fingers through it. I think of that sometimes. Not as much as I used to."

I tiptoed closer, not wanting to disturb them.

"Do you still miss him?" May asked, curious about boys as always.

"Less and less," Lucy admitted, a tiny lilt of hope in her voice. "When I got here, I thought I would die from the ache. I kept dreaming up ways to escape the palace and get back to him, but that would never really happen. I couldn't leave my dad, and even if I got outside the walls, there's no way I could have found my way back."

I knew a little about Lucy's past, how her family gave themselves as servants to a family of Threes in exchange for the money to pay for an operation for Lucy's mother. Lucy's mom eventually died, and when the mother found out her son was in love with Lucy, she sold Lucy and her father to the palace.

I peeked through the door to find May and Lucy on the bed. The balcony doors were open, and the delicious Angeles air wafted in. May fell into the palace look so naturally, her day dress hanging perfectly on her frame as she sat braiding parts of Lucy's hair back and letting the rest fall free. I'd never seen Lucy without her hair pulled up tight into a bun. She looked lovely like this, young and carefree.

"What's it like to be in love?" May asked.

Part of me ached. Why hadn't she ever asked me? Then I remembered, as far as May knew, I'd never been in love.

Lucy's smile was sad. "It's the most wonderful and terrible

thing that can ever happen to you," she said simply. "You know that you've found something amazing, and you want to hold on to it forever; and every second after you have it, you fear the moment you might lose it."

I sighed softly. She was absolutely right.

Love is beautiful fear.

I didn't want to let myself think too much about losing things, so I walked inside.

"Lucy! Look at you!"

"Do you like it?" She reached back, touching the delicate braids.

"It's wonderful. May used to braid my hair all the time, too. She's very talented."

May shrugged. "What else was I supposed to do? We couldn't afford to have dolls, so I used Ames instead."

"Well," Lucy said, turning to face her, "while you're here, you will be our little doll. Anne, Mary, and I are going to make you look as pretty as the queen."

May tilted her head. "No one's as pretty as her." Then she quickly turned to me. "Don't tell Mom I said that."

I chuckled. "I won't. For now, though, we have to get ready. It's almost time for tea."

May clapped her hands together excitedly and went to settle in front of the mirror. Lucy pulled her hair up, managing to keep the braids together as she made her bun, putting her cap on to cover most of it. I couldn't blame her for wanting it to stay as it was a little bit longer.

"Oh, a letter came for you, miss," Lucy said, handing an

envelope to me with great care.

"Thank you," I replied, unable to keep the shock out of my voice. Most of the people I expected to hear from were currently with me. I tore it open and read the brief note, its deliberate scratch completely familiar.

America,

I have found out belatedly that the families of the Elite were recently invited to the palace, and that Father, Mother, and May have left to visit you. I know that Kenna is far too pregnant to travel, and Gerad is much too young. I'm trying to understand why this invitation wasn't extended to me. I'm your brother, America.

My only guess is that Father chose to exclude me. I certainly hope it wasn't you. We are on the edge of great things, you and I. Our positions can be very helpful to each other. If any other special privileges are ever offered to your family, you ought to remember me, America. We can help each other.

Did you happen to mention me to the prince? Just curious.

Write soon.

Kota

I debated crumpling it up and tossing it in the trash. I had hoped Kota might be getting over his caste climbing and learn to be content with the success he had. No such luck, it seemed. I threw the letter in the back of a drawer, choosing to forget about it entirely. His jealousy wasn't going to spoil this visit.

Lucy rang for Anne and Mary, and we all had a wonderful time getting ready. May's effervescent attitude kept us all in good spirits, and I found myself singing while we dressed. Not long after, Mom came by, asking all of us to double-check that she looked all right.

She did, of course. She was shorter and curvier than the queen, but she was every bit as regal in her dress. As we walked downstairs, May clutched my arm, looking sad.

"What's wrong? You're excited to meet the queen, aren't you?" I asked.

"I am. It's just . . ."

"What?"

She sighed. "How am I supposed to go back to khakis after all this?"

The girls were animated, and everyone was sparkling with energy. Natalie's sister, Lacey, was about May's age, and they sat in a corner, talking. I could see how Lacey resembled her sister. Physically, they were thin, blond, and lovely. But where May and I were opposites personality-wise, Natalie and Lacey were so similar. I would have described Lacey as a bit less whimsical, however. Not quite as clueless as her sister.

The queen made her rounds, speaking to all the mothers, asking questions in her sweet way. I was in a small group listening to Elise's mother talk about her family back in New

Asia when May tugged on my dress, pulling me away.

"May!" I hissed. "What are you doing? You can't act like that, especially when the queen's present!"

"You have to see!" she insisted.

Thank goodness Silvia wasn't here. I wouldn't put it past her to admonish May for something like this, even though May didn't know any better.

We made our way to the window, and May pointed outside. "Look!"

I peered past the shrubs and fountains and saw two figures. The first was my father, speaking with his hands as he either explained or asked something. The second was Maxon, pausing to think before responding. They walked slowly, and sometimes my dad would put his hands in his pockets or Maxon would tuck his behind his back. Whatever this conversation was, it seemed intense.

I glanced around. The women were all still engrossed with the experience, with the queen herself, and no one seemed to notice us.

Maxon stopped, stood in front of my father, and spoke deliberately. There was no aggression or anger, but he looked determined. After a pause, Dad held out his hand. Maxon smiled and shook it eagerly. A moment later, they both seemed lighter, and Dad slapped Maxon on the back. Maxon seemed to stiffen a bit at that. He wasn't used to being touched. But then Dad put his arm around Maxon's shoulder, the way he did with me and Kota, the way he did with all his kids. And Maxon seemed to like that very much.

"What was that about?" I asked aloud.

May shrugged. "It looked important though."

"It did."

We waited to see if Maxon had a conversation with anyone else's father; but if he did, they didn't go to the gardens.

CHAPTER 8

THE HALLOWEEN PARTY WAS AS amazing as Maxon had promised. When I walked into the Great Room with May by my side, I was stunned by the sheer beauty before me. Everything was golden. Ornaments on the walls, glittering jewels in the chandeliers, cups, plates, even the food— everything had hints of gold in it. It was nothing short of magnificent.

Popular music was playing through a sound system, but in the corner a small band waited to play the songs for the traditional dances we'd learned. Cameras—both for photography and video—dotted the room. No doubt this would be the highlight of Illéa programming tomorrow. There couldn't be a celebration equal to this one. I briefly wondered what it would be like if I was still here at Christmastime.

Everyone's costumes were gorgeous. Marlee was dressed

as an angel and dancing with that guard I ran into, Officer Woodwork. She even had wings that looked like they'd been made out of iridescent paper floating behind her. Celeste's dress was short and made of feathers, with a large plume behind her head announcing she was a peacock.

Kriss was standing with Natalie, and they seemed to have coordinated. Natalie's dress had flowers blossoming on the bodice, and her full skirt was fluttery blue tulle. Kriss's dress was as golden as the room and covered with cascading leaves. Guessing, I'd say they were spring and fall. It was a cute idea.

Elise's Asian heritage was being taken full advantage of. Her silken dress was an exaggeration of the demure ones she tended to favor. The draping sleeves were incredibly dramatic, and I was in awe of her ability to walk with the ornate headdress she was wearing. Elise didn't typically stand out, but tonight she looked lovely, almost regal.

Around the room, all the family and friends were in costume, too, and the guards were equally dashing. I saw a baseball player, a cowboy, someone in a suit with a name tag that said GAVRIL FADAYE, and one guard so bold as to put on a lady's dress. A few girls were near him, laughing up a storm. But many of the guards were in the dress version of their uniforms, which was simply pressed white pants and their blue jackets. They had on gloves but no hats, and these features helped distinguish them from the guards who were actually on duty, surrounding the perimeter of the room.

"So, what do you think?" I asked May, but when I turned, I saw she had disappeared into the crowd, already exploring.

I laughed to myself as I surveyed the room, trying to find her puffy little dress. When she said she wanted to go to the party as a bride—"the kind we see on TV"—I had thought it was a joke. She looked absolutely adorable in her veil though.

"Hello, Lady America," someone whispered in my ear.

I started and turned to see Aspen in his dress uniform beside me.

"You scared me!" I put my hand over my heart as if that would slow it. Aspen only chuckled.

"I like your costume," he said jovially.

"Thank you. I do, too." Anne had made me into a butterfly. My dress was tapered from front to back in a fluttering material edged in black that floated around me. A tiny mask that looked like wings covered my eyes, making me feel mysterious.

"Why didn't you dress up?" I asked. "Couldn't you think of anything?"

He shrugged. "I prefer the uniform."

"Oh." It seemed sad to waste a perfectly good reason to be extravagant. Aspen had even fewer opportunities than I did in that department. Why not live it up?

"I just wanted to say hello, see how you were."

"Good," I said quickly. I felt so awkward.

"Oh." He sounded unsatisfied. "All right then."

Maybe after his little speech the other day, he expected more of an answer, but I wasn't ready to say anything yet. He gave me a bow and went off to see another guard who embraced him like a brother. I wondered if being a guard gave him a sense of family the way the Selection had done for me.

Marlee and Elise found me moments later and dragged me onto the dance floor. As I swayed, trying not to hit anyone, I caught Aspen standing on the edge of the floor, talking with Mom and May. Mom ran her hand over Aspen's sleeve, like she was straightening it out, and May was beaming. I could imagine them telling him how handsome he looked in his uniform, how proud his mother must be. He smiled back, and I could see how pleased he was, too. Aspen and I were rarities, a Five and Six pulled out of our monotonous lives and placed in the palace. The Selection had been so life changing that I sometimes forgot to appreciate the experience.

I danced in a circle with some of the other girls and guards until the music quieted and the DJ spoke.

"Ladies of the Selection, gentlemen of the guard, and friends and relatives of the royal family, please welcome King Clarkson, Queen Amberly, and Prince Maxon Schreave!"

The band swelled with music, and we all curtsied and bowed as they came in together. The king was apparently dressed as a king, simply that of another country. I didn't catch the reference. The queen's dress was a blue so deep it almost appeared black, with glittering jewels across it. She looked like the night sky. And Maxon, comically, was a pirate. His pants were torn in places, and he wore a loose shirt with a vest and a bandanna over his hair. To add to the effect, he hadn't shaved in a day or two, and a shadow of dark blond fuzz covered the bottom half of his face like a smile.

The DJ asked us to clear the floor, and the king and queen had a first dance together. Maxon stood to one side beside Kriss and Natalie, whispering things to each in turn and making them laugh. Finally I saw that he was doing a sweep of the room. I didn't know if he was looking for me or not, but I didn't want to be caught staring at him. I fluffed out my dress and stared at his parents instead. They looked very happy.

I thought about the Selection and how crazy it seemed, but I couldn't argue with the outcome. King Clarkson and Queen Amberly were suited for each other. He seemed forceful, and she combated that with a calming nature. She was a quiet listener, and he always seemed to have something to say. Though the whole thing should be archaic and wrong, it worked.

Did they ever grow apart during their Selection the way I felt Maxon might be growing apart from me? Why had he not made a single attempt to see me in the midst of dating the rest of the girls? Maybe that was why he was speaking with Dad, to explain to him why he'd have to let me go. Maxon was a polite person, so that seemed like something he would do.

I surveyed the crowd, looking for Aspen. In the process, I saw that Dad had finally arrived and was standing arm in arm with Mom on the opposite side of the room. May had found her way to Marlee and was tucked right in front of her. Marlee held her arms across May's chest in a sisterly gesture, and their white dresses shone in the lights. It didn't surprise me at all that they got so close in less than a day. I sighed. Where was Aspen?

In a last effort, I peeked behind me. There he was, just over my shoulder, waiting by me as always. When our eyes met, he gave me a quick wink, and it lifted my entire mood.

After the king and queen finished, we all crowded onto the dance floor. Guards shuffled around, pairing up with girls easily. Maxon was still standing on the side of the room with Kriss and Natalie. I hoped maybe he'd come ask me to dance. I certainly didn't want to ask him.

Gathering my nerve, I smoothed my dress and walked in his direction. I decided that I would at least present him with an opportunity to ask me. I made my way across the floor, planning to jump into their conversation. When I got close enough to do that, Maxon turned to Natalie.

"Would you like to dance?" he asked.

She laughed and tilted her blond head to the side like it was the most obvious thing in the world, and I breezed past them, my eyes trained on a table of chocolates, as if that was my goal the entire time. I kept my back to the room as I ate the delicious treats, hoping no one could see how deeply I was blushing.

Perhaps a half-dozen songs in, Officer Woodwork appeared next to me. Like Aspen, he had opted to stay in his uniform.

"Lady America," he said with a bow. "May I have this dance?"

His voice was bright and warm, and his enthusiasm washed over me. I took his hand easily.

"Absolutely, sir," I replied. "I should warn you, though, I'm not very good."

"That's fine. We'll take it slow." His smile was so inviting that I couldn't be worried about my poor dancing skills, and I happily followed him to the floor.

The dance was an upbeat one, which suited his mood. He spoke through the entire thing, and it was hard to keep up. So much for taking it slow.

"It seems you've fully recovered from me nearly running you over," he joked.

"It's a shame you didn't do any damage," I shot back. "If I was in a splint, I wouldn't have to dance at least."

He laughed. "I'm glad you're as funny as everyone says you are. I hear you're a favorite of the prince, too." He made it sound as if it was common knowledge.

"I don't know about that." Part of me was sick of people saying that. Another part yearned for it still to be true.

Over Officer Woodwork's shoulder, I saw Aspen dancing with Celeste. Something knotted in my chest at the sight.

"Sounds like you get along well with most everyone. Someone even said that during the last attack you took your maids with you to the hiding place for the royal family. Is that true?" He sounded amazed. At the time, it seemed like a completely normal thing to protect the girls I loved, but to everyone else it came across as daring or strange.

"I couldn't leave them behind," I explained.

He shook his head in awe. "You're a true lady, miss."

I blushed. "Thank you."

I was left gasping for breath after the song, so I took a seat at one of the many tables sprinkled around the room. I drank orange punch and fanned myself with a napkin, watching others dancing on the floor. I found Maxon with Elise. They looked happy as they spun around in circles. He'd danced with Elise twice now and still hadn't sought me out.

It took awhile to find Aspen on the floor since so many men were in uniform, but I finally spotted him in a corner, talking with Celeste. I watched as she winked at him, her lips turned up in a flirtatious smile.

Who does she think she is? I stood to go and tell her to stop but realized what that would mean for both Aspen and myself before I took a step forward. I sat back down and continued to sip my punch. By the time the song ended, though, I was on the move and had situated myself close enough to Aspen for it to be appropriate for him to ask me to dance.

And he did, which was good, because I didn't think I could have been patient.

"What in the world was that?" I asked quietly but with obvious outrage in my voice.

"What was what?"

"Celeste was running her hands all over you!"

"Somebody's jealous," he sang into my ear.

"Oh, stop it! She's not supposed to be acting like that; it's against the rules!" I looked around to make sure no one could see how intimately we were talking, particularly my parents. I noticed Mom sitting and talking with Natalie's mother. Dad had disappeared.

"This from you," he said, rolling his eyes playfully. "If we aren't together, you can't tell me who I'm not allowed to talk to."

I made a face. "You know it's not like that."

"So what is it like?" he whispered. "I don't know if I'm supposed to be holding on or letting go." He shook his head. "I don't want to give up, but if there's nothing for me to hope for, then tell me."

I could see the effort behind him keeping his face so calm, the lingering sadness in his voice. And I hurt, too. Thinking about letting this end brought a stabbing pain to my chest.

I sighed and confessed. "He's been avoiding me. He'll say hello, but he's been very devoted to dating the other girls recently. I think I must have imagined that he actually liked me."

He stopped dancing for a moment, shocked at what I was saying. He quickly picked back up, studying my face for a moment.

"I didn't realize that was what was going on," he said softly. "I mean, you know I want us to be together, but I didn't want you to get hurt."

"Thanks." I shrugged. "I feel stupid more than anything."

Aspen pulled me in a little closer, still keeping a respectful distance though I knew he didn't want to. "Trust me, Mer, any man who passes up the chance to be with you is the stupid one."

"You tried to pass me up," I reminded him.

"That's how I know," he replied with a smile. I was glad we could joke about that now.

I looked over Aspen's shoulder and found Maxon dancing with Kriss. Again. Wasn't he even going to ask me once?

Aspen leaned in. "You know what this dance reminds me of?"

"Tell me."

"Fern Tally's sixteenth birthday party."

I gave him a look like he was crazy. I remembered Fern's sixteenth birthday. Fern was a Six, and sometimes we got help from her when Aspen's mom was too busy to fit us in. Her sixteenth birthday party came about seven months after Aspen and I had started dating. We were both invited, and it wasn't much of a party. A cake and water, the radio turned on because she didn't own any music discs, and the lights dimmed in her unfinished basement. The big thing was that it was the first party I'd been to that wasn't a "family" party. It was just the local kids alone in a room, and that was exciting. However, it in no way compared to the splendor of what was happening around us now.

"How in the world is this party like that one?" I asked disbelievingly.

Aspen swallowed once and spoke. "We danced. Remember? I was so proud to have you there, in my arms, in front of other people. Even if you did look like you were having a seizure." He winked at me.

The words stirred my heart. I did remember that. I lived off that moment for weeks.

In an instant a thousand secrets that Aspen and I had built and saved flooded my mind: the names we'd picked out for our imaginary children, our tree house, his ticklish spot on the back of his neck, the notes we'd written and hidden away, my failed efforts in making homemade soap, games of tic-tac-toe played with our fingers on his stomach . . . games where we couldn't remember our invisible moves . . . games he always let me win.

"Tell me you'll wait for me. If you'll wait for me, Mer, I can handle anything else," he breathed into my ear.

The music switched to a traditional song, and a nearby officer asked for a dance. I was swept away, leaving both Aspen and myself without any answers.

The night went on, and I found myself peeking over at Aspen more than once. Though I tried to seem casual about it, I bet anyone really paying attention might have noticed, particularly my dad, if he had been in the room. But he seemed more interested in touring the palace than in dancing.

I tried to distract myself with the party and must have danced with everyone in the room except for Maxon. I was sitting down resting my tired feet when I heard his voice beside me.

"My lady?" I turned to see him. "May I have this dance?"

That feeling, that indefinable something, coursed through me. As dejected as I'd felt, as embarrassed as I'd been, when he offered me that moment, I had to take it.

"Of course." He took my hand and walked me out to the floor, where the band was starting a slow song. I felt a rush of happiness. He didn't seem upset or uncomfortable. On the contrary, Maxon held me so close I could smell his cologne and feel his stubble against my cheek.

"I was wondering if I was going to get a dance at all," I commented, trying to sound playful.

Maxon managed to pull me even closer. "I was saving this one. I've put in time with all the other girls, so my obligations are over. Now I can enjoy the rest of the evening with you."

I blushed the way I always did when he said things like that to me. Sometimes his words were like single lines of poetry. After the last week, I didn't think I'd ever hear him speak to me that way again. It made my pulse race.

"You look lovely, America. Much too beautiful to be on the arm of a scraggly pirate."

I giggled. "How could you have possibly dressed to match? Come as a tree?"

"At the very least, some kind of shrubbery."

I laughed again. "I would pay money to see you dressed as a shrubbery!"

"Next year," he promised.

I looked at him. *Next year?*

"Would you like that? For us to have another Halloween

party next October?" he asked.

"Will I even be here next October?"

Maxon stopped dancing. "Why wouldn't you?"

I shrugged. "You've been avoiding me all week, dating the other girls. And . . . I saw you talking to my dad. I thought you might be telling him why you had to kick out his daughter." I swallowed the lump in my throat. I was *not* going to cry here.

"America."

"I get it. Someone has to go, and I'm a Five, and Marlee's the people's favorite—"

"America, stop," he said gently. "I'm such an idiot. I had no idea you'd see it that way. I thought you felt secure in your standing."

I was missing something here.

Maxon sighed. "Honestly? I was trying to give the other girls a sporting chance. From the beginning, I've really only looked at you, wanted you." I ducked my head for a moment, overcome by his deep stare. "When you told me how you felt, I was so relieved that a part of me didn't believe it. I still have a hard time accepting that it was real. You'd be surprised how infrequently I get something I truly want." Maxon's eyes were hiding something, some sadness he wasn't prepared to share. But he shook it away and continued explaining, starting to sway to the music again.

"I was afraid I was wrong, that you would change your mind any second. I've been looking for a suitable alternative, but the truth is . . ."—Maxon looked me in the eyes again, unwavering—"there's only you. Maybe I'm not really looking, maybe they aren't right for me. It doesn't matter. I just know I want you. And that terrifies me. I've been waiting for you to take back the words, to beg to leave."

It took me a moment to find my breath. Suddenly all that time away looked different. I could understand that feeling—that it was too good to be true, too good to trust. I felt like that every day with him.

"Maxon, that's not going to happen," I whispered into his neck. "If anything, you're going to realize I'm not good enough."

His lips were at my ear. "Darling, you're perfect."

My arm on his back drew him toward me, and he did the same, until we were closer to each other physically than we'd ever been. In the back of my mind, I realized we were in a crowded room, that somewhere my mother was probably fainting at the sight, but I didn't care. For that moment, it felt like we were the only two people in the world.

I pulled back to look at Maxon, noticing that I needed to get the moisture out of my eyes to do so. But I liked these tears.

Maxon explained everything. "I want us to take our time. After I announce the dismissal tomorrow, that will appease the public and my father, but I don't want to rush you at all. I want you to see the princess's suite. It adjoins mine, actually," he said quietly. Something about being that close to him all the time made my bones feel weak.

"I think you should start deciding what you want in there. I want you to feel completely at home. You'll have to pick a few more maids, too, and figure out if you want your family in the palace or just nearby. I'll help you with everything." A tiny beat of my heart whispered, *What about Aspen?* But I was so taken in by Maxon that I barely even heard it.

"Soon, when it's proper for me to end the Selection, when I propose to you, I want it to be as easy as breathing for you to say yes. I promise to do everything in my power between now and that moment to make it that way. Anything you need, anything you want, say the words. I will do everything I can for you."

I was overwhelmed. He understood me so well, how nervous I was about making this commitment, how frightening it was for me to become a princess. He was going to give me every last second he could and, in the meantime, lavish me with everything possible. I had another one of those moments when I couldn't believe this was all happening.

"That's not fair, Maxon," I mumbled. "What in the world am I supposed to be able to give you?"

He smiled. "All I want is your promise to stay with me, to be mine. Sometimes it feels like you can't possibly be real. Promise me you'll stay."

"Of course. I promise."

With that I rested my head on his shoulder, and we slow danced through song after song. Once May caught my eye, and she looked like she was about to die with happiness watching us together. Mom and Dad stood looking on, and Dad shook his head as if to say *And you thought he was sending you home.*

Something occurred to me.

"Maxon?" I asked, turning my face toward him.

"Yes, darling?"

I smiled at the name. "Why were you talking with my dad?"

Maxon smiled. "He is aware of my intentions. And you should know that he approves wholeheartedly, so long as you're happy. That seemed to be his only stipulation. I assured him that I'd do everything I could to see that you were, and I told him you seemed happy here already."

"I am."

I felt Maxon's chest rise. "Then he and I both have everything we need."

Maxon's hand moved slightly and settled low on my back, encouraging me to stay close. In that touch I knew so many things. I knew that this was real, that it was happening, and that I could let myself believe it. I knew I'd let go of the friendships I'd made here if I had to, though I was sure Marlee wouldn't mind losing in the slightest. And I knew I'd let the torch I held for Aspen burn out. It would be slow, and I would have to tell Maxon, but I would do it.

Because now I was his. I knew it. I'd never been so sure.

For the first time I could see it. I saw the aisle, the guests waiting, and Maxon standing at the end of it all. With that touch, it all made perfect sense.

The party went on late into the night, when Maxon dragged the six of us to the balcony at the front of the palace for the best view of the fireworks. Celeste was stumbling up the marble steps, and Natalie had acquired some poor guard's hat. Champagne was being passed around, and Maxon was celebrating our engagement prematurely with a bottle he'd kept all to himself.

As the fireworks lit up the sky in the background, Maxon raised his bottle in the air.

"A toast!" he exclaimed.

We all raised our glasses and waited expectantly. I noticed Elise's glass was smeared with the dark lipstick she'd been wearing, and even Marlee held a glass quietly, choosing to sip rather than gulp.

"To all you beautiful ladies. And to my future wife!" Maxon called.

The girls hooted, thinking this toast might be especially for each of them, but I knew better. As everyone tipped their glasses back, I watched Maxon—my almost fiancé—who gave me a tiny wink before taking another swig of champagne. The glow and excitement of the entire evening was overwhelming, like a fire of happiness was swallowing me whole.

I couldn't imagine anything strong enough to take that happiness away.

CHAPTER 9

I BARELY SLEPT. BETWEEN GETTING in so late and the excitement over what was coming, it was impossible. I curled closer to May, comforted by her warmth. I'd miss her so much once she left, but at least I had the prospect of her living here with me to look forward to.

I wondered who would be leaving today. It didn't seem polite to ask, so I didn't; but if pressed, I would guess it was Natalie. Marlee and Kriss were popular with the public—more popular than I was—and Celeste and Elise had connections. I had Maxon's heart, and that left Natalie without much to hold on to.

I felt bad because I really didn't have anything against Natalie. If anything, I wished Celeste would go. Maybe Maxon would send her home since he knew how much I disliked her, and he did say he wanted me to be comfortable here.

I sighed, thinking of everything he'd said last night. I'd never imagined this was possible. How did I, America Singer—a Five, a nobody—fall for Maxon Schreave—a One, *the* One? How did this happen when I'd spent the last two years bracing myself for life as a Six?

A tiny part of my heart throbbed. How would I explain this to Aspen? How would I tell him that Maxon had chosen me and that I wanted to be with him? Would he hate me? The thought made me want to cry. No matter what, I didn't want to lose Aspen's friendship. I couldn't.

My maids didn't knock when they came in, which was typical. They always tried to let me rest as long as I could, and after the party, I certainly needed it. But instead of going to prep things, Mary went around to May and gently rubbed her shoulder to wake her.

I rolled over to see Anne and Lucy with a garment bag. A new dress?

"Miss May," Mary whispered, "it's time to get up."

May slowly roused. "Can't I sleep?"

"No," Mary said sadly. "There's some important business this morning. You need to go to your parents right away."

"Important business?" I asked. "What's going on?"

Mary looked to Anne, and I followed her eyes. Anne shook her head, and that seemed to be the end of it.

Confused but hopeful, I got out of bed, encouraging May to do the same. I gave her a big hug before she went to Mom and Dad's room.

Once she left, I turned back to my maids. "Can you

explain now that she's gone?" I asked Anne. She shook her head. Frustrated, I huffed. "Would it help if I commanded you to tell?"

She looked at me, a clear solemnity in her eyes. "Our orders come from much higher. You'll have to wait."

I stood at the door to my bathroom and watched them move. Lucy's hands were shaking as she pulled out fistfuls of rose petals for my bath, and Mary's eyebrows were knit together as she lined up my makeup and the pins for my hair. Lucy sometimes trembled for no reason at all, and Mary tended to do that with her face when she was concentrating. It was Anne's look that made me scared.

She was always put together, even in the most frightening and taxing of situations, but today she looked as if her body was full of sand, her whole frame low with worry. She kept stopping and rubbing her forehead as if she could smooth away the anxiety in her face.

I looked on as she pulled my dress out of the garment bag. It was understated, simple . . . and jet-black. I looked at that dress and knew it could only mean one thing. I started crying before I even knew who I was mourning.

"Miss?" Mary came to help me.

"Who died?" I asked. "Who died?"

Anne, steady as ever, pulled me upright and wiped the tears from under my eyes.

"No one has died," she said. But her voice wasn't comforting; it was commanding. "Be grateful for that when this is all over. No one died today."

She gave me no further explanation and sent me straight to my bath. Lucy tried to keep herself under control; but when she finally broke into tears, Anne asked her to go get me something light to eat, and she jumped on the command obediently. She didn't even curtsy as she left.

Lucy eventually returned with some croissants and apple slices. I wanted to sit and eat slowly, stretching out my time, but one bite was all it took for me to know that food was not my friend today.

Finally Anne placed my name pin on my chest, the silver shining beautifully against the black of my dress. There was nothing left for me to do but face this unimaginable fate.

I opened my door but found myself frozen. Turning back to my maids, I breathed out my fear. "I'm scared."

Anne put her hands on my shoulders and spoke. "You are a lady now, miss. You must handle this like a lady."

I gave a small nod as she released me, unclenched my hands from the door, and walked away. I wish I could have said my head was high; but honestly, lady or not, I was terrified.

To my immense surprise, when I reached the foyer, the rest of the girls were waiting, all wearing dresses and expressions similar to my own. A wave of relief hit me. I wasn't in trouble. If anything, we all were, so at least I wouldn't be going through whatever this was alone.

"There's the fifth," a guard said to his counterpart. "Follow us, ladies."

Fifth? No, that wasn't right. It was six. As we walked down the stairs, I quickly scanned the girls. The guard *was* right. Only five. Marlee wasn't here.

My first thought was that Maxon had sent Marlee home, but wouldn't she have come by my room to say good-bye? I tried to think of a relationship between all this secrecy and Marlee's absence, and nothing I came up with made sense.

At the bottom of the stairs, an assembly of guards waited, along with our families. Mom, Dad, and May seemed anxious. Everyone did. I looked at them, hoping for some sort of clarity, but Mom shook her head while Dad gave me a shrug. I scanned the uniformed men for Aspen. He wasn't there.

I saw a pair of guards escorting Marlee's parents to the back of our line. Her mother was hunched with worry, and she leaned into her husband, his face heavy, as if he had aged years in a single night.

Wait. If Marlee was gone, why were they here?

I turned as a burst of light flooded the foyer. For the first time since I'd been at the palace, the front doors were both opened wide, and we were paraded outside. We crossed the short circular driveway and headed past the massive walls that fenced us into the grounds. As the gates creaked open, the deafening sound of a massive crowd greeted us.

A large platform had been set up in the street. Hundreds, maybe thousands of people were crowded together, children sitting on the shoulders of their parents. Cameras were positioned around the platform, and production people were running in front of the crowds, capturing the scene. We were led to a small section of stadium seats, and the crowd cheered for us as we walked out. I could see the shoulders of every girl in front of me relax as the people in the streets called out our names and threw flowers at our feet.

I lifted my hand in a wave as people called my name. I felt so silly for worrying. If the people were this happy, then nothing bad could be happening. The staff at the palace really needed to rethink the way they handled the Elite. All that anxiety for nothing.

May giggled, happy to be a part of the excitement, and I was relieved to see her back to herself. I tried to keep up with all the well-wishers, but I was distracted by the two odd structures waiting on the platform. The first was a ladder-like contraption in the shape of an *A*; the second was a large wooden block with loops on either end. With a guard at my side, I climbed into my seat in the middle of the front row and tried to figure out what was going on.

The crowd erupted again as the king, queen, and Maxon emerged. They too were dressed in dark clothes and wore sober expressions. I was close to Maxon, so I turned his way. Whatever was happening, if he looked at me and smiled, I knew it would be fine. I kept willing him to glance at me, to give me some sort of acknowledgment. But Maxon's face was hard.

A moment later the crowd's cheers turned into cries of disdain, and I turned to see what made them so unhappy.

My stomach twisted as I watched my world shatter.

Officer Woodwork was being dragged out in chains. His lip was bleeding, and his clothes were so dirty he looked like he'd spent the night rolling in mud. Behind him,

Marlee—her beautiful angel costume lacking its wings and covered in grime—was also in chains. A suit coat covered her hunched shoulders, and she squinted into the light. She took in the massive crowd, finding my eyes for a split second before she was pulled forward again. She searched once more, and I knew who she was seeking out. To my left, I saw Marlee's parents watching, gripping each other tightly. They were visibly crushed, gone from this place, as if their very hearts had abandoned them.

I looked back to Marlee and Officer Woodwork. The anxiety in their faces was obvious, yet they walked with a certain pride. Only once, when Marlee tripped over the hem of her dress, did that veneer crack. Beneath it, terror awaited.

No. No, no, no, no, no.

As they were led up onto the platform, a man in a mask began speaking. The crowd hushed for him. Apparently, this—whatever it was—had happened before, and the people here knew how to respond. But I didn't; my body lurched forward, and my stomach heaved. Thank goodness I hadn't eaten.

"Marlee Tames," the man called, "one of the Selected, a Daughter of Illéa, was found last night in an intimate moment with this man, Carter Woodwork, a trusted member of the Royal Guard."

The crier's voice was full of an inappropriate amount of self-importance, as if he was reciting the cure for some deadly disease. The crowd booed again at his accusations.

"Miss Tames has broken her vow of loyalty to our prince

Maxon! And Mr. Woodwork has essentially stolen property of the royal family through his relations with Miss Tames! These offenses are treason to the royal family!" He was shrieking out his statements, willing the crowd to agree. And they did.

But how could they? Didn't they know this was Marlee? Sweet, beautiful, trusting, giving Marlee? She made a mistake, maybe, but nothing deserving of this much hatred.

Carter was being strapped up to the A-shaped frame by another masked man, his legs spread wide and his arms pulled into a position that mimicked the structure. Padded belts were wrapped around his waist and legs, tightened to a point that looked uncomfortable even from here. Marlee was forced to kneel in front of the large wooden block as a man ripped the coat from her back. Her wrists were bound down to the loops on either side, palms up.

She was crying.

"This is a crime punishable by death! But, in his mercy, Prince Maxon is going to spare these two traitors their lives. Long live Prince Maxon!"

The crowd chanted after the man. If I had been in my right mind, I would have known I was supposed to call out, too, or at least applaud. The girls around me did, and so did our parents, even if they were in shock. But I wasn't paying attention. All I saw were Marlee's and Carter's faces.

We had been given front-row seats for a reason—to show us what would happen if we made such a stupid mistake—but from here, not more than twenty feet from the platform,

I could see and hear everything that really mattered.

Marlee was staring at Carter, and he was looking right back at her, craning his neck to do so. The fear was unmistakable, but there was also this look on her face, as if she was trying to reassure him that he was worth all this.

"I love you, Marlee," he called to her. It was barely audible over the crowd, but it was there. "We're going to be okay. It'll be okay, I promise."

Marlee couldn't speak in her fear, but she nodded back at him. In that moment, all I could think of was how beautiful she looked. Her golden hair was messy and her dress a disaster, and she'd lost her shoes at some point; but, my God, she looked radiant.

"Marlee Tames and Carter Woodwork, you are both hereby stripped of your castes. You are the lowest of the low. You are Eights!"

The crowd cheered, which seemed wrong. Weren't there any Eights standing here who hated being referred to that way?

"And to inflict upon you the shame and pain you have brought on His Majesty, you will be publicly caned with fifteen strikes. May your scars remind you of your many sins!"

Caned? What did that even mean?

My answer came a second later. The two masked men who had bound Carter and Marlee pulled long rods out of a bucket of water. They swiped them in the air a few times, testing them out, and I could hear the sticks whistling as they cut at the air. The crowd applauded this warm-up with the same frenzy and adoration they had just given the Selected.

In a few seconds, Carter's backside would be humiliatingly struck, and Marlee's precious hands . . .

"No!" I cried. "No!"

"I think I'm going to be sick," Natalie whispered as Elise made a weak moan into her guard's shoulder. But nothing stopped.

I stood up and lunged toward Maxon's seat, falling over my father's lap.

"Maxon! Maxon, stop this!"

"You have to sit down, miss," my guard said, trying to wrangle me back into my chair.

"Maxon, I beg you, please!"

"It's not safe, miss!"

"Get off me!" I yelled at my guard, kicking him as hard as I could. Try as I may, he held on tight.

"America, please sit down!" my mother urged.

"One!" cried the man on the stage, and I saw the cane fall on Marlee's hands.

She let out the most pathetic whimper, like a dog that had been kicked. Carter made no sound.

"Maxon! Maxon!" I yelled. "Stop it! Stop it, please!"

He heard me; I knew he did. I saw him slowly close his eyes and swallow one time, as if he could push the sound out of his head.

"Two!"

Marlee's cry was pure anguish. I couldn't imagine her pain—and there were still thirteen more strikes to go.

"America, sit!" Mom insisted. May was between her and Dad, her face averted, her cries almost as pained as Marlee's.

"Three!"

I looked at Marlee's parents. Her mother buried her head in her hands, her father's arms wrapped around her, as if he could protect her from everything they were losing in that moment.

"Let me go!" I yelled at my guard to no avail. "MAXON!" I screamed. My tears were blurring my vision, but I could see him enough to know he'd heard me.

I looked at the other girls. Shouldn't we do something? Some appeared to be crying, too. Elise was bent over, a palm pressed to her forehead, looking as if she might pass out. No one seemed angry though. Shouldn't they be?

"Five!"

The sound of Marlee's shrieks would haunt me for the rest of my life. I'd never heard anything like it. Or the sickening echo of the crowd cheering it on, as if this was merely entertainment. Or Maxon's silence, allowing this to happen. Or the crying of the girls around me, accepting it.

The only thing that gave me any sort of hope was Carter. Even though he was sweating from the trauma and shaking with pain, he managed to pant out comforting words to Marlee.

"It'll be . . . over soon," he managed.

"Six!"

"Love . . . you," he stammered.

I couldn't handle this. I tried to claw at my guard, but his thick sleeves protected him. I shrieked as he gripped me tighter.

"Get your hands off my daughter!" Dad yelled, pulling the guard's arms. With that space, I wiggled myself until I was facing him and thrust my knee up as hard as I could.

He let out a muffled cry and fell back, my dad catching him on the way down.

I hopped over the railing, clumsy in my dress and heeled shoes. "Marlee! Marlee!" I screamed, running as quickly as I could. I almost got to the steps; but two guards caught up with me, and that was a fight I couldn't win.

From the angle behind the stage, I saw that they'd exposed Carter's backside, and his skin was already torn, pieces hanging sickeningly. Blood was trickling down, ruining what used to be his dress pants. I couldn't imagine the state of Marlee's hands.

The thought sent me into an even deeper hysteria. I screamed and kicked at the guards, but all that accomplished was the loss of one of my shoes.

I was dragged inside as the man cried out for the next strike, and I didn't know whether to be grateful or ashamed. On the one hand, I didn't have to see it all; on the other, I felt like I'd abandoned Marlee in the worst possible moment of her life.

If I had been a true friend, wouldn't I have done better than that?

"Marlee!" I screamed. "Marlee, I'm sorry!" But the crowd was so frenzied, and she was crying so much, I didn't think she heard me.

CHAPTER 10

I THRASHED AND SHRIEKED ALL the way back. The guards had to hold me so tightly that I knew I'd be covered in bruises later, but I didn't care. I had to fight.

"Where's her room?" I heard one ask, and twisted to see a maid walking down the hall. I didn't recognize her, but she clearly knew me. She escorted the guards to my door. I heard my maids shouting in protest at the way I was being handled.

"Calm down, miss; that's no way to behave," a guard said with a grunt as they threw me onto my bed.

"Get the hell out of my room!" I screamed.

My maids, all of them in tears, rushed over to me. Mary started trying to get the dirt from my fall off my dress, but I slapped her hands away. They knew. They knew, and they didn't warn me.

"You, too!" I yelled at them. "I want all of you out! NOW!"

They recoiled at my words, and the tremors running down Lucy's little body almost made me regret saying them. But I had to be alone.

"We're sorry, miss," Anne said, pulling the other two back. They knew how close I was to Marlee.

Marlee . . .

"Just go," I whispered, turning to bury my face in my pillow.

Once the door clicked shut, I slipped off my remaining shoe and climbed deeper into bed, finally making sense of a hundred tiny details. So this was the secret she had been too afraid to share. She didn't want to stay because she wasn't in love with Maxon, but she didn't want to leave and be separated from Carter.

A dozen moments suddenly made sense: why she chose to stand in certain places or stared toward doors. It was Carter; he was there. The time the king and queen of Swendway came and she refused to get out of the sun . . . Carter. It was Marlee he was waiting for when I ran into him outside the bathroom. It was always him, standing silently by, perhaps sneaking a kiss here and there, waiting for a time when they could truly be together.

How much must she have loved him to be so careless, to risk so much?

How could this even be real? It didn't seem possible. I knew that there would be a punishment for something like this, but that it happened to Marlee, that she was gone. . . . I couldn't understand it.

My stomach writhed. It so easily could have been me. If Aspen and I hadn't been so careful, if someone had over-heard our conversation on the dance floor last night, that could have been us.

Would I ever see Marlee again? Where would she be sent? Would her parents have anything to do with her? I didn't know what Carter was before the draft made him a Two, though my guess was he was a Seven. Seven was low, but it was better than Eight by a long shot.

I couldn't believe she was an Eight. This *could not* be real.

Would Marlee ever be able to use her hands again? How long did such wounds take to heal? And what about Carter? Would he even be able to walk after that?

That could have been Aspen.

That could have been me.

I felt so sick. I had a cruel sense of relief that it *wasn't* me, and the guilt of that relief was so heavy it was hard to breathe. I was a terrible person, a terrible friend. I was ashamed.

There was nothing left to do but cry.

I spent the morning and most of the afternoon curled in a ball on my bed. My maids brought me lunch, but I couldn't touch it. Mercifully, they didn't insist on staying and let me be alone in my sadness.

I couldn't pull myself together. The more I thought over

what had happened, the sicker I felt. I couldn't get the sound of Marlee screaming out of my head. I wondered if a time would come when I'd forget.

A hesitant knock came at the door. My maids weren't here to open it, and I didn't feel like moving, so I didn't. After a brief pause the visitor came in anyway.

"America?" Maxon said quietly.

I didn't answer.

He shut the door and walked across the room to stand by my bed.

"I'm sorry," he said. "I didn't have a choice."

I stayed still, unable to speak.

"It was that or kill them. The cameras found them last night and circulated the footage without us knowing," he insisted.

He didn't talk for a while, maybe thinking that if he stood there long enough, I'd find something I wanted to say to him.

Finally he knelt beside me. "America? Look at me, darling?"

The endearment made my stomach turn. I did look at him though.

"I had to. I *had* to."

"How could you just stand there?" My voice sounded funny. "How could you not do anything?"

"I told you once before that part of this job is looking calm, even when you aren't. It's something I've had to master. You will, too."

My brow folded together. He couldn't still think I wanted that now? Apparently, he did. As he slowly took in my expression, his fell into absolute shock.

"America, I know you're upset, but please? I told you; you're the only one. Please don't do this."

"Maxon," I said slowly, "I'm sorry, but I don't think I can do this. I could never stand by and watch someone get hurt like that, knowing it was my judgment that sent them there. I can't be a princess."

He drew in a staggered breath, probably the closest thing to a truly sad emotion I'd ever seen from him.

"America, you're basing the rest of your life on five minutes of someone else's. Things like that rarely happen. You wouldn't have to do that."

I sat up, hoping it would help me see matters more clearly. "I just . . . I can't even think right now."

"Then don't," he urged. "Don't let this make a decision for the both of us when you're so upset."

Somehow those words sounded like a trick.

"Please," he whispered intensely, clutching my hands. The desperation in his voice made me look at him. "You promised you'd stay with me. Don't give up, not like this. Please."

I let out a breath and nodded.

His relief was palpable. "Thank you."

Maxon sat there, holding on to my hand like a lifeline. It didn't feel like it did yesterday.

"I know . . . ," he started. "I know that you're hesitant

about the job. I always knew that would be hard for you to embrace. And I'm sure this makes it harder. But . . . what about me? Do you still feel sure about me?"

I fidgeted, uncertain of what to say. "I told you I couldn't think."

"Oh. Right." His absolute dejection was clear. "I'll let you be for now. We'll talk soon though."

He leaned forward like he might kiss me. I looked down, and he cleared his throat. "Good-bye, America."

Then he was gone.

And I broke down all over again.

Maybe minutes or hours later, my maids came in and found me bawling. I rolled over, and there was no way they could miss the pleading in my eyes.

"Oh, my lady," Mary cried, coming to embrace me. "Let's get you ready for bed."

Lucy and Anne began working on the buttons of my dress while Mary cleaned my face and smoothed my hair.

My maids sat around me, comforting me as I cried. I wanted to explain that it was more than Marlee, that it was this sick ache over Maxon, too; but it was embarrassing to admit how deeply I cared, how wrong I'd been.

Then my heartbreak doubled when I asked for my parents, and Anne told me that all the families had been escorted away quickly. I didn't even get to say good-bye.

Anne stroked my hair, gently shushing me. Mary was at my feet, rubbing my legs comfortingly. Lucy simply held her hands to her heart, as if she felt it all with me.

"Thank you," I whispered between sniffles. "I'm sorry about earlier."

They exchanged glances. "There's nothing to apologize for, miss," Anne insisted.

I wanted to correct her, because I'd certainly crossed the line with how I treated them, but another knock came at the door. I tried to think of how to politely say I didn't want to see Maxon right now, but when Lucy hopped up to answer it, Aspen's face was on the other side.

"I'm sorry to disturb you, ladies, but I heard the crying and wanted to make sure you were all right," he said.

He crossed the floor toward my bed, a bold move considering the day we'd all had.

"Lady America, I'm very sorry about your friend. I heard she was something special. If you need anything, I'm here." The look in Aspen's eyes communicated so much: that he was willing to sacrifice any number of things to make this better if he could, that he wanted to take it all away if only for my sake.

What an idiot I'd been. I'd almost given up the one person in the world who really knew me, really loved me. Aspen and I had been building a life together, and the Selection nearly destroyed it.

Aspen was home. Aspen was safe.

"Thank you," I replied quietly. "Your kindness means a great deal to me."

Aspen gave me an almost imperceptible smile. I could tell he wanted to stay, and I wanted that as well; but with my maids bustling around, it couldn't happen. I remembered thinking the other day that I would always have Aspen, and I was happy to find that it was absolutely true.

CHAPTER 11

HEY KITTEN,

I'M SO SORRY WE DIDN'T GET TO SAY GOOD-BYE. THE KING SEEMED TO THINK IT WOULD BE SAFEST FOR THE FAMILIES TO LEAVE AS SOON AS POSSIBLE. I TRIED TO GET TO YOU, I PROMISE. IT JUST DIDN'T HAPPEN.

I WANTED TO LET YOU KNOW WE GOT HOME SAFELY. THE KING LET US KEEP OUR CLOTHES, AND MAY IS SPENDING EVERY SPARE MOMENT IN THOSE DRESSES. I SUSPECT SHE'S SECRETLY HOPING SHE NEVER GROWS ANOTHER INCH SO SHE CAN USE HER BALL GOWN AT HER WEDDING. IT REALLY LIFTS HER SPIRITS. I'M NOT SURE I'LL EVER FORGIVE THE ROYAL FAMILY FOR MAKING TWO OF MY CHILDREN WATCH THAT FIRSTHAND, BUT YOU KNOW HOW RESILIENT MAY IS. IT'S YOU I'M WORRIED ABOUT. WRITE US SOON.

MAYBE THIS ISN'T THE RIGHT THING TO SAY, BUT I WANT YOU TO KNOW: WHEN YOU RAN FOR THE STAGE, I'VE NEVER BEEN SO PROUD OF YOU IN ALL MY LIFE. YOU'VE ALWAYS BEEN BEAUTIFUL; YOU'VE ALWAYS BEEN TALENTED. AND NOW I KNOW THAT YOUR

MORAL COMPASS IS PERFECTLY ALIGNED, THAT YOU SEE CLEARLY
WHEN THINGS ARE WRONG, AND YOU DO EVERYTHING YOU CAN TO
STOP IT. AS A FATHER, I CAN'T ASK FOR MORE.
I LOVE YOU, AMERICA. AND I'M SO, SO PROUD.
DAD

How was it that Dad always knew what to say? I kind of wanted someone to rearrange the stars so they spelled out his words. I needed them big and bright, and somewhere I could see them when things felt dark. *I love you. And I'm so, so proud.*

The Elite were given the option of breakfast in their rooms, and I took it. I wasn't ready to see Maxon yet. By the afternoon I was a bit more put together and decided to go down to the Women's Room for a while. If nothing else, there was at least a television, and I could stand to be distracted.

The girls seemed surprised when I walked in, which I guessed was to be expected. I did tend to hide from time to time, and if there was ever a moment to do that, it was now. Celeste was lounging on a couch, flipping through a magazine. Illéa didn't have newspapers like I'd heard other countries did. We had the *Report*. Magazines were the closest things we had to printed news, and people like me could never afford them. Celeste always seemed to have one on hand, and, for some reason, that irritated me today.

Kriss and Elise were at a table drinking tea and talking as

Natalie stood in the back, looking out a window.

"Oh, look," Celeste said to no one in particular. "Here's another one of my ads."

Celeste was a model. The idea of her flipping through pictures of herself drove my irritation deeper.

"Lady America?" someone called. I turned and saw the queen and some of her attendants in the corner. She looked like she was doing needlework.

I curtsied, and she waved me over. My stomach did a flip as I considered my behavior yesterday. I'd never intended to offend her and was suddenly afraid I'd done just that. I felt the eyes of the other girls on me. The queen usually spoke to us as a group, rarely one-on-one.

I gave another curtsy as I approached. "Majesty."

"Please sit, Lady America," she said kindly, motioning to an empty chair across from her.

I obliged, still very nervous.

"You put up quite a fight yesterday," she commented.

I swallowed. "Yes, Your Majesty."

"You were very close to her?"

I choked back my sadness. "Yes, Your Majesty."

She sighed. "A lady ought not to behave in such a way. The cameras were so focused on the action at hand that they missed your conduct. Still, it doesn't behoove you to lash out like that."

It wasn't the order of a queen. It was the reprimand of a mother. That made it a thousand times worse. It was like she felt responsible for me, and I'd let her down.

I bowed my head. For the first time, I truly felt bad about how I reacted.

She reached over and rested her hand on my knee. I looked up to her face, shocked by the casual touch.

"All the same," she whispered, "I'm glad you did it." And she smiled at me.

"She was my best friend."

"That doesn't stop because she's gone, sweetheart." Queen Amberly patted my leg kindly.

It was exactly what I needed: motherly affection.

Tears bit at the corners of my eyes. "I don't know what to do," I whispered. I nearly let everything spill out right there about how I was feeling, but I was conscious of the eyes of the other girls on me.

"I told myself I wouldn't get involved," she stated, and sighed. "Even if I wanted to, I'm not sure there's much to say."

She was right. What words could undo all that had happened?

The queen leaned in to me and spoke sweetly. "Still, go easy on him."

I knew she meant well, but I really didn't want to discuss her son. I nodded and rose. She smiled at me kindly and gestured that I was free to go. I wandered over to sit with Elise and Kriss.

"How are you doing?" Elise asked sympathetically.

"I'm fine. It's Marlee I'm worried about."

"At least they're together. They'll make it as long as they have each other," Kriss commented.

"How do you know Marlee and Carter are together?"

"Maxon told me," she replied, as if it was common knowledge.

"Oh," I said, disappointed.

"I can't believe he didn't tell you, of all people. You and Marlee were so close. Besides, you're his favorite, right?" she said.

I glanced at Kriss, then at Elise. They both carried a look of concern in their eyes but also maybe a sense of relief.

Celeste laughed. "She's obviously not anymore," she muttered, not bothering to look up from her magazine. Clearly, my fall was to be expected.

I changed the subject back to Marlee. "I still can't believe Maxon put them through that. It was disturbing how calm he was about it."

"But what she did was wrong," Natalie remarked. There wasn't anything judgmental about her tone, only a quiet acceptance, like she was following instructions.

Elise spoke up. "He could have had them killed. The law is on his side in that one. He showed them mercy."

"Mercy?" I scoffed. "You call having your skin torn apart in public merciful?"

"Yes, all things considered," she continued. "I bet if we could ask Marlee, she'd choose caning over *dying*."

"Elise is right," Kriss said. "I agree that it was absolutely terrible, but I would rather have that than death."

"Please," I sneered, my anger coming to the surface. "You're a Three. Everyone knows your dad's a famous professor, and you've lived your whole life in libraries, completely comfortable. You'd never survive the beating, let alone a life as an Eight afterward. You'd be begging to die."

Kriss glared at me. "Don't pretend that you know anything about what I can and cannot tolerate. Just because you're a Five, you think you're the only one who's ever suffered?"

"No, but I'm sure I've experienced far worse than you," I said, my voice rising in anger, "and *I* couldn't take what Marlee went through. I'm saying I doubt you'd fare any better."

"I'm braver than you think, America. You have no idea the things I've sacrificed over the years. And if I make a mistake, I own up to the consequences."

"Why should there be any consequences at all?" I posed. "Maxon keeps saying how difficult the Selection is for him, how hard it is to make the choice, and then one of us falls for someone else. Shouldn't he be thanking her for making his decision easier?"

Natalie, seeming distressed, tried to interject. "I heard the funniest thing yesterday!"

"But the law—" Kriss called over her.

"America has a point," Elise countered quickly, and the ordered conversation crumbled.

We were speaking over one another, trying to make our opinions heard, justifying why we thought what happened was wrong or right. This was a first, but something I'd been expecting from the start. With this many girls together, competing against one another, there was no way we wouldn't fight eventually.

Then, in a disconnected voice, Celeste mumbled to her magazine as we continued to argue, "Got what she deserved. Whore."

The following silence was as charged as our quarrel.

Celeste looked over her shoulder just in time to see me lunge at her. She screamed as I landed on her, knocking us both into a coffee table. I heard something, probably a cup of tea, smash onto the floor.

I'd closed my eyes midjump, and when I opened them, Celeste was underneath me, trying to grab at my wrists. I pulled back my right arm and slapped her as hard as I could across her face. The burning sensation in my hand was nearly overwhelming, but it was worth it to hear the satisfying smack that erupted when it made contact.

Celeste immediately let out a shriek and started clawing at me. For the first time I regretted not keeping my nails long like the other girls did. She made a few cuts on my arm, which only angered me more, and I struck her again. This time I cut her lip. In response to the pain, she reached for something—the saucer from her cup of tea—and slammed it against the side of my head.

Thrown off, I tried to grab at her again, but people were pulling us apart. I was so consumed, I hadn't noticed someone calling for the guards. I took a swing at one of them, too. I was tired of being manhandled.

"Did you see what she did to me?" Celeste cried.

"You keep your mouth shut!" I screamed. "Don't you ever talk about Marlee again!"

"She's crazy! Don't you hear her? Did you see what she did?"

"Let me go!" I said, struggling against the guard.

"You're psychotic! I'm going to tell Maxon right now. You can kiss the palace good-bye!" she threatened.

"No one's seeing Maxon right now," the queen said sternly. She looked into Celeste's eyes and then into mine. Her disappointment was clear. I hung my head. "You're both going to the hospital wing."

The hospital wing was a long, pristine corridor with beds against the walls. Pinned by the head of each bed was a curtain to wrap around for privacy. Cabinets of medical supplies were scattered throughout.

Wisely, Celeste and I were placed at opposite ends of the wing, with Celeste being closer to the entrance and me near a window in the back. She'd pulled her curtain partially around her bed almost immediately so she wouldn't have to see me. I couldn't blame her. I did have a rather smug look on my face. Even while the nurse tended to the sore spot behind my hairline where Celeste had hit me, I couldn't bring myself to grimace.

"Now, hold this ice here, and that will help keep the swelling down," she offered.

"Thanks," I replied.

The nurse looked up and down the wing quickly, seeming to check that no one could hear us. "Good for you," she whispered. "Most everyone's been waiting for something like this to happen."

"Really?" I asked, my voice as low as hers. I probably shouldn't have been smiling this much.

"I can't begin to count the horror stories I've heard about that one," she said, nodding her head toward Celeste's curtained bed.

"Horror stories?"

"Well, she provoked that one girl who hit her."

"Anna? How do you know?"

"Maxon's a good man," she said simply. "He made sure she was checked out here before she went home. She told us what Celeste said about her parents. It was so filthy, I can't repeat it." The look on her face conveyed her disgust.

"Poor Anna. I knew it had to be something like that."

"One girl came in with her feet bleeding after someone slipped glass in her shoes in the night. We can't prove it was Celeste, but who else would do something so mean?"

"I never heard about that." I gasped.

"She looked terrified that she might get worse. I suppose she chose to keep her mouth shut. And Celeste hits her maids. Not with anything more than her hands, but they come in for ice from time to time."

"No!" All the maids I'd encountered were sweet girls. I couldn't imagine any of them doing something that would provoke getting hit at all, let alone regularly.

"Suffice to say, your antics are making the rounds already. You're a hero around here," the nurse said with a wink.

I didn't feel like a hero.

"Wait," I said suddenly. "You said Maxon had Anna checked out before he sent her home?"

"Yes, miss. He's very concerned that you're all taken care of."

"What about Marlee? Did she come here? How was she when she left?"

Before the nurse could answer, I heard Celeste's pouty voice pierce the room.

"Maxon, sweetheart!" she called as he marched through the doorway.

We shared a brief moment of eye contact before he approached Celeste's bed. The nurse walked away, leaving me alone and aching to know if she'd actually seen Marlee.

The sound of Celeste's whiny voice was almost too irritating to bear. I heard Maxon murmur his condolences, comforting the poor thing before extricating himself. He made his way around her curtain and focused his eyes on me, seeming exhausted as he walked down the wing.

"You're lucky my father had the cameras barred from the palace, otherwise there'd be hell to pay for your actions." He ran his hand through his hair, exasperated. "How am I supposed to defend this, America?"

"Are you going to kick me out, then?" I played with a piece of my dress while I waited for his answer.

"Of course not."

"What about her?" I asked, nodding my head toward Celeste's bed.

"No. You're all stressed after yesterday, and I can't hold that against you. I'm not sure my father will accept that excuse, but that's what I'm going to say."

I paused. "Maybe you should tell him it was my fault. Maybe you should just send me home."

"America, you're overreacting."

"Look at me, Maxon," I urged. I felt the lump rising in my throat and fought to speak past it. "I've known from the beginning I don't have what it takes, and I thought that I could—I don't know—change, or somehow make it work; but I can't stay here. I can't."

Maxon moved to sit on the edge of my bed. "America, you might hate the Selection, and you might be mad about what happened to Marlee; but I know that you care about me enough not to just abandon me in this."

I reached for his hand. "I also care enough about you to tell you you're making a mistake."

I could see the pain in Maxon's face as he held my hand tighter, as if he could hold me there and keep me from disappearing. Hesitantly, he leaned in and whispered, "It's not always so difficult. And I want to show that to you, but you have to give me time. I can prove that there are good things to this, but you have to wait."

I inhaled to contradict him, but he cut me off. "For weeks,

America, you've asked me for time, and I gave it to you without question because I had faith in you. Please, I need you to have a little bit of faith in me, too."

I didn't know what Maxon could possibly show me that might change my mind, but how could I not give him more time when he'd done that for me?

I sighed. "Fine."

"Thank you." The relief in his voice was obvious. "I have to get back, but I'll come see you soon."

I nodded. Maxon stood and left, stopping briefly to tell Celeste good-bye. I watched him go and wondered if trusting him was a bad idea.

CHAPTER 12

BOTH CELESTE'S AND MY INJURIES were minimal, so we were
sent back to our rooms within an hour. They staggered our
release times so we didn't have to leave together, and thank
goodness for that.

As I turned the corner at the top of the stairs, I saw a guard
coming toward me. Aspen. Even though he was bigger after
being bulked up from training, I knew his walk and his
shadow and a thousand other things that were ingrained in
my heart.

As he approached, he stopped to give me an unnecessary
bow.

"Jar," he whispered, and rose again, continuing on his
path.

I stood there for a split second, confused, and then realized what he meant. Fighting the urge to run, I moved down the hall eagerly.

I opened the door and was both surprised and relieved to find that all three of my maids were out.

I went over to the jar on my bedside table and found that the one little penny in there had company. I opened the lid and pulled out the folded sheet of paper. How clever of him. My maids probably wouldn't have noticed it; and if they had, they never would have intruded on my privacy.

I unfolded the note and read a very clear list of instructions. It seemed Aspen and I had a date tonight.

The directions Aspen gave me were complicated. I took a roundabout way to get to the first floor, where I was to look for the door next to the five-foot-high vase. I remembered that vase from walking around the palace before. What flower in the world needed a container that big?

I found the door and looked around to double-check that no one saw me. I'd never managed to find myself so free from the eyes of the guards. Not a one in sight. I opened the door slowly and crept inside. The moon shone through the window, giving the room sparse light and making me feel a little nervous.

"Aspen?" I whispered into the darkness, feeling silly and scared all at once.

"Just like old times, eh?" his voice called, though I couldn't see him.

"Where are you?" I squinted, trying to find his form.

Then the shadow of the heavy drape by the window shifted in the moonlight, and Aspen appeared from behind it.

"You startled me," I complained jokingly.

"Wouldn't be the first time, won't be the last." I heard the smile in his voice.

I walked over to him, knocking into every obstacle along the way it seemed.

"Shhh!" he complained. "The entire palace is going to know we're in here if you keep pushing things over." But I could tell he was playing.

"Sorry," I said, laughing quietly. "Can't we turn on a light?"

"No. If someone sees it shining under the door, we might get caught. This corridor isn't checked a lot, but I want to be smart."

"How did you even know about this room?" I reached out, making contact with Aspen's arms at last. He pulled me in for a hug and then started walking me toward the back corner.

"I'm a guard," he said simply. "And I'm very good at what I do. I know the entire grounds of the palace, inside and out. Every last pathway, all the hiding spots, and even most of the secret rooms. I also happen to know the rotations of the guards, which areas are usually the least checked, and the points in the day when the guards are at their fewest. If you ever want to sneak around the palace, I'm the guy to do it with."

"Unbelievable," I mumbled. We sat behind the broad back of a couch, the floor blanketed in a patch of moonlight.

Finally I could make out Aspen's face.

I questioned him seriously. "Are you sure this is safe?" If he hesitated at all, I was planning to bolt that very second. For both our sakes.

"Trust me, Mer. An extraordinary number of things would have to happen for someone to find us here. We're safe."

I was still worried, but I needed to be comforted so badly, I went along.

He wrapped an arm around me and pulled me in close. "How are you doing?"

I sighed. "Okay, I guess. I've been sad a lot, and angry. Mostly I wish I could undo the last two days and get Marlee back. Carter, too, and I didn't even know him."

"I did." He sighed. "He's a great guy. I heard he was telling Marlee he loved her the whole time and trying to help her get through it."

"He was," I confirmed. "At least in the beginning anyway. I got hauled off before it was over."

Aspen kissed my head. "Yeah, I heard about that, too. I'm proud you went out with a fight. That's my girl."

"My dad was proud, too. The queen said I shouldn't act that way, but she was glad I did. It's been confusing. Like it was almost a good idea but not really, and then it didn't fix anything anyway."

Aspen held me closer. "It was good. It meant a lot to me."

"To you?"

"Yeah," he whispered, seeming reluctant to share. "Every

once in a while I wonder if the Selection has changed you. You've been so taken care of, and everything is so fancy. I keep wondering if you're the same America. That let me know that you are, that they haven't gotten to you."

"Oh, they're getting to me all right, but not like that. Mostly this place reminds me that I wasn't born to do this."

I ducked my head into Aspen's chest, the safe place where I'd always hidden when things were bad.

"Listen, Mer, the thing about Maxon is that he's an actor. He's always putting on this perfect face, like he's so above everything. But he's just a person, and he's as messed up as anyone is. I know you care about him or you wouldn't have stayed here. But you have to know now that it's not real."

I nodded. Maxon with his talk about putting on a calm face. Was that what he was always doing? Was he acting when he was with me? How was I supposed to be able to tell?

Aspen continued. "It's better you know now. What if you got married and then found out it was like this?"

"I know. I've been thinking about that myself." Maxon's words on the dance floor played themselves on repeat in my head. He seemed so sure of our future, prepared to give me so much. I sincerely thought the only thing he wanted was for me to be happy. Couldn't he see how *unhappy* I was now?

"You've got a big heart, Mer. I know you can't just get over things, but it's okay to *want* to. That's all."

"I feel so stupid," I whispered, wanting to cry.

"You're not stupid."

"I am, too."

"Mer, do you think I'm smart?"

"Of course."

"That's because I am. And I'm way too smart to be in love with a stupid girl. So you can drop that right now."

I gave a tiny laugh and let Aspen hold on to me.

"I feel like I've hurt you so much. I don't understand how you can still possibly be in love with me," I confessed.

He shrugged. "It's just the way it is. The sky is blue, the sun is bright, and Aspen endlessly loves America. It's how the world was designed to be. Seriously, Mer, you're the only girl I ever wanted. I couldn't imagine being with anyone else. I've been trying to prepare myself for that, just in case, and . . . I can't."

We sat there, holding each other for a moment. Every little tickle of Aspen's fingers, the warmth of his breath in my hair felt like medicine for my heart.

"We shouldn't stay much longer," he said. "I'm pretty confident in my abilities, but I don't want to push it."

I sighed. It felt like we'd only just gotten here, but he was probably right. I moved to stand, and Aspen jumped up to help me. He pulled me in for one last hug.

"I know it's hard to believe, but I'm really sorry Maxon turned out to be such a bad guy. I wanted you back, but I didn't want you to get hurt. Especially not like that."

"Thanks."

"I mean it."

"I know you do." Aspen had his faults, but he didn't have it in him to be a liar. "It's not over though. Not if I'm still here."

"Yeah, but I know you. You'll ride it out so your family gets money and you can see me, but he'd have to reverse time to fix this."

I let out a long breath. It felt like he might be right. Maxon's hold on me was slipping away, shrugging off my skin like a coat.

"Don't worry, Mer. I'll take care of you."

Aspen didn't have any way to prove that at the moment, but I believed him. He'd do anything for the people he loved, and I knew without question that I was the person he loved the most.

The next morning I let my mind wander to Aspen all through getting ready, breakfast, and my hours in the Women's Room. I was blissfully detached until the slap of a pile of papers on the table in front of me jarred me back to the real world.

I looked up to see Celeste, still sporting a puffy lip. She pointed to one of her gossip magazines opened to a two-page spread. It didn't even take a full second for me to recognize Marlee's face, even though it was twisted with pain from the caning.

"Thought you should see this," Celeste said before she walked away.

I wasn't exactly sure what she meant, but I was so eager to know anything about Marlee, I dived in.

O f all our country's great traditions, perhaps none is looked upon with such excitement as the Selection. Created specifically to bring joy to a saddened nation, it seems everyone still gets a little giddy watching the great love story of a prince and his future princess unfold. When Gregory Illéa took the throne more than eighty years ago and his elder son, Spencer, died suddenly, the entire country mourned the loss of such an enigmatic and promising young man. When his younger son, Damon, was set to inherit the throne, many wondered if he was ready even to train for the task at nineteen. But Damon knew he was prepared to step into adulthood and set out to prove it via the greatest commitment in life: marriage. Within months the Selection was born, and the spirits of the country were lifted by the possibility of an average girl becoming the first princess of Illéa.

However, since then we have been forced to wonder at the effectiveness of the competition. While a romantic idea at heart, some say it's unfair to force princes to marry women beneath them, though no one can deny the absolute poise and beauty of our current queen, Amberly Station Schreave. Some of us still remember the rumors of Abby Tamblin Illéa, who allegedly poisoned her husband, Prince Justin Illéa, only a few years into their marriage before agreeing to marry his cousin, Porter Schreave, thus keeping the royal line intact.

While that rumor has never been confirmed, what we can say for sure is that the behavior of the women in the palace this time around is nothing short of scandalous. Marlee Tames, now an Eight, was caught with a guard undressing her in a closet Monday night after the Halloween Ball that was billed to be the highlight of the Selection programming. Its splendor was completely overshadowed by Miss Tames's reckless behavior, sending the palace into a frenzy the very next morning.

But beyond Miss Tames's inexcusable actions, the girls remaining at the palace might not be crownworthy either. An unnamed source tells us that some of the Elite are constantly bickering, rarely making the effort to perform the duties they're required to. Everyone remembers Anna Farmer's dismissal in early September after deliberately attacking the lovely Celeste Newsome, a model from Clermont. And our source confirms that that isn't the only physical interaction to take place at the palace between the Elite, forcing this reporter to question the pool of girls chosen for Prince Maxon.

When asked for a comment on these rumors, King Clarkson only said, "Some of the girls come from less-refined castes and aren't used to the proper behavior expected at the palace. Clearly Miss Tames wasn't prepared for life as a One. My wife has a particular indefinable quality about her and is one of the rare exceptions to the rule of lower castes. She has always sought to raise herself to a level befitting a queen, and it would be quite a challenge to find someone more suited for the throne than she. But for some of the lower castes remaining in the current Selection, it would be difficult to say we weren't expecting this from them."

While Natalie Luca and Elise Whisks are both Fours, they have always been the height of refinement when presented to the public, particularly Lady Elise, who is quite sophisticated. We are forced to assume our king is referring to America Singer, the only Five who made it past day one of the Selection. Miss Singer has had an average run at the Selection. She's pretty enough, but not quite what Illéa was expecting for its new princess. From time to time her interviews on the *Capital Report* are entertaining, but we need a new leader, not a comedienne.

In further disturbing news, we have heard reports that Miss Singer attempted to release Miss Tames during her caning, which in this reporter's eyes makes her an accessory to the treacherous activities in which Miss Tames was partaking by being unfaithful to our prince.

With all of these reports (and with Miss Tames no longer in the top spot) one question remains: Who should be the new princess?

A quick poll of readers has confirmed what we've suspected all along.

We congratulate Miss Celeste Newsome and Miss Kriss Ambers for their neck-and-neck places on the top of our public poll. Elise Whisks takes the third spot, with Natalie Luca not too far behind. In a wide gap between fourth and fifth places, America Singer comes (unsurprisingly) in last.

I think I speak for all of Illéa when I encourage Prince Maxon to take his time finding us a good princess. We narrowly avoided disaster by Miss Tames exposing her true nature before a crown was placed on her head. Whoever you love, Prince Maxon, make sure she's worthy. We want to love her, too!

CHAPTER 13

I RAN FROM THE ROOM. Of course Celeste wasn't doing me a favor. She was showing me my place. Why was I even bothering with this? The king was expecting me to fail, the public didn't want me, and I was sure I couldn't be a princess.

I made my way upstairs quickly and quietly, trying not to draw attention to myself. There was no telling who that magazine's unnamed source was.

"My lady," Anne said when I walked through the doorway. "I thought you'd be downstairs until lunch for sure."

"Could you leave, please?"

"I'm sorry?"

I huffed, trying not to lose my patience. "I need to be alone. Please?"

Without a word, they curtsied and left me. I went to the piano. I would distract myself until I couldn't think about this anymore. I played a handful of songs that I knew by heart, but that was too easy. I needed to really focus.

I stood up and dug through the bench for something more challenging. I burrowed past pages of sheet music until the edge of a book peeked out at me. Illéa's diary! I'd completely forgotten it was down here. This would be a great distraction. I carried the book over to the bed and opened it, taking in the ancient pages as they flipped through my hands.

The diary opened to the page with the Halloween picture, the stiff photo acting as a natural bookmark, and I reread the entry.

THE CHILDREN CELEBRATED HALLOWEEN THIS YEAR WITH A PARTY. I SUPPOSE IT'S ONE WAY TO FORGET WHAT'S GOING ON AROUND THEM, BUT TO ME IT ALL FEELS FRIVOLOUS. WE'RE ONE OF THE FEW FAMILIES REMAINING WHO HAS ENOUGH MONEY TO DO SOMETHING FESTIVE, BUT THIS CHILD'S PLAY SEEMS WASTEFUL.

I looked at the picture again, wondering about the girl in particular. How old was she? What was her job? Did she like being Gregory Illéa's daughter? Did it make her very popular?

I turned the page and realized that it wasn't a new entry but a continuation of the Halloween post.

I GUESS I THOUGHT THAT AFTER CHINA INVADED WE'D SEE THE ERROR OF OUR WAYS. IT'S BEEN OBVIOUS TO ME,

PARTICULARLY RECENTLY, JUST HOW LAZY WE'VE BECOME.
REALLY, IT'S NO WONDER CHINA CAME IN SO EASILY,
AND IT'S NO WONDER IT TOOK SO LONG FOR US TO GET
IN A POSITION TO FIGHT BACK. WE'VE LOST THAT SPIRIT
THAT DROVE PEOPLE ACROSS OCEANS AND THROUGH
DEVASTATING WINTERS AND CIVIL WAR. WE GOT LAZY.
AND WHILE WE WERE SITTING BACK, CHINA TOOK THE
REINS.

IN THE LAST FEW MONTHS IN PARTICULAR, I'VE
FELT DRIVEN TO GIVE MORE THAN MONEY TO THE WAR
EFFORTS. I WANT TO LEAD. I HAVE IDEAS, AND PERHAPS
SINCE I'VE DONATED SO GENEROUSLY, NOW IS THE TIME
TO OFFER THEM UP. WHAT WE NEED IS CHANGE. I CAN'T
HELP BUT WONDER IF I MIGHT BE THE ONLY PERSON WHO
CAN PROVIDE IT.

I got chills. I couldn't help but compare Maxon to his
predecessor. Gregory seemed inspired. He was trying to take
something broken and make it whole. I wondered what he'd
say about the monarchy if he was here today.

When Aspen slid my door open that night, I was nearly
bursting at the seams to tell him what I'd read. But I
remembered that I'd already mentioned to my dad that the
diary existed, and even that was going past what I'd sworn
to do.

"How have you been?" he asked, kneeling by my bed.

"All right, I suppose. Celeste showed me this article

today." I shook my head. "I'm not sure I want to get into it. I'm so tired of her."

"I guess with Marlee gone, he won't be sending anyone home for a while, huh?"

I shrugged. I knew the public had been looking forward to an elimination, and what happened with Marlee was more dramatic than anything anyone expected.

"Hey," he said, risking a touch in the light of the wide-open door. "It's going to be all right."

"I know. I just miss her. And I'm confused."

"Confused about what?"

"Everything. What I'm doing here, who I am. I thought I knew. . . . I don't even know how to explain it right." That seemed to be the problem lately. Every thought that passed through my head was sloppy. I couldn't line up anything.

"You know who you are, Mer. Don't let them try to change you." His voice was so sincere, and for a minute I did feel sure. Not because I had any answers, but because I had Aspen. If I ever lost sight of who I really was, I knew he'd be there to guide me back.

"Aspen, can I ask you something?" He nodded. "This is kind of strange, but if being the princess didn't mean I had to marry someone, if it was just a job someone could pick me for, do you think I could do it?"

Aspen's green eyes grew wide for a second, taking in the enormity of that question. To his credit, I could see him considering the possibility.

"Sorry, Mer. I don't. You don't have it in you to be as

calculating as they are." There was an apology in his expression, but I wasn't offended that he thought I couldn't do it. I was a bit surprised at his reasoning though.

"Calculating? How so?"

He sighed. "I'm everywhere, Mer. I hear things. There's a lot of turmoil down South, in the areas with a heavy concentration of lower castes. From what the older guards say, those people never particularly agreed with Gregory Illéa's methods, and there's been unrest down there for a long time. Rumor has it, that was part of why the queen was so attractive to the king. She came from the South, and it appeased them for a while. Not so much anymore it seems."

I thought again about bringing up the diary, but I didn't. "That doesn't explain what you meant by calculating."

He hesitated. "I was in one of the offices the other day, before all the Halloween stuff. They were mentioning rebel sympathizers in the South. I was told to see these letters to the postal wing safely. It was over three hundred letters, America. Three hundred families who were getting knocked down a caste for not reporting things or for helping someone the palace saw as a threat."

I sucked in a breath.

"I know. Can you imagine? What if it was you, and all you knew how to do was play the piano? Suddenly you're supposed to know how to do clerical work, how to find those jobs even? It's a pretty clear message."

I nodded. "Do you . . . Does Maxon know?"

"I think he has to. He's not that far off from running the country himself."

In my heart, I didn't want to believe that he'd *agreed* with this, but it seemed likely he was aware of what was going on. He was expected to fall in line.

Could *I* do that?

"Don't tell anyone, okay? A slip like that could cost me my job," Aspen warned.

"Of course. It's already forgotten."

Aspen smiled at me. "I miss being with you, away from all this. I miss our old problems."

I laughed. "I know what you mean. Sneaking out of my window was so much better than sneaking around a palace."

"And scrounging to find a penny for you was better than having nothing to give you at all." He tapped on the glass jar by my bed, the one that used to hold hundreds of pennies that he'd given me for singing to him in the tree house back home, payment that he thought I deserved. "I had no idea you'd saved them all until the day before you left."

"Of course I did! When you were away, they were all I had to hold on to. Sometimes I used to pour them over my hand on the bed, just to scoop them up again. It was nice to have something you touched." Our eyes met, and everything else felt distant for the moment. It was comforting finding myself in that bubble again, the place that Aspen and I had created for ourselves years ago. "What did you do with all of them?"

I had been so mad at him when I left, I'd given them back. All except for the one that stuck to the bottom of the jar.

He smiled. "They're at home, waiting."

"For what?"

His eyes glittered. "That, I cannot say."

I sighed through my smile. "Fine, keep your secrets. And don't worry about not giving me anything. I'm just happy you're here, that you and I can at least fix things, even if it's not what it used to be."

But clearly, for Aspen, that wasn't enough. He reached down to the bottom of his sleeve and tore off one of his golden buttons. "I literally have nothing else to give you, but you can hold on to this—something I've touched—and think of me anytime. And you can know that I'm thinking of you, too."

As silly as it seemed, I wanted to cry. It was unavoidable, the natural instinct to compare Aspen to Maxon. Even now, when thinking of choosing one or the other felt like something very distant, I measured them side by side.

It seemed very easy for Maxon to give me things—to resurrect a holiday for my sake, to make sure I had the best of everything—because he had the entire world at his disposal. Here Aspen was, giving me precious stolen moments and the tiniest trinket to connect us to each other, and it felt like he'd given me so much more.

I remembered suddenly that Aspen had always been this way. He sacrificed sleep for me, he risked getting caught out after curfew for me, he scrounged together pennies for me. Aspen's generosity was harder to see because it wasn't as grand as Maxon's, but the heart behind what he gave was so much bigger.

I sniffed back the lingering urge to cry. "I don't know how to do this right now. I feel like I don't know how to do anything. I . . . I haven't forgotten you, okay? It's still here."

I put my hand to my chest, partly to show Aspen what I meant and partly to soothe the strange longing there. He understood.

"That's enough for me."

CHAPTER 14

I SURREPTITIOUSLY WATCHED MAXON THE next morning at breakfast. I wondered how much he knew about the people losing their castes in the South. Only once did he glance my way, but he didn't seem to be looking at me so much as at something near me.

Anytime I felt uncomfortable, I'd reach down and touch Aspen's button, which I'd laced on a tiny ribbon and made into a bracelet. He would get me through my time here.

Toward the end of the meal, the king stood and we all turned to him. "As there are so few of you now, I thought it would be nice for us to have tea tomorrow night before the *Report*. Since one of you will be our new daughter-in-law, the queen and I would like to make more opportunities to speak with you, learn your interests and such."

I felt a little nervous. Relating to the queen was one thing, but I wasn't sure how I felt about the king. While the other girls watched him eagerly, I sipped my juice.

"Please come an hour before the *Report* to the lounge on the first floor. If you're not familiar, don't worry. The doors will be open, and there will be some music playing. You'll hear us before you see us," he said with a chuckle. The others giggled lightly in return.

Soon after, girls started making their way to the Women's Room. I sighed. Sometimes that room, huge as it was, made me feel claustrophobic. I usually tried to interact with people or use the time to read. This would be a Celeste day. I was going to park myself in front of the television and zone out.

It was easier said than done. The girls seemed particularly chatty today.

"I wonder what the king wants to know about us," Kriss gabbed.

"We just have to remember everything Silvia taught us about poise," Elise commented.

"I hope my maids have a good dress for tomorrow night. I don't want to have to go through what I did for Halloween. They're so scatterbrained sometimes." Celeste sounded put out.

"I wish the king would grow a beard," Natalie said wistfully. I peeked over my shoulder to see her stroking an imaginary beard on her own chin. "I think he'd look good."

"Yes, I can see that," Kriss said graciously before moving on.

I shook my head and tried to focus on the ridiculous show

in front of me, but no matter how I tried, I couldn't tune out the words of the other girls.

By lunch I was a ball of nerves. What would he want to say to me—the girl from the lowest caste left in the competition? What would he want to discuss with the girl he expected so little from?

King Clarkson was right. I heard the floating melody from the piano long before I found the lounge. The musician was good. Better than me, that was for sure.

I hesitated before walking in. I decided to pause before I spoke, really think about my words. I realized I wanted to prove him wrong. I wanted to prove that reporter wrong, too. Even if I lost, I didn't want to go home a loser. I was surprised by how much this suddenly meant to me.

I stepped through the doorway, and the first thing I saw was Maxon standing along the back wall of the room talking to Gavril Fadaye. Gavril was sipping wine as opposed to tea, and he'd suddenly lost Maxon's attention. I saw Maxon's eyes rake over me, and I could have sworn his lips made the shape of a *Wow*.

I turned my head and blushed, walking away. I took the risk of glancing at him again and saw that he was watching me move. It was hard to think rationally when he looked at me that way.

King Clarkson was talking to Natalie in one corner, and Queen Amberly was with Celeste in another. Elise was sipping her tea, and Kriss was walking around the room. I watched as she passed Maxon and Gavril, giving Gavril a warm smile. She said something, which they both chuckled at, and kept walking, peeking over her shoulder at Maxon once as she did so.

After that she made her way to me. "You're late," she jokingly scolded.

"I was feeling a little nervous."

"Oh, it's nothing to worry about. It was actually kind of fun."

"You're already done?" If the king was finished speaking with at least two girls, I'd have less time to compose myself than I thought.

"Yes. Sit with me. We can have some tea while you wait."

Kriss pulled me over to a table, and a maid approached us immediately, setting tea, milk, and sugar in front of us.

"What did he ask you?" I pressed.

"Actually, it was very conversational. I don't think he's trying to get any information exactly, more like he's trying to get a feeling for our personalities. I made him laugh once!" she gushed. "It went really well. And you're naturally funny, so if you just talk like you would to anyone else, you'll be fine."

I nodded before picking up my tea. She made it sound all right. Maybe the king had to compartmentalize himself. When it came to dealing with threats to the country, he had to be decisive, cold. He had to act quickly and deliberately. This was just tea with a bunch of girls. There was no need for him to be that way with us.

The queen had moved away from Celeste and was now speaking softly to Natalie. The look on Natalie's face was adoring. For a while I'd been irritated by her dreamy disposition; but she was simple, and it was refreshing.

I sipped my tea again. King Clarkson drifted over to Celeste, and she gave him a seductive smile. It was a little disturbing. Where were her boundaries?

Kriss leaned over to touch my dress. "That fabric is amazing. With your hair, you look like a sunset."

"Thank you," I said, blinking my eyes. The light had caught on her necklace, an explosion of silver on her throat, and it blinded me for a moment. "My maids are very talented."

"Absolutely. I like mine, but if I become princess, I'm stealing yours!"

She laughed, maybe meaning her words as a joke, maybe not. Either way, something about my maids hemming her clothes bothered me. I forced a smile though.

"What's so funny?" Maxon asked, walking over.

"Just girl talk," Kriss said flirtatiously. She was really on tonight. "I was trying to calm America. She's nervous about speaking to your father."

Thank you for that, Kriss.

"You don't have a thing to worry about. Be natural. You already look fantastic." Maxon gave me an easy smile. He was clearly trying to open up our lines of communication again.

"That's what I said!" Kriss exclaimed. They shared a quick

look, and there was this feeling of them being on a team. It was strange.

"Well, I'll leave you to your girl talk. Good-bye for now." Maxon gave us both a short bow and went over to join his mother.

Kriss sighed and watched Maxon go. "He's really something." She gave me a quick smile and went to talk to Gavril.

I watched the elaborate dance of the room, couples coming together to speak, separating to find new partners. I was even happy to have Elise join me in my corner, though she didn't say much.

"Oh, ladies, the time has gotten away from us," the king called. "We need to make our way downstairs."

I looked up at the clock, and he was right. We had about ten minutes to get down to the set and prepare ourselves.

It didn't seem to matter how I felt about being a princess, or how I felt about Maxon, or how I felt about anything. The king clearly thought I was so unlikely a candidate that he didn't even want to bother speaking with me. I was excluded, perhaps on purpose, and no one even noticed.

I held it together through the *Report*. I even made it through dismissing my maids. But once I was alone, I broke down.

I wasn't sure how I'd explain myself when Maxon came knocking, but that ended up not mattering. He never showed. And I couldn't help but wonder whose company he was enjoying instead.

CHAPTER 15

MY MAIDS WERE GIFTS. THEY didn't ask about the puffy eyes or the tear-stained pillows. They merely helped me pull myself together. I allowed myself to be pampered, grateful for the attention. They were wonderful to me. Would they be this nice to Kriss if she managed to win and took them away?

I watched them as I debated, and I was surprised to notice a tension among them. Mary seemed mostly fine, maybe a little worried. But Anne and Lucy looked like they were deliberately avoiding eye contact with each other and not speaking unless they absolutely had to.

I couldn't begin to guess at what was happening, and I didn't know if it was my place to ask. They never intruded on my sadness or anger. I supposed it was only right that I do the same for them.

I tried not to let the silence bother me as they did my hair and dressed me for a long day in the Women's Room. I ached to put on one of the luxurious pants that Maxon had given me for Saturday use, but this seemed like a bad time for that. If I was heading down, I wanted to be a lady about it. Points to me for effort.

As I settled in for another day of tea and books, the others chatted about the night before. Well, all of them except for Celeste, who had more gossip magazines waiting to be read. I wondered if the one in her hands said anything about me.

I was debating trying to take it when Silvia came in with a thick pile of paper in her arms. Great. More work.

"Good morning, ladies!" Silvia crooned. "I know you usually wait for guests on Saturdays, but today the queen and I have a special assignment for you."

"Yes," the queen said, walking over to us. "I know this is short notice, but we have visitors coming next week. They will be touring the country and stopping by the palace to meet all of you."

"As you know, the queen is usually in charge of receiving such important guests. You all saw how she graciously hosted our friends from Swendway." Silvia gestured over to Queen Amberly, who smiled demurely.

"However, the visitors we have coming from the German Federation and Italy are even more important than the Swendish royal family. And we thought this visit would be an excellent exercise for you all, especially since we've been so focused on diplomacy lately. You will work in teams to prepare a reception for your respective guests, including a meal, entertainment, and gifts," Silvia explained.

I gulped as she continued.

"It is very important for us to maintain the relationships we have as well as to forge new ones with other countries. We have outlines of proper etiquette for interacting with these guests, as well as guides for what's typically frowned on when hosting events for them. However, the actual execution is in your hands."

"We wanted to make it as fair as possible," the queen said. "I think we've done a good job of putting you all on the same field. Celeste, Natalie, and Elise, you will be organizing one reception. Kriss and America, you will take care of the other. And since you have one less person, you will have one more day. Our visitors from the German Federation will be coming on Wednesday, and we'll be receiving guests from Italy on Thursday."

There was a short moment of silence as we took that in.

"You mean we have four days?" Celeste screeched.

"Yes," Silvia said. "But a queen has to do this work alone and sometimes on far less notice."

The panic was palpable.

"Can we have our papers, please?" Kriss asked, holding out her hand. Instinctively, I put mine out as well. Within seconds we were devouring the pages.

"This is going to be tough," Kriss said. "Even with the extra day."

"Don't worry," I assured her. "We're going to win."

She laughed nervously. "How can you be so sure?"

"Because," I said decisively, "there's no way I'm letting Celeste do better than me."

It took two hours to read through the packet and one more to digest everything it said. There were so many different things to consider, so many details to plan. Silvia claimed she would be at our disposal, but I had a feeling asking for help would make her think we couldn't do a good enough job on our own, so that was out.

The setup was going to be challenging. We weren't allowed to use red flowers because they were associated with secrecy. We weren't allowed to use yellow flowers because they were associated with jealousy. And we weren't allowed to use purple *anything* because that color was associated with bad luck.

The wine, food, everything had to be opulent. Luxury wasn't seen as showing off; it was meant to make a statement about the palace. If it wasn't good enough, our guests might leave unimpressed and completely unwilling to meet with us again. On top of all that, the regular things we were supposed to have learned—speaking clearly, proper table manners, and the like—had to be adapted to a culture of which neither Kriss nor I had any knowledge besides what was printed in our packets.

It was incredibly intimidating.

Kriss and I spent the day taking notes and brainstorming while the others did the same thing at a nearby table. As the afternoon wore on, our groups started complaining back and forth about who had the worse situation, and after a while it was actually kind of funny.

"You two at least get another day to work," Elise said.

"But Illéa and the German Federation are already allies. The Italians might hate everything we do!" Kriss worried.

"Do you know we're supposed to wear dark colors for ours?" Celeste complained. "It's going to be a very . . . rigid event."

"We probably don't want it to be floppy anyway," Natalie said, doing a little shimmy. She laughed at her own joke, and I smiled before moving on.

"Well, ours is supposed to be superfestive. And you all have to wear your best jewelry," I instructed. "You need to make a great first impression, and appearances are very important."

"Thank goodness I'll get to look good at one of these stupid things." Celeste sighed, shaking her head.

In the end, it was clear we were all struggling. After everything that had happened with Marlee and then being somewhat dismissed by the king, I felt strangely comforted to know we were miserable together. But it would be a lie to say that paranoia didn't take over before the end of the day. I was convinced that one of the other girls—Celeste in particular—might try to sabotage our reception.

"How loyal are your maids?" I asked Kriss at dinner.

"Very. Why?"

"I wonder whether we should store some things in our

rooms instead of in the parlor. You know, so the other girls don't try to take our ideas." It was only a tiny lie.

She nodded. "That's a good idea. Especially since we go second, and it would look like we copied them."

"Exactly."

"You're so smart, America. It's no wonder Maxon liked you so much." And she went back to eating.

I didn't miss her casual use of the past tense. Maybe while I'd been worrying about being good enough to be a princess and feeling completely unsure I wanted to be one at the same time, Maxon was forgetting all about me.

I convinced myself that she was just trying to make herself feel more confident about her standing with Maxon. Besides, it had only been a few days since Marlee was caned. How much could she possibly know?

The piercing scream of a siren jerked me from my sleep. The sound was so foreign, I couldn't even begin to process what it was. All I knew was that my heart was pounding in my chest from the sudden rush of adrenaline.

Before a second had passed, the door to my room flew open and a guard ran in.

"Damn it, damn it, damn it," he repeated.

"Huh?" I said groggily as he raced over to me.

"Get up, Mer!" he urged, and I did as he said. "Where are your damn shoes?"

Shoes. So I was going somewhere. Only then did the sound make sense to me. Maxon had told me once before that there was an alarm for when the rebels came, but it had been thoroughly dismantled in a recent attack. It finally must have been repaired.

"Here," I said, finding and slipping my feet into them. "I need my robe." I pointed to the end of the bed, and Aspen grabbed it, trying to open it for me. "Don't bother, I'll carry it."

"You need to hurry," he said. "I don't know how close they are."

I nodded, heading for the door, Aspen's hand on my back. Before I hit the hallway, he jerked me toward him. I found myself in a deep, rough kiss. Aspen's hand was behind my head, holding my lips to his for one long moment. Then, as if he forgot the danger, his other hand pulled my waist to his, and the kiss deepened. It had been a long time since he'd kissed me this way—between my fickle heart and the fear of being caught, there was no reason to. But I could feel an urgency tonight. Something might go wrong, and this could be our last kiss.

He wanted to make it count.

We stepped apart, barely taking a second to look at each other one more time. He put his hand around my arm and pushed me out the door. "Go. Now."

I dashed for the secret passage hidden at the end of the hall. Before I pushed the wall, I looked behind me and caught sight of Aspen's back as he ran around the corner.

There was nothing I could do but run myself, so I did. As quickly as I could manage, I made my way down the steep, dark stairs to the safe room reserved for the royal family.

Maxon had told me once that there were two kinds of rebels: Northern and Southern. The Northern ones were pesky, but the Southern ones were deadly. I hoped whatever I was running from was more interested in disturbing us than in killing.

As I descended the stairs, the cold set in. I wanted to throw on my robe, but I worried I might trip. I felt steadier as the light of the safe room came into view. I leaped from the last step, and I could see a figure standing out among the shapes of the guards. Maxon. Though it was late, he was still in his suit pants and his shirt, slightly rumpled but presentable.

"Am I the last?" I asked, pulling on my robe as I approached.

"No," he answered. "Kriss is still out there. So is Elise."

I looked behind me at the darkened corridor that seemed to go on forever. In either direction, I could make out the skeletons of three or four stairways stemming from their secret origins in the palace above. They were empty.

If anything Maxon had told me was true, his feelings for Kriss and Elise were limited. But there was no mistaking the concern for them in his eyes. He rubbed his temple and craned his neck, as if that would really help in the dark. We looked past each other, watching the stairs as guards milled around the door, clearly anxious to close it.

Suddenly he sighed and put his hands on his hips. Then, with no warning at all, he embraced me. I couldn't help but clutch him to my chest.

"I know you're still probably upset, and that's fine. But I'm happy you're safe."

Maxon hadn't touched me since Halloween. It hadn't even been a week, but for some reason, it felt like an eternity. Maybe because so much had happened that night, and even more had happened since.

"I'm glad you're safe, too."

He held me tighter. Suddenly he gasped. "Elise."

I turned to see her thin figure coming down the stairs. Where was Kriss?

"You should go inside," Maxon gently urged. "Silvia is waiting."

"We'll talk soon."

He gave me a small, hopeful smile and nodded. I headed into the room, with Elise following right behind. As she walked in, I saw she was crying. I put an arm around her shoulder, and she did the same to me, happy to have the company.

"Where were you?" I asked.

"I think my maid is sick. She was a little slow to help me. And then I was so frightened by the alarm, I got confused for a moment and couldn't remember where to go. I pushed on four different walls before I found the right one." Elise shook her head at her forgetfulness.

"Don't worry," I said, hugging her. "You're safe now."

She nodded her head to herself, trying to slow her breathing. Of the five of us, she was easily the most delicate.

As we went deeper, I saw the king and queen sitting close together, both of them in robes and slippers. The king had a small stack of papers on his lap, as if he was going to use the time down here to work. The queen had a maid massaging one of her hands, and they both wore serious expressions.

"What, no company this time?" Silvia joked, drawing our attention to her.

"They weren't with me," I said, suddenly worried about the safety of my maids.

She smiled gently. "I'm sure they're fine. This way."

We followed her to a row of cots set up against an uneven wall. The last time I was in this place, it was clear that the people who maintained the room weren't prepared for the chaos of all the Selected girls down here. They'd made progress since then, but it wasn't completely up-to-date. There were six beds.

Celeste was curled up on the one closest to the king and queen, though we were still quite a ways from them. Natalie had settled in next to her and was braiding thin pieces of her own hair.

"I expect you to sleep. You all have a serious week ahead of you, and I can't have you planning if you're deliriously tired." Silvia went away, probably to look for Kriss.

Elise and I both sighed. I couldn't believe they were going to make us go through with the whole reception thing. Wasn't this stressful enough? We let go of each other and made our way to neighboring cots. Elise was quick to tuck herself into the blankets, obviously worn out.

"Elise?" I said quietly. She peeked up at me. "If you need anything, let me know, okay?"

She smiled. "Thank you."

"Sure thing."

She rolled back over, and it looked like she was asleep within seconds. I knew it was true when she didn't turn over at the bustle of noise coming from the door. I glanced back and saw Maxon carrying Kriss into the safe room, with Silvia close by. Immediately after she was through, the door was sealed shut.

"I tripped," she explained to Silvia, who was fretting over her. "I don't think I broke my ankle, but it really hurts."

"There are bandages in the back. We can at least wrap it," Maxon instructed. Silvia walked away quickly, passing us as she went hunting for bandages.

"Sleep! Now!" she ordered.

I sighed, and I wasn't the only one. Natalie took it in stride, but Celeste seemed very irritated. I checked myself then. If my behavior was anything like hers, it needed to change. Though I didn't want to, I crawled into my cot and faced the wall.

I tried not to think about Aspen fighting upstairs, or my maids maybe not making it to their hiding place fast enough. I tried not to worry about the upcoming week, or the possibility of the rebels being Southern and trying to slaughter people above us as we rested.

But I did think about all of that. And it was so exhausting, I eventually found sleep on my cold, hard cot.

I didn't know what time it was when I woke up, but it must have been hours since we'd come to the safe room. I rolled over, looking at Elise. She was sleeping peacefully. The king was reading his papers, whipping them through his hands so quickly, he appeared to be mad at them. The queen's head rested on the back of her chair. She looked even more beautiful when she slept.

Natalie was still asleep, or at least she looked that way. But Celeste was awake, propped up on one arm and looking across the room. Her eyes held a fire that she usually reserved for me. I followed her gaze over to the opposite wall, where she was watching Kriss and Maxon.

They sat side by side, his arm wrapped around her shoulder. Kriss had her legs curled to her chest, looking as if she was trying to keep warm, even though she was wearing a robe. Her left ankle was wrapped in gauze and didn't appear to be bothering her at the moment. They spoke quietly with smiles on their faces.

I didn't want to watch, so I rolled back over.

By the time Silvia tapped me on my shoulder to wake me, Maxon was already gone. So was Kriss.

CHAPTER 16

As I emerged from the stairwell that had ushered me to safety the night before, it was all too apparent that the Southerners had been here. In the short hallway that led to my room, there was a pile of debris that I had to climb over to get to my door.

Typically, the worst of the mess was gone by the time we were released from the safe room. This time, however, it looked like there had been too much for the staff to get to, and we would have been down there all day. Still, I wished they'd tried a little harder. I spied a group of maids working to scrub away giant letters on a far wall.

WE'RE COMING

The line was repeated down the hall, sometimes written in mud, other times in paint; and one appeared to be done in blood. Chills ran through me, and I wondered what that meant.

As I stood there, my maids dashed up to me. "Miss, are you all right?" Anne asked.

I was startled by their sudden appearance. "Um, yes. Fine." I looked back to the words on the wall.

"Come away, miss. We'll get you ready," Mary insisted.

I followed obediently, slightly stunned from everything I saw and too confused to do anything else. They worked deliberately, the way they did when they tried to soothe me with the routine of getting dressed. Something about their steady hands—even Lucy's—was calming.

By the time I was ready, a maid came to escort me outside, where we would apparently be working this morning. The smashed glass and chilling graffiti were easy to forget about in the Angeles sun. Even Maxon and the king were standing at a table with advisers, reviewing piles of documents and making decisions.

Under a tent, the queen read over papers, pointing out details to a nearby maid. Near her, Elise, Celeste, and Natalie sat at a table discussing plans for their reception. They were so engrossed, it looked like they'd completely forgotten the rough night.

Kriss and I sat on the opposite side of the lawn, under a similar tent, but our work was going slowly. I was having a hard time talking to her as I fought to get the image of her sharing a moment with Maxon out of my head. I watched as she underlined sections in the papers Silvia gave us and scribbled notes in the margin.

"I think I might have figured out how to do our flowers," she commented without looking up.

"Oh. Good."

I let my eyes wander over to Maxon. He was trying to look busier than he was. Anyone really watching could see how the king pretended not to hear his comments. I didn't understand that. If the king was worried about Maxon being a good leader, the thing to do was to truly instruct him, not keep him from doing anything because he worried his son would make a mistake.

Maxon shuffled some papers and looked up. He caught my eye and waved. As I went to raise my hand, I saw Kriss enthusiastically wave back from the corner of my eye. I focused on the papers again, fighting a blush.

"Isn't he handsome?" Kriss asked.

"Sure."

"I keep imagining how children would look with his hair and my eyes."

"How's your ankle?"

"Oh," she said with a sigh. "It hurts a little, but Doctor Ashlar says I'll be fine by the reception."

"That's good," I said, finally looking up at her. "Wouldn't want you hobbling around when the Italians come." I was trying to sound friendly, but I could tell she was questioning my tone.

She opened her mouth to speak but then quickly looked

away. I followed her gaze and saw that Maxon was heading over to the refreshment table the butlers had set up for us.

"I'll be right back," she said quickly, and limped toward Maxon faster than I would have thought possible.

I couldn't help but watch. Celeste had walked over, too, and they were all talking quietly as they poured water or grabbed finger sandwiches. Celeste said something, and Maxon laughed. It looked like Kriss was smiling, but she was clearly too bothered by Celeste interrupting her time to be genuinely amused.

I was almost grateful for Celeste at that moment. She might have been a hundred things that irritated me, but she was also impossible to intimidate. I could use some of that.

The king bellowed something to one of his advisers, and my head snapped in his direction. I missed exactly what he'd said, but he sounded irritated. Over his shoulder, I caught a glimpse of Aspen, walking his rounds.

He looked my way briefly, risking a fast wink. I knew that was meant to ease my worries, and it did a little. Still, I couldn't help but wonder what he went through last night that led to the slight limp in his step and the bandaged gash by his eye.

As I was debating whether there was a way to inconspicuously ask him to come see me tonight, a call rang out from just inside the palace doors.

"Rebels!" a guard yelled. "Run!"

"What?" another guard called back, confused.

"Rebels! Inside the palace! They're coming!"

The guard's words made the threat on the walls this morning flash through my mind: WE'RE COMING.

Things started moving very quickly. The maids ushered the queen toward the far side of the palace, some pulling her hands to make her move faster while others dutifully raced behind her, blocking her from an attack.

Celeste's red dress blazed as she followed the queen, rightly assuming that was probably the safest way to go. Maxon scooped up Kriss and her injured foot, turning to place her in the arms of the nearest guard, who happened to be Aspen.

"Run!" he screamed at Aspen. "Run!"

Aspen, faithful to a fault, bolted, carrying Kriss like she weighed nothing at all.

"Maxon, no!" she cried over Aspen's shoulder.

I heard a loud pop from inside the opened doors to the palace and screamed. As several of the guards reached under their dark uniforms and pulled out guns, I understood what that sound was. Two more pops came, and I found myself frozen, watching the flurry of bodies move around me. The guards pushed people to the sides of the palace, urging them to move out of the way as a swarm of people in rugged pants and sturdy jackets raced outside, running with backpacks or satchels packed to the brim. Another shot came.

Finally realizing that I needed to move, I turned and ran without thinking.

With the rebels flooding out of the palace, the logical thing to do seemed to be to run away from them. But that put me heading toward the great forest with a pack of vicious people chasing me. I ran and slipped a few times in the flats I was wearing, and I considered taking them off. In the end, I decided slippery shoes were better than none.

"America," Maxon called. "No! Come back!"

I risked peeking back and saw the king grabbing Maxon by the neck of his suit jacket, pulling him away. I could see the terror in Maxon's eyes as he stared after me. Another shot was fired.

"Stand down!" Maxon shrieked. "You'll hit her! Cease fire!"

There were some more shots, and Maxon continued to scream his orders until I was too far away to make them out. I ran through the open field and realized then that I was alone in this. Maxon was being held back by his father, and Aspen was doing his duty. Any guard coming for me would be behind the rebels. All I could do was run for my life.

Fear made me fast, and I was surprised by how well I avoided the undergrowth once I hit the woods. The ground was dry, parched from months with no rain, and it was solid. I vaguely felt my legs getting scratched, but I didn't slow down to see how bad it was.

I was sweating, and my dress was sticking to my chest as I moved. It was cooler in the woods, and steadily getting darker, but I was hot. At home I sometimes ran for fun, to play with Gerad or just to feel the ache of exertion. But I'd been sitting in the palace for months, eating real food for the first time, and I could feel it now. My lungs burned, and my legs were throbbing. Still, I ran.

After I got far enough in the woods, I looked over my shoulder to check how close the rebels were. I couldn't hear them with the blood pounding in my ears, and when I checked, I couldn't see them either. I decided this was my best chance to hide, before they caught sight of the bright dress in the dim woods.

I didn't stop until I saw a tree that looked wide enough to conceal me. Once I was behind it, I noticed that there was a branch low enough to grab and climb, too. I took off my shoes, tossing them away, hoping they wouldn't lead the rebels right to me. I climbed, though not very high, and turned my back to the tree, making myself as small as I could.

I focused hard on slowing my breath, fearing the sound would give me away. But even after I did that, for a moment it was quiet. I figured I'd lost them. I didn't move, waiting to be sure. Seconds later, I heard a loud rustling.

"We should have come at night," someone—a girl—huffed. I flattened myself against the tree, praying nothing would snap.

"They wouldn't have been outside at night," a man replied.

They were still running, or trying to, and it sounded like they were having a rough go of it.

"Let me carry some," he offered. It sounded like they were getting very close.

"I can do it."

I held my breath and watched as they passed right under my tree. Just when I thought I might be safe, the girl's bag ripped, and a pile of books fell to the forest floor. What was she doing with so many books?

"Damn it," she cursed, getting down on her knees. She was wearing a denim jacket with some kind of flower embroidered on it over and over again. She had to be burning in that.

"Told you to let me help."

"Shut up!" The girl pushed at the boy's legs. In that playful gesture, I could see how much affection there was between them.

In the distance, someone whistled.

"Is that Jeremy?" she asked.

"Sounds like him." He bent and picked up a few books.

"Go get him. I'll be right behind you."

He looked unsure but agreed, kissing her forehead before jogging off.

The girl gathered the rest of her books, using a knife to cut the strap off her bag and bind them together.

I felt a sense of relief as she rose, assuming she would start moving. But she flipped her hair back out of her face, raising her eyes to the sky.

And she saw me.

No amount of quiet or stillness would help me now. If I screamed, would the guards come? Or were the rest of the rebels too close for that to matter?

We stared at each other. I waited for her to call the others, hoping that whatever they had planned for me wasn't too painful.

But she didn't make a sound except to let out a single quiet laugh, amused at our situation.

Another whistle sounded, slightly different from the last, and we both glanced in the direction it came from before looking at each other again.

And then, in the least expected of all possible gestures, she swung one leg behind the other, lowering herself in a graceful curtsy. I looked on, completely stunned. She rose, smiling, and ran off toward the whistle. I watched her back as a hundred tiny sewn flowers disappeared into the brush.

When it felt like more than an hour had passed, I decided I could get down. I stood at the foot of the tree, realizing I didn't know where my shoes were. I walked around the base of the trunk, trying to locate the little white slippers to no avail. Giving up, I decided I should make my way back to the palace.

Looking around, it became clear that that wasn't going to happen. I was lost.

CHAPTER 17

I SAT AT THE BASE of the tree, legs folded up to my chest, waiting. Mom always said that was what we were supposed to do when we were lost. It gave me time to think about what had happened.

How was it possible that rebels had gotten into the palace two days in a row? *Two days in a row!* Had things gotten so much worse on the outside since the Selection had begun? Based on what I'd seen back in Carolina and had experienced at the palace, this was unprecedented.

My legs had a bunch of scratches on them, and now that I wasn't hiding, I could finally feel the sting. There was also a small bruise halfway up my thigh that I wasn't sure how I'd acquired. I was thirsty; and as I settled down, I felt worn-out from the emotional, mental, and physical strain of the day. I let my head rest against the tree, closing my eyes. I didn't intend to fall asleep. But I did.

Sometime later, I heard the distinct sound of footsteps. My eyes flashed open, and the forest was darker than I remembered. How long had I been asleep?

My first instinct was to climb back up the tree, and I ran around to the other side, stepping on the torn remnants of the rebel girl's bag. But then I heard people calling my name.

"Lady America!" someone said. "Where are you?"

"Lady America?" another voice called. Then, after a while, in a loud voice, a command came. "Be sure to look everywhere. If they've killed her, they might have hung her or tried to bury her. Pay attention."

"Yes, sir," men chorused back.

I peeked around the tree, focusing on the sound. I squinted, trying to make out the figures moving through the shadows, unsure they could really be here to save me. But one guard, his slight limp not slowing him at all, made me finally sure that I was safe.

A small patch of fading sunlight fell across Aspen's face, and I ran. "I'm here!" I yelled. "I'm over here!"

I ran straight into Aspen's arms, for once not caring about who saw. "Thank goodness," he breathed into my hair. Then, turning toward the other figures, "I've got her! She's alive!"

Aspen bent down and picked me up, cradling me. "I was terrified we were going to find your body somewhere. Are you hurt?"

"My legs a little."

A second later, several guards were surrounding us, congratulating Aspen on a job well done.

"Lady America," the one in charge said, "are you injured at all?"

I shook my head. "Just some scratches on my legs."

"Did they try to hurt you?"

"No. They never caught up to me."

He looked a bit shocked. "None of the other girls could have outrun them, I don't think."

I smiled, finally at ease. "None of the other girls is a Five."

Several of the guards chuckled, Aspen included.

"Good point. Let's get you back." He went in front of us and called out to the other guards, "Be on the lookout. They could still be lingering in the area."

As we moved, Aspen talked to me quietly. "I know you're fast and smart, but I was terrified."

"I lied to the officer," I whispered.

"What do you mean?"

"They did catch up with me, eventually."

Aspen looked at me in horror.

"They didn't do anything, but this one girl saw me. She curtsied and ran off."

"Curtsied?"

"I was surprised, too. She didn't look angry or threatening at all. In fact, she just looked like a normal girl."

I thought over Maxon's comparison of the two rebel groups and knew this girl must be a Northerner. There was absolutely no aggression in her, only a drive to do her task.

And there was no doubt that the attack last night was from the Southern rebels. Did that mean something, that the attacks weren't only back-to-back, but by different groups? Were the Northerners watching us, waiting for us to be this drained? Thinking about them spying on the palace so intently was a little frightening.

At the same time, the attack was almost funny. Did they simply walk in the front doors? How many hours were they in the palace collecting their treasures? Which reminded me.

"She had books, lots of them," I said.

Aspen nodded. "That seems to happen a lot. No clue what they're doing with them. My guess is kindling. I think it's cold where they stay."

"Hmm," I replied, not really answering. If I needed kindling, I could think of much easier places to get it than the palace. And the way the girl was so desperate to gather up the books made me sure it was something more than that.

It took nearly an hour of slow, steady trekking to get back to the palace. Even though he was injured, Aspen never let his hold on me slip. In fact, he looked to be enjoying the walk despite the extra labor. I liked it, too.

"The next few days might be busy for me, but I'll try to come see you soon," Aspen whispered as we crossed the wide, grassy lawn leading up to the palace.

"Okay," I answered quietly.

He smiled a little as he looked forward, and I joined him, taking in the view. The palace was glittering in the evening sun, with windows lit up on every story. I'd never seen it like this. It was beautiful.

For some reason I thought Maxon would be there, waiting by the back doors for me. He wasn't. No one was. Aspen was instructed to take me to the hospital wing so Dr. Ashlar could tend to my legs while another guard went off to tell the royal family I'd been found alive.

My homecoming was a nonevent. I was alone in a hospital bed with bandaged legs, and that was how I stayed until I fell asleep.

I heard someone sneeze.

I opened my eyes, confused for a second before remembering where I was. I blinked, looking around the room.

"I didn't mean to wake you," Maxon said in hushed tones. "You should go back to sleep." He was propped up in a chair by my bed, so close he could rest his head by my elbow if he wanted to.

"What time is it?" I rubbed my eyes.

"Almost two."

"In the morning?"

Maxon nodded. He watched me carefully, and I was suddenly very worried about how I looked. I had washed my face and pulled my hair up when I came back, but I was pretty sure I had a pillow imprinted on my cheek.

"Don't you ever sleep?" I asked.

"I do. I'm just on edge a lot."

"Occupational hazard?" I sat up a bit more.

He gave me a thin smile. "Something like that."

There was a long pause as we sat there, unsure of what to say next.

"I thought of something today, when I was in the woods," I said casually.

He smiled a bit more at how easily I brushed off the incident. "Oh, really?"

"It was about you."

He inched closer, his brown eyes focused on mine. "Do tell."

"Well," I started, "I was thinking about how you were last night when Elise and Kriss weren't in the hall, how worried you were. And then today I saw you try to run after me when the rebels came."

"I tried. I'm so sorry." He shook his head, ashamed that he hadn't done more.

"I'm not upset," I explained. "That's the thing. When I was out there alone, I thought about how worried you probably were, how worried you are about the others. And I can't pretend to know how you feel about all of us, but I know that you and I aren't exactly a highlight right now."

He chuckled. "We've seen better days."

"But you still ran after me. You handed Kriss off to a guard because she couldn't run. You're trying to keep us all safe. So why would you ever hurt one of us?"

He sat silently, not sure where I was going.

"I understand now. If you're that concerned with our safety, you couldn't have wanted to do that to Marlee. I'm sure you would have stopped it if you could."

He sighed. "In a heartbeat."

"I know."

Tentatively, Maxon reached across the bed for my hand. I let him take it. "Do you remember how I said I had something I wanted to show you?"

"Yes."

"Don't forget, okay? It's coming. This position requires a lot of things, and they aren't always pleasant. But sometimes . . . sometimes you can do great things."

I didn't understand what he meant, but I nodded.

"I suppose it will have to wait until you're done with this project though. You're a bit behind."

"Ugh!" I pulled my hand from Maxon's to cover my eyes. I'd completely forgotten about the reception. I looked back at him. "Are they still going to make us do that? There've been two rebel attacks, and I spent the majority of my day lost in the woods. We're going to mess it up."

Maxon's face was sympathetic. "You'll have to push through."

I let my head flop back on the pillow. "It's going to be a disaster."

He chuckled. "Don't worry. Even if you don't do as well as the others, I don't have it in me to kick you out."

Something in that sounded funny. I sat back up. "Are you saying that if the others do worse, one of *them* could be kicked out?"

Maxon hesitated a moment, clearly unsure how to respond.

"Maxon?"

He sighed. "I have about two weeks before they expect another cut. This is supposed to be a big part of it. You and Kriss have the harder setup. A new relationship, fewer people to do the work; and while the culture is very celebratory, the Italians are easy to offend. Add to that the fact that you've hardly been able to do any work at all . . ."

I wondered if the blood was visibly draining from my face.

"I'm not supposed to help, but if you need something, please say so. I can't send either of you home."

When we'd had our first fight, a stupid spat over Celeste, I thought a piece of me shattered for Maxon. And then when Marlee left so abruptly, I thought it did again. I was sure that every time something blocked my way, bits of my heart were crumbling to nothing. But I was wrong.

There, lying in the hospital wing, my heart broke for the first time over Maxon Schreave. And the ache was unthinkable. Up until then I could convince myself that I'd imagined everything I'd seen between him and Kriss, but now I knew for sure.

He liked her. Maybe as much as he liked me.

I nodded at his offer for help, unable to say anything else.

I told myself to tug my heart back, that he couldn't have it. Maxon and I started all this as friends, and maybe that's all we were meant to be: close friends. But I was crushed.

"I should go," he said. "You need sleep. You had a very long day."

I rolled my eyes. That wasn't the half of it.

Maxon stood and straightened his suit. "I wanted to say so

much more to you. I really thought I'd lost you today."

I shrugged. "I'm fine. Really."

"I can see that now, but there were several hours today when I was forced to brace myself for the worst." He paused, measuring his words. "Usually, of all the girls, you're the easiest to talk to about what we are. But I have a feeling that perhaps that's not the wisest thing to do right now."

Ducking my head, I gave a slight nod. I couldn't try to talk about my feelings for a person who obviously had a crush on someone else.

"Look at me, America," he asked gently.

I did.

"I'm fine with that. I can wait. I just want you to know . . . I'm not able to find words big enough to express how relieved I am that you're here, in one piece. I've never been so grateful for anything."

I was stunned into silence, the way I always was when he touched the shy places of my heart. A corner of myself worried at how easily I trusted his words.

"Goodnight, America."

CHAPTER 18

IT WAS MONDAY NIGHT. OR Tuesday morning. It was so late, it was hard to tell.

Kriss and I had worked all day finding appropriate swaths of fabric, having butlers hang them, choosing our clothes and jewelry, picking china, creating a rough draft of the menu, and listening to a language coach speak lines in Italian to us in the hope that some of it would stick. At least I had the advantage of knowing Spanish, which helped me pick it up faster; they were so similar. Kriss was just doing all she could to keep up.

I ought to have been exhausted, but all I could think about were Maxon's words.

What had happened with Kriss? Why was she all of the sudden so close to him? Should I even care this much?

But this was Maxon.

And try as I might to pull away, I still cared about him. I wasn't ready to give up completely.

There had to be a way to figure this out. As I debated everything that was happening, attempting to separate my issues from one another, it looked like all the pieces fell into one of four categories.

My feelings about Maxon. Maxon's feelings about me. Whatever was going on between Aspen and me. And my feelings about actually becoming a princess.

Of all the things swimming in my head right now, it actually felt like the princess thing might be the easiest to tackle. At least in that area, I had something the other girls didn't. I had Gregory.

I went over to my piano stool, drew out his diary, and hoped with all my heart that he would have some wisdom for me. He hadn't been born into royalty; he must have had to adjust. Based on what he'd said in his Halloween entry, he was already preparing for a big change in his future.

I pulled up the covers, protecting the words from the world, and dove in.

I WANT TO EMBODY THE OLD-FASHIONED AMERICAN IDEAL. I HAVE A BEAUTIFUL FAMILY, AND I'M VERY WEALTHY; AND BOTH OF THOSE THINGS SUIT THIS IMAGE BECAUSE THEY WEREN'T HANDED TO ME. ANYONE WHO SEES ME NOW KNOWS HOW HARD I WORKED FOR WHAT I HAVE.

BUT THE FACT THAT I'VE BEEN ABLE TO USE MY

POSITION, TO GIVE SO MUCH WHERE OTHERS EITHER
HAVE NOT OR COULD NOT, HAS CHANGED ME FROM SOME
FACELESS BILLIONAIRE INTO A PHILANTHROPIST. STILL,
I CANNOT REST ON THIS. I NEED TO DO MORE, TO BE
MORE. WALLIS IS IN CHARGE, NOT ME, AND I NEED TO
FIGURE OUT HOW TO PROPERLY GIVE THE PUBLIC WHAT
THEY NEED WITHOUT BEING SEEN AS A USURPER. A TIME
MAY COME WHEN I WILL LEAD AND CAN DO WHAT I SEE
FIT. FOR NOW I WILL PLAY BY THE RULES AND GO AS
FAR AS I CAN WITH THAT.

I tried to glean some actual wisdom from his words. He said to use your position. He said to play by the rules. He said not to be afraid.

Maybe that should have been enough, but it wasn't. It didn't even feel close to helpful. Since Gregory failed me, there was only one other man I could count on. I went over to my desk, pulled out a pen and paper, and scribbled a brief letter to my father.

CHAPTER 19

THE NEXT DAY FLEW BY, and suddenly Kriss and I were arriving at the other girls' reception in conservative gray dresses.

"What's the plan?" Kriss asked as we walked down the hall.

I considered for a moment. I disliked Celeste and wouldn't mind seeing her fail, but I wasn't sure I wanted her to do it on this grand a scale. "Be polite, but not helpful. Watch Silvia and the queen for cues. Absorb everything we can . . . and work all night to make ours better."

"All right." She sighed. "Let's go."

We were on time, as was crucial to the culture, and the girls were already a mess. It was like Celeste was sabotaging herself. Where Elise and Natalie were in respectable deep blues, Celeste's dress was practically white. Put a veil on her, and this was a wedding. Not to mention how revealing it was, especially when she stood next to any of the German women. Most of them were wearing sleeves to their wrists despite the warm weather.

Natalie had been put in charge of the flowers and missed the detail that lilies were traditionally used at funerals. All the flower arrangements had to be removed hastily.

Elise, though clearly more agitated than she usually was, appeared to be the image of calm. To our guests, she would look like the star.

It was intimidating, trying so hard to communicate with the women from the German Federation—who spoke very broken English—particularly when I had so much Italian in my brain. I tried to be hospitable; and despite their severe appearance, the ladies were actually quite friendly.

It became clear pretty quickly that the true threat of disaster was Silvia and her clipboard. While the queen graciously aided the girls in hosting the German guests, Silvia walked the perimeter of the room, her sharp eyes missing nothing. It seemed she had pages of notes before the event had ended. Kriss and I quickly realized that our only hope was to have Silvia fall in love with our reception.

The next morning, Kriss came to my room with her maids, and we got ready together. We wanted to make an effort to look similar enough so it was clear we were in charge but not so much alike we looked silly. It was kind of fun having so many girls in my room. The maids all knew one another, and they talked animatedly behind us as they worked. It reminded me of how things had felt when May was here.

Hours before our guests were supposed to arrive, Kriss and I made our way to the parlor to double-check everything one last time. Unlike the other reception, we were forgoing place cards and letting our guests sit wherever they liked. The band came to practice in the space, and as a lucky bonus, it seemed our choice of fabrics to cover the bland walls made for great acoustics.

I straightened Kriss's necklace as we quizzed each other on the conversational phrases one last time. She sounded very natural speaking Italian.

"Thank you," she said.

"*Grazie*," I answered.

"No, no," she replied, facing me. "I mean thank you. You did an amazing job on this, and . . . I don't know. I thought that after Marlee, you might give up. I was afraid that I'd be doing this alone, but you've worked so hard. You've done great."

"Thanks. You have, too. I don't know if I would have survived if I had to work with Celeste. You made it almost easy." Kriss smiled. I meant it, too. She was tireless. "And you're right; it's been hard without Marlee, but I wouldn't quit. This is going to be great."

Kriss bit her lip and considered for a moment. Quickly, as if she might lose her nerve, she spoke. "So you're still competing then? You still want Maxon?"

It wasn't like I didn't know what we were all doing here, but none of the other girls had spoken about it like that. I was caught off guard for a moment, wondering if I should answer her. And, if I did, what would I say?

"Girls!" Silvia trilled, rushing in through the doorway. I'd never been so grateful to see that woman. "It's nearly time. Are you ready?"

Behind her, the queen came in, a soothing calm to balance Silvia's energy. She studied the room, admiring our work. It was a huge relief to see her smile.

"Almost ready," Kriss said. "We just have a few details to take care of. One we specifically need you and the queen for."

"Oh?" Silvia said curiously.

The queen approached us then, her dark eyes warm with pride. "It's beautiful. And you both look stunning."

"Thank you," we chorused. The pale-blue dresses with large gold accents had been my idea. Festive and lovely, but not too over the top.

"Well, you might notice our necklaces," Kriss said. "We thought that if they were similar, it would help people identify us as hosts."

"Excellent idea," Silvia said, scribbling on her clipboard.

Kriss and I smiled at each other. "Since you are both hosts here, too, we thought you should have ones as well," I said as Kriss pulled the boxes off the table.

"You didn't!" The queen gasped.

"For . . . for me?" Silvia asked.

"Of course," Kriss said sweetly, handing over the jewelry.

"You've both been so helpful. This is your project, too," I added.

I could see how touched the queen was by our gesture, but Silvia was completely speechless. I suddenly wondered if anyone at the palace ever gave her any kind of attention. Yes, we'd thought up the idea yesterday as a way to get Silvia on our side, but I was glad we'd done it for more than just that now.

Silvia might be overwhelming, but she did try to do all this instruction for our benefit. I vowed to do a better job of thanking her.

A butler told us our guests were arriving, and Kriss and I stood on either side of the double doors to welcome people as they came. The band started playing softly in the background, maids began circulating with hors d'oeuvres, and we were ready.

Elise, Celeste, and Natalie were walking toward us, surprisingly on time. Once they caught sight of our setup— the billowing fabric covering the drab walls, the sparkling centerpieces towering on our tables, the overflowing flowers— there was a clear ache in the eyes of Elise and Celeste. Natalie, however, was too excited to be bothered.

"It smells like the gardens," she said with a sigh, practically dancing into the room.

"A bit too much like it," Celeste added. "You're going to give people a headache." Leave it to her to find fault with something beautiful.

"Try to sit at different tables," Kriss suggested as they poured past. "The Italians are here to make friends."

Celeste sucked her teeth, acting as if this was putting her

out. I wanted to tell her to pull it together: We had been on our best behavior for her reception. But then I heard the warm buzzing conversation of the Italian women as they came down the hall and forgot all about her.

The best way to describe the Italian ladies was statuesque. They were tall, golden skinned, and absolutely beautiful. As if that wasn't enough, they were all so good-natured. It was like they carried the sun inside their souls and let it shine out on everything around them.

The Italian monarchy was even younger than Illéa's. They had been closed off to our attempts at friendship for decades, according to the packet I'd read, and this was the only time they'd ever reached out to us. This meeting was the first step toward a closer relationship with a growing government. It had been frightening to think about until the moment they walked through the doorway, and their kindness melted my worries. They kissed Kriss and me on both cheeks and yelled *"Salve!"* I happily tried to match their level of enthusiasm.

I botched some of my Italian phrases, but our visitors were gracious, laughing off my mistakes and helping to correct me. Their English was impressive, and we doted on one another's hairstyles and dresses. It seemed we'd made a good first impression appearance-wise, and that helped me relax.

I ended up settling in for most of the party next to Orabella and Noemi, two of the princess's cousins.

"This is delicious!" Orabella cried, raising her glass of wine.

"We're glad you like it," I replied, worrying that I was

coming across as too shy. They were so loud when they talked.

"You must have some!" she insisted. I hadn't had anything to drink since Halloween, and I wasn't very fond of alcohol in the first place. I didn't want to be rude, though, so I took the glass she handed me and sipped.

It was incredible. Champagne was all bubbles; but the deep, red wine had several flavors overlapping, each coming to the forefront in its own time.

"Mmmm." I sighed.

"Now, now," Noemi said, drawing my attention to her. "This Maxon, he is handsome. How can I get into the Selection?"

"A heap of paperwork," I joked.

"That's all? Where's my pen?"

Orabella cut in. "I will take some of this paper, too. I would love to take Maxon home with me."

I laughed. "Trust me, it's a bit of a mess in here."

"You need more wine," Noemi insisted.

"Absolutely!" Orabella seconded, and they called over a butler to refill my glass.

"Have you ever been to Italy?" Noemi asked.

I shook my head. "Before the Selection, I'd never even left my province."

"You must come!" Orabella insisted. "You can stay with me anytime."

"You always hog the company," Noemi complained. "She stays with me."

I felt the wine warming me all over, and their excitement was making me almost too happy.

"So, is he a good kisser?" Noemi asked.

I choked a little on the sip I was taking, pulling the glass away to laugh. I was trying not to give too much away, but they knew.

"How good?" Orabella demanded. When I didn't answer, she waved her hand. "Have some more wine!" she exclaimed.

I pointed an accusing finger at them, realizing what they were doing. "You two are nothing but trouble!"

They threw back their heads laughing, and I couldn't help but join them. Admittedly, girl talk was much more tempting when we weren't all competing for the same boy, but I couldn't get too drawn into this.

I stood to leave before I ended up passed out under the table. "He's very romantic. When he wants to be," I said. They clapped and laughed as I walked away, smiling at how playful they were.

After I got some water and food in me, I played some of the folk songs I'd learned on my violin, and most of the room sang along. Out of the corner of my eye, I spotted Silvia taking notes and tapping her foot to the beat at the same time.

When Kriss got up and proposed a toast to the queen and Silvia for their help, the room applauded them. When I raised my glass to our guests, they shrieked with delight, downing their glasses and then throwing them against the walls. Kriss and I weren't expecting that and shrugged before tossing ours as well.

The poor maids scuttled around to clean the shattered pieces as the band started up again and the whole room began to dance. Perhaps the highlight was Natalie on top of the table, doing some kind of dance that made her look like an octopus.

Queen Amberly sat in a corner, speaking jovially with the Italian queen. I felt a rush of accomplishment at the sight and was so engrossed, I nearly jumped when Elise addressed me.

"Yours is better," she said reluctantly but genuinely. "You two really pulled together an incredible reception."

"Thanks. I was worried for a while—we got off to such a bad start."

"I know. That makes it even more impressive. It looks like you two have been working for weeks." She looked around the room, staring longingly at the bright decor.

I put a hand on her shoulder. "You know, Elise, anyone could see yesterday that you worked the hardest on your team. I'm sure Silvia will make sure Maxon knows that."

"You think?"

"Of course. And I promise, if this is some sort of a competition and you lose, I'll tell Maxon myself what a good job you did."

She squinted her already thin eyes. "You would do that?"

"Sure. Why not?" I said with a smile.

Elise shook her head. "I really admire you for how you

are. Honest, I guess. But you need to realize we're competing, America." My smile disappeared. "I wouldn't lie and say anything bad about you, but I wouldn't go out of my way to tell Maxon you did something good. I can't."

"It doesn't have to be that way," I said quietly.

She shook her head. "Yes, it does. This isn't just some prize. This is a husband, a crown, a future. And you probably have the most to gain or lose by it."

I stood there, completely stunned. I thought we were friends. Except for Celeste, I really trusted these girls. Was I too blind to see how hard they were fighting?

"That doesn't mean I don't like you," she went on. "I like you a lot. But I can't cheer for you to win."

I nodded, still taking in her words. It was obvious I wasn't as mentally in this as she was. One more thing that made me doubt my ability to do this job.

Elise smiled over my shoulder, and I turned to see the Italian princess coming toward us.

"Pardon me. Can I have the hostess, please?" she asked in her lovely accent.

Elise gave her a curtsy before heading back to the dancing. I tried to shake off that conversation and focus on the person I was meant to impress.

"Princess Nicoletta, I'm sorry we haven't gotten to speak much today," I said, giving her a curtsy myself.

"Oh, no! You've been very busy. My cousins, they love you!"

I laughed. "They're very funny."

Nicoletta pulled me into a corner of the room. "We've been hesitant to make bonds with Illéa. Our people are much . . . freer than yours."

"I can see that."

"No, no," she said seriously. "I mean, in *personal* freedoms. They enjoy more than you. You have the castes still, yes?"

Suddenly understanding that this was more than a friendly conversation, I nodded.

"We watch, of course. We see what happens here. The riots, the rebels. It seems people are not happy?"

I wasn't sure what to say. "Your Majesty, I don't know if I'm the best person to talk to about this. I don't really control anything."

Nicoletta took my hands. "But you could."

A shiver ran through me. Was she saying what I thought?

"We saw what happened to the girl. The blonde?" she whispered.

"Marlee." I nodded. "She was my best friend."

She smiled. "And we saw you. There's not much footage, but we saw you run. We saw you fight."

The look in her eyes mirrored the way Queen Amberly had looked at me this morning. There was unmistakable pride there.

"We are very much interested in forming a bond with a powerful nation, if that nation can change. Unofficially, if there is anything we can do to help you acquire the crown, let us know. You have our full support."

She crammed a piece of paper into my hand and walked

away. As she turned her back, she shouted out something in Italian, and the room roared with delight. I didn't have pockets, so I quickly shoved the note in my bra, praying that no one would notice.

Our reception went on much longer than the first, and I suspected it was because our guests were too happy to actually leave. Still, for as lengthy as it was, the whole thing passed in a blur.

Hours later, I headed back to my room completely worn out. I was much too full to even think about dinner, and though it was early in the evening, the idea of going straight to bed was very appealing.

Before I could even look at my bed, however, Anne walked up to me with a surprise. I gasped and took the letter from her hand immediately. I had to give the postal workers at the palace credit; they were very fast.

I tore open the envelope and went to the balcony, soaking up my father's words and the last few rays of sunshine at the same time.

DEAR AMERICA,

YOU'LL NEED TO WRITE A LETTER TO MAY SOON. WHEN SHE SAW THIS WAS INTENDED FOR MY EYES ONLY, SHE WAS VERY DISAPPOINTED. I HAVE TO SAY, I WAS A LITTLE CAUGHT OFF GUARD MYSELF. I DON'T KNOW WHAT I WAS EXPECTING, BUT CERTAINLY NOT WHAT YOU ASKED.

FIRST, IT'S TRUE. WHEN WE CAME TO VISIT, I SPOKE WITH MAXON, AND HE WAS VERY CLEAR ABOUT HIS INTENTIONS TOWARD

YOU. I DON'T THINK HE HAS IT IN HIM TO BE LESS THAN GENUINE, AND I BELIEVED (AND STILL DO) THAT HE CARES ABOUT YOU VERY MUCH. I THINK IF THE WHOLE PROCESS WAS SIMPLER, HE'D HAVE CHOSEN YOU ALREADY. PART OF ME THINKS THE SLOWNESS IS ON YOUR SIDE. AM I WRONG?

THE SIMPLE ANSWER IS YES. I APPROVE OF MAXON, AND IF YOU WANT TO BE WITH HIM, I SUPPORT THAT. IF YOU DON'T, I SUPPORT THAT, TOO. I LOVE YOU, AND I WANT YOU TO BE HAPPY. MAYBE THAT MEANS YOU LIVE IN OUR SCRUBBY LITTLE HOUSE INSTEAD OF A PALACE. I'M FINE WITH THAT.

AS FOR YOUR OTHER QUESTION, I HAVE TO SAY YES TO THAT, TOO.

AMERICA, I KNOW YOU DON'T SEE MUCH IN YOURSELF, BUT YOU NEED TO START. WE TOLD YOU FOR YEARS YOU WERE TALENTED, BUT YOU DIDN'T BELIEVE IT UNTIL YOUR BOOKINGS WENT UP. I REMEMBER THE DAY YOU SAW THE FULL WEEK AND KNEW IT WAS BECAUSE OF YOUR VOICE AND THE WAY YOU PLAY, AND YOU WERE SO PROUD. IT WAS LIKE YOU WERE SUDDENLY AWARE OF EVERYTHING YOU COULD DO. AND WE'VE SAID FOR AS LONG AS I CAN REMEMBER THAT YOU ARE BEAUTIFUL, BUT I'M NOT SURE YOU EVER TRULY SAW YOURSELF THAT WAY UNTIL YOU WERE PICKED FOR THE SELECTION.

YOU HAVE IT IN YOU TO LEAD, AMERICA. YOU HAVE A GOOD HEAD ON YOUR SHOULDERS; YOU ARE WILLING TO LEARN; AND, PERHAPS MOST IMPORTANTLY, YOU SHOW COMPASSION. THAT IS SOMETHING PEOPLE IN THIS COUNTRY YEARN FOR MORE THAN YOU KNOW.

IF YOU WANT THE CROWN, AMERICA, TAKE IT. TAKE IT. BECAUSE IT SHOULD BE YOURS.

AND YET . . . IF YOU DON'T WANT THAT BURDEN, I COULD
NEVER BLAME YOU. I WOULD WELCOME YOU HOME WITH OPEN ARMS.
I LOVE YOU.
DAD

The tears spilled out quietly. He genuinely thought I could
do it. He was the only one. Well, he and Nicoletta.

Nicoletta!

I'd forgotten completely about the note. I fished inside my
dress and pulled it out. It was a telephone number. She didn't
even put her name on it.

I couldn't imagine how much she was risking to make
that offer.

I held the tiny piece of paper and the letter from my dad in
my hands. I thought of Aspen's certainty that I couldn't be a
princess. I remembered the last-place spot in the public poll.
I thought of Maxon's cryptic promise earlier this week. . . .

I closed my eyes and tried to search within myself.

Could I really do this? Could I be the next princess of
Illéa?

CHAPTER 20

THE DAY AFTER THE ITALIAN reception we gathered in the Women's Room after breakfast. The queen was absent, and none of us knew what that meant.

"I bet she's helping Silvia write up the final report," Elise guessed.

"I don't think she's supposed to have much of a say," Kriss countered.

"Maybe she's hung over," Natalie offered as she pressed her fingers to her temples.

"Just because you are doesn't mean she is," Celeste spat.

"She might not be feeling well," I said. "She tends to get sick a lot."

Kriss nodded. "I wonder why that is."

"Didn't she grow up in the South?" Elise asked. "I hear the air and water aren't very clean down there. Maybe it's because of how she was raised."

"I hear everything is bad below Sumner," Celeste added.

"She's probably just resting," I interjected. "There's a *Report* tonight, and she simply wants to be ready. She's smart. It's barely ten, and I need a nap."

"Yeah, we should all take naps," Natalie said wearily.

A maid entered with a small platter and walked quietly across the room, almost too nimble to be noticed.

"Wait," Kriss said. "You don't think they'll talk about the reception stuff on the *Report*, do you?"

Celeste groaned. "I hated that stupid thing. You and America lucked out."

"You're joking, right? Do you have any . . ."

Kriss's words dropped off as the maid stopped just to my left, revealing a small, folded note on the platter.

I felt everyone's eyes on me as I tentatively picked up the letter and read it.

"Is that from Maxon?" Kriss asked, trying not to seem as interested as she was.

"Yes." I didn't look up.

"What's it say?" she probed.

"That he needs to see me for a moment."

Celeste laughed. "Sounds like you're in trouble."

I sighed and stood to follow the maid from the room. "Guess there's only one way to find out."

"Maybe he's finally kicking her out," Celeste whispered loudly enough for me to hear.

"You think?" Natalie asked a little too excitedly.

A chill went through me. Maybe he *was* kicking me out! If he wanted to talk to me or spend time with me, wouldn't he have said it differently?

Maxon was waiting in the hallway, and I walked up timidly. He didn't look upset, but he did seem tense.

I braced myself. "So?"

He took my arm. "We have fifteen minutes. What I'm about to show you, you can't share with anyone. Do you understand?"

I nodded.

"All right then."

We darted up the stairs, all the way to the third floor. Gently but quickly, Maxon pulled me down the hallway to a set of white double doors. "Fifteen minutes," he reminded.

"Fifteen minutes."

He took a key out of his pocket and unlocked one of the doors, holding it open so I could go in before him. The room was wide and bright, with lots of windows and two doors opening onto a balcony along the wall. There was a bed, a massive armoire, and a table with chairs; but other than that the room was empty. No paintings on the walls, no pieces on the inlaid shelves. Even the paint was a little drab.

"This is the princess's suite," Maxon said quietly.

My eyes widened.

"I know it's not much to look at right now. The princess is supposed to choose the decor, so once my mother moved to the queen's suite, the room was stripped."

Queen Amberly had slept here. Something about the room felt magical.

Maxon came up behind me and started pointing. "Those doors go to the balcony. And over there"—he pointed to the other end of the room—"those doors go to the princess's personal study. Right here"—he noted a door to our right—"this goes to my room. Can't have the princess too far off."

I felt myself blush thinking of sleeping here with Maxon so close.

He stepped toward the armoire. "And this? Behind this piece of furniture is the escape to the safe room. You can get to other places in the palace this way, too, but that's its main purpose." He sighed. "This is a slight misuse, but I thought it would be worth it."

Maxon placed his hand on a hidden latch, and the armoire and the panel of wall behind it swung forward. I saw him smile at the space behind it. "Right on time."

"I wouldn't miss it," another voice said.

I sucked in a breath. There was no way that voice belonged to who I thought it did. I stepped to see around the hulking piece of furniture and Maxon's smiling face. There, dressed in very plain clothes and with her hair pulled into a bun, was Marlee.

"Marlee?" I whispered, sure I had to be dreaming. "What are you doing here?"

"I've missed you so much!" she cried, and ran to me with her arms open. With her hands out, I could see clearly the red, healing welts on her palms. It really was Marlee.

She wrapped me in a hug, and we crumpled to the ground, I was so overcome. I couldn't stop from crying and asking over and over what in the world she was doing here.

When I quieted down long enough, Maxon got my attention. "Ten minutes. I'll be waiting outside. Marlee, you can leave the way you came."

She gave him her word, and Maxon left us alone.

"I don't understand," I said. "You were supposed to go south. You were supposed to be an Eight. Where's Carter?"

She smiled through my misunderstanding. "We've been here the whole time. I just started working in the kitchens; and Carter's still on the mend, but I think he'll be in the stables soon."

"On the mend?" So many questions were racing through my mind, I wasn't sure why that one popped out.

"Yes, he walks and can sit and stand, but it's hard for him to do anything too strenuous. He's helping in the kitchens until he's fully healed. He's going to be fine though. And look at me," she said, holding out both hands. "We've been very well taken care of. They aren't pretty, but at least they don't hurt anymore."

I carefully touched the swollen lines on her palms, sure they couldn't actually be painless. But she didn't flinch, and after a moment I slid my hand into hers. It felt funny, but at the same time completely natural. Marlee was here. And I was holding her hand.

"So Maxon's had you in the palace the whole time?"

She nodded. "After the caning, he was afraid we would be hurt if we were left on our own, so he kept us here. Two other servants, a brother and sister who had family in Panama, were sent instead. We're going by new names, and Carter is growing out his beard, so after a while we'll blend in. Not a lot of people know we're in the palace in the first place, just a few of the cooks I work with, one of the nurses, and Maxon. I don't even think the guards know because they have to answer to the king, and he wouldn't be pleased to find out."

She shook her head before quickly moving on. "Our little apartment is small, basically just enough room for our bed and some shelves; but at least it's clean. I'm trying to sew us a new bedspread, but I'm not—"

"Hold on. *Our* bed? As in, you share one?"

She smiled. "We got married two days ago. I told Maxon the morning we were caned that I loved Carter and that he was the one I wanted to marry, and I apologized for hurting him. He didn't care, of course. He came to me two days ago saying there was some big event happening and that if we wanted to get married, this was the time."

I counted back. Two days ago was when the German Federation had come. The entire palace staff was either helping serve them or preparing for the ladies from Italy.

"Maxon gave me away. I'm not sure I'll ever see my parents again. The more distance they have from me, the better."

I could tell she was pained to say so, but I understood why. If it had been me and I was suddenly an Eight, the kindest thing I could do for my family was disappear. It would take time, but people would forget. Eventually, my parents would recover.

To push away her sad thoughts, she fanned out her left hand, and I noticed the little band across her finger for the first time. It was twine tied in a simple knot, but it was a clear statement: I'm taken.

"I think I'm going to have to get him to give me a new one soon; I'm already fraying this one. I guess if he works in the stables, I'll have to make him a new ring every day." She playfully shrugged. "Not that I mind."

My mind had jumped to another question that I worried might be rude to ask, but I knew I would never be able to have this kind of conversation with my mom or Kenna. "So, have you . . . you know?"

It took her a moment to understand, but then she laughed. "Oh! Yes, we have."

We both giggled. "How is it?"

"Honestly? A little uncomfortable at first. The second time was better."

"Oh." I didn't know what else to say.

"Yeah."

There was a bit of a pause.

"I've been really lonely without you. I miss you." I played with the little piece of twine on her finger.

"I miss you, too. Maybe once you're the princess, I can sneak up here all the time."

I snorted. "I'm not so sure that'll happen."

"What do you mean?" she asked, her face turning serious.

"You're still his favorite, right?"

I shrugged.

"What happened?" The question was laced with concern, and I didn't want to admit that it had started with losing her. It wasn't her fault.

"Just things."

"America, what's going on?"

I sighed. "After you got caned, I was upset with Maxon. It took me a while to realize that he wouldn't have done something like that if he could have stopped it."

Marlee nodded. "He tried so hard, America. And when he couldn't, he did everything he could to make the situation better. So don't be mad at him."

"I'm not anymore, but I'm also not sure I want to be the princess. I don't know if I could do what he did. And then there was this poll in a magazine Celeste showed me. The people don't like me, Marlee. I'm at the bottom.

"I'm not sure I have what it takes. I was never a good choice, and it seems like I'm plummeting. And now . . . now . . . I think Maxon wants Kriss."

"Kriss? When did that happen?"

"I have no idea, and I don't know what to do. Part of me thinks it's a good thing. She'd make a better princess; and if he really likes her, I want him to be happy. And he's supposed to do another elimination really soon. When he called me out today, I thought I might be going home."

Marlee laughed. "You're so ridiculous. If Maxon didn't have feelings for you, he'd have sent you home a long time ago. The reason you're still here is because he refuses to lose hope."

Something between a choke and a laugh came out of my mouth.

"I wish we could talk more, but I should go," she said. "We're taking advantage of guards changing to do this."

"I don't care that it's short. I'm just glad to know you're okay."

She pulled me in for a hug. "Don't give up yet, all right?"

"I won't. Maybe you could send me a letter or something sometime?"

"That might work. We'll see." She let me go, and we stood together. "If they polled me, I would have voted for you. I've always thought it should be you."

I blushed. "Go on, now. Say hello to your husband for me."

She smiled. "I will." Nimbly, she went over to the armoire and found the latch. For some reason, I thought the caning would break her, but she was stronger now. She even carried herself differently. Marlee turned to blow me a kiss and disappeared.

I quickly exited the room and found that Maxon was waiting in the hallway. At the sound of the door, he looked up from his book, smiling, and I went over to sit by him.

"Why didn't you tell me sooner?"

"I had to make sure they were safe first. My father doesn't know I did this; and until I knew it wouldn't endanger them, I had to keep it to myself. I'm hoping to arrange for you to see her more, but that will take time."

I felt my shoulders lighten, as if the bricks of worry I'd been carrying around were falling off all at once. The happiness at seeing Marlee, the assurance that Maxon was as kind as I thought he was, and the general relief that this meeting wasn't about him sending me home were overwhelming.

"Thank you," I whispered.

"Of course."

I wasn't sure what else to say. After a moment Maxon cleared his throat.

"I know that you are averse to doing the difficult parts of this job, but there are a lot of opportunities here. I think you could do great things. I can tell you see the prince in me now, but that had to come eventually if you were ever going to truly be mine."

My eyes held his. "I know."

"I can't read you anymore. I used to be able to see it in the beginning when you didn't really care for me; and when things changed between us, you looked at me differently. Now there are moments when I think it's there and others when it seems like you're already gone."

I nodded.

"I'm not asking you to say you love me. I'm not asking for you to suddenly decide you want to be a princess. I just need to know if you want to be here at all."

That was the question, wasn't it? I still didn't know if I could do the job, but I wasn't sure I wanted to give up on it. And seeing this kindness in Maxon shifted my heart. There was still so much to consider, but I couldn't give up. Not now.

Maxon's hand was resting on his leg, and I slid mine under his. He gave me a welcoming squeeze. "If you'll still have me, I want to stay."

Maxon let out a relieved sigh. "I'd like that very much."

I returned to the Women's Room after a quick stop in the bathroom. No one said anything until I sat down, and it was Kriss who was bold enough to ask.

"What was that all about?"

I looked not just to her, but to all the watching eyes. "I'd rather not say."

With my puffy face, a response like that was enough to make it seem like nothing good could have come from the meeting; but if that was what I had to say to protect Marlee, then I was fine with it.

What really stung was Celeste pressing her lips together to hide her smile, Natalie's raised eyebrows as she pretended to read her borrowed magazine, and the hopeful glance between Kriss and Elise.

The competition was deeper than I had guessed.

CHAPTER 21

WE WERE SPARED THE HUMILIATION of dealing with the aftermath of our receptions on the *Report*. The visits from our foreign friends were mentioned in passing, but the actual events were kept from the public. It wasn't until the next morning that Silvia and the queen came to speak to us about our performances.

"It was a very daunting task we gave you, and it absolutely could have gone horribly wrong. I'm pleased to say, however, that both teams did very well." Silvia looked at each of us appraisingly.

We all sighed, and I reached for Kriss's hand as she did the same. As confused as I was about her and Maxon, I knew there was no way I could have made it through that without her.

"If I'm honest, one event was slightly better than the other, but you should all be proud of your accomplishments. We received thank-you letters from our longtime friends in the German Federation for your gracious hosting," Silvia said, looking at Celeste, Natalie, and Elise. "There were a few minor hiccups, and I don't think any of us truly enjoy such serious affairs, but they certainly did.

"And as for you two," Silvia turned toward Kriss and me. "The ladies from Italy enjoyed themselves immensely. They were quite impressed with your style, and the food; and they made a special point to ask for the wine you served, so, bravo! I wouldn't be surprised if Illéa gained a wonderful new ally based on that welcome. You're to be commended."

Kriss squeaked, and I let out a nervous laugh, happy enough that it was over, let alone that we'd beat the others.

Silvia went on to talk about how she would be writing up an official report to hand over to the king and Maxon but said that none of us had a thing to worry about. As she spoke, a maid scurried into the room and ran over to the queen, whispering in her ear.

"Absolutely, they may," the queen said, suddenly standing and walking forward.

The maid rushed back and opened the door for the king and Maxon. I knew men weren't supposed to come into this room without the queen's permission, but it was comical to see it in action.

As they entered, we stood to curtsy, but they didn't seem to care about formalities.

"Dear ladies, we are sorry to intrude, but we have urgent news," the king informed us.

"I'm afraid we've had a development with the war in New Asia," Maxon said firmly. "The situation is so dire that Father and I are leaving this very moment to see if we can do any good."

"What's wrong?" the queen asked, clutching her chest.

"It's nothing to worry about, my love," the king said confidently. But that couldn't be a completely honest statement if they had to rush out of here so suddenly.

Maxon walked over to his mother. They had a brief, whispered conversation before she kissed his forehead. He hugged her and stepped away. The king then began rattling off a list of instructions to the queen while Maxon came to say good-bye to each of us.

His good-bye to Natalie was so short it almost didn't happen. Natalie didn't seem too bothered, and I didn't know what to make of that. Was she actually not worried by Maxon's lack of affection, or was she so bothered that she was forcing herself to be calm?

Celeste draped herself across Maxon and exploded into the worst display of fake crying that I'd ever seen. It reminded me of May when she was younger, thinking tears would magically bring money for us to have what we wanted. When he went to untangle himself, she planted a kiss on his lips that he promptly—and in as polite a manner as possible—wiped away after his back was turned.

Elise and Kriss were so close that I heard his good-byes to them.

"Call ahead and tell them to go easy on us," he said to Elise. I'd almost forgotten that the main reason she was still here was that she had family ties to leaders in New Asia. I wondered if this war going downhill would cost her her spot.

Then I suddenly realized that I had no clue what Illéa stood to lose if we lost this war.

"If you get me a phone, I will talk to my parents," she promised.

Maxon nodded and kissed Elise's hand, then walked over to Kriss.

She immediately laced her fingers in his.

"Will you be in danger?" she asked quietly, her voice beginning to shake.

"I don't know. During our last trip to New Asia, the situation wasn't nearly so tense. I can't be sure this time." His voice was so tender, I felt they should have been having this conversation in private. Kriss lifted her gaze to the ceiling and sighed, and in that quick second Maxon looked over to me. I averted my eyes.

"Please be careful," she whispered. A tear fell onto her cheek.

"Of course, my dear." Maxon gave her a silly little salute, which made her laugh a bit. He then kissed her cheek and put his lips to her ear. "Please try to keep my mother entertained. She worries."

He pulled back to look into her eyes, and Kriss nodded once and let his hands go. The second they were no longer touching, a tremor went through her body. Maxon's hands twitched for a second, like he was going to embrace her, but then he stepped away and started to walk toward me.

As if Maxon's words of last week weren't enough, here was physical proof of their relationship. By the look of it, they had something very sweet and real. One glimpse of Kriss with her face in her hands was proof of how much she cared for him. Either that, or she was an incredible actress.

I tried to gauge his expression when he looked at me versus the way he had looked at Kriss. Was it the same? Was there less warmth there?

"Try not to get into any trouble while I'm gone, all right?" he said teasingly.

He didn't joke with Kriss. Did *that* mean something?

I raised my right hand. "I promise to be on my best behavior."

He chuckled. "Excellent. One less thing to worry about."

"What about us? Should we worry?"

Maxon shook his head. "We should be able to smooth over whatever's going on. Father can be very diplomatic and—"

"You are such an idiot sometimes," I said as Maxon's brow furrowed. "I mean about you. Should we worry about you?"

His face was very serious then and did nothing to help my fears.

"Flying in and flying out. If we can make it to the

ground . . ." Maxon swallowed once, and I saw how frightened he was.

I wanted to ask something else, but I didn't know what to say.

He cleared his throat. "America, before I go . . ."

I looked up to Maxon's face and felt the tears rising.

"I need you to know that everything—"

"Maxon," the king barked. Maxon lifted his head and waited for his father's instructions. "We need to go."

Maxon nodded. "Good-bye, America," he said quietly, and lifted my hand to his lips. As he did so, he noted the little homemade bracelet I wore. He studied it, seeming confused, then kissed my hand tenderly.

That little feather of a kiss sent me back to a memory that felt years old. He had kissed my hand like that my first night in the palace when I'd yelled at him, when he'd let me stay anyway.

The other girls' eyes were glued to the king and Maxon as they left, but I was watching the queen. Her entire body seemed weak. How many times would her husband and only child be put in danger before she cracked?

The moment the door shut behind her family, Queen Amberly blinked a few times, inhaled deeply, and pulled herself up to her full height.

"Forgive me, ladies, but this sudden news will require a lot of work from me. I think it's best if I go to my room so I can focus." She was fighting so hard. "How about I have lunch delivered here so you can eat at your leisure, and I will join you all for dinner tonight?"

We nodded. "Excellent," she said, and turned to leave. I knew she was strong. She'd grown up in a poor neighborhood in a poor province, working in a factory until she was chosen for the Selection. Then, once she was queen, she suffered miscarriage after miscarriage before she finally had a child. She would make it to her room looking like a lady, as her position demanded. But she would cry once she was alone.

After the queen left, Celeste went, too. Then I decided I didn't have to stay either. I went to my room, wanting to be alone and to think.

I kept wondering about Kriss. How had she and Maxon suddenly connected? Not too long ago, he was making me promises about our future. He couldn't have been that interested in her if he was saying such intimate things to me. It must have happened after that.

The day passed quickly. After dinner, as my maids quietly helped me prepare for bed, a single sentence lifted me from my reflections.

"Do you know who I found in here this morning, miss?" Anne asked as she gently pulled a brush through my hair.

"Who?"

"Officer Leger."

I froze, but only for a fraction of a second. "Oh?" I said. I kept my eyes on my reflection as they continued.

"Yes," Lucy said. "He said he was doing a sweep of your room. Something about security." She looked a little confused.

"It was strange though," Anne said, echoing Lucy's expression. "He was in his plain clothes, not his uniform. He shouldn't be doing security work on his time off."

"He must be very dedicated," I commented in a disconnected tone.

"I think he is," Lucy said with awe. "Whenever I see him around the palace, he's always noticing things. He's a very good soldier."

"True," Mary said matter-of-factly. "Some of the men who come through here really aren't fit for the job."

"And he looks good in his plain clothes. Most of them look terrible once you get them out of their uniforms," Lucy commented.

Mary giggled and blushed, and even Anne cracked a smile. It had been a long time since they'd seemed so relaxed. On another day, in another moment, it might be fun to gossip about the guards. Not today though. All I could think about was that there was a letter in my room from Aspen. I wanted to peek over my shoulder at my jar, but I didn't dare.

It felt like an eternity before they left me alone. I forced myself to be patient and wait a few minutes to make sure they didn't come back. Finally I darted over to my bed and clutched my jar. Sure enough, a tiny slip of paper was waiting for me.

Maxon is gone. This changes everything.

CHAPTER 22

"HELLO?" I WHISPERED, FOLLOWING THE instructions Aspen had left for me the day before. I cautiously walked into a room lit only by the fading daylight spilling in through the gossamer curtains, but it was enough for me to see the excitement on Aspen's face.

I closed the door behind me, and he immediately ran over and scooped me up.

"I've missed you."

"I missed you, too. I was so busy with that reception, I barely had time to breathe."

"Glad it's over. Did you have a hard time getting here?" he joked.

I giggled. "Seriously, Aspen, you're way too good at your job." It was almost comical how simple his idea was. The queen was a little more relaxed when it came to running the palace. Or maybe she was distracted. Either way, she'd made dinner an option: in your room or downstairs. My maids prepped me for the meal, but instead of heading to the dining room, I walked across the hall to Bariel's old room. It was too easy.

He smiled as he took in my praise and sat me down in the back corner of the room on some pillows he'd already piled there. "Are you comfortable?"

I nodded and expected him to sit too, but he didn't. Instead he pushed over a large couch, which blocked the door from sight, and then pulled in a table that brushed the top of our heads as we sat on the floor. Finally he grabbed a bundle he'd left on top of the table—it smelled like food—and settled next to me.

"Almost like home, huh?" He moved behind me so I was between his legs. The position was so familiar and the space was so small that it did feel a little like our old tree house. It was like he'd taken a piece of something I thought was gone forever and placed it neatly in my hands.

"It's even better." I sighed, leaning into him. After a minute I felt his fingers combing down my hair. It gave me shivers.

For a while we sat there in silence, and I closed my eyes and focused on the sound of Aspen's breathing. Not so long ago, I'd done the same thing with Maxon. But this was different. If I had to, I thought I could pick Aspen's breathing out of a crowd. I knew him so well. And, clearly, he knew me. This tiny bit of peace was everything I'd been aching for, and Aspen made it real.

"What are you thinking about, Mer?"

"Lots of things." I sighed. "Home, you, Maxon, the Selection, everything."

"What are you thinking about all of that?"

"Mostly how confused I get about them. Like how I'll think I understand what's happening to me, and then something shifts, and my feelings change."

Aspen was quiet for a moment, and his voice sounded pained when he asked, "Do your feelings about me change a lot?"

"No!" I said, pushing myself closer to him. "If anything, you're the one constant. I know that if everything turns upside down, you'll still be here, in the exact same place. Everything gets so crazy that my love for you gets pushed to the background, but I know it's always there. Does that make sense?"

"It does. I know I make this whole thing more complicated than it already is. I'm glad to know I'm not completely out of the running though."

Aspen wrapped his arms around me, like he could hold me there forever.

"I haven't forgotten us," I promised.

"Sometimes I feel like Maxon and I are in our own version of the Selection. It's just him and me, and one of us will get you in the end; and I can't decide who's worse off. Maxon doesn't exactly know we're competing, so he might not be able to try as hard. But then, I have to hide, so it's not like I can give you everything he can. It's not really a fair fight either way."

"You shouldn't think about it that way."

"I don't know how else to see it, Mer."

I exhaled. "Let's not talk about that."

"All right. I don't like talking about him anyway. What about all the other stuff you're confused about? What's going on?"

"Do you like being a soldier?" I asked, turning toward him.

He nodded enthusiastically as he reached down and opened the food. "I love it, Mer. I thought I'd hate every minute, but it's fantastic." He popped a chunk of bread into his mouth and kept talking. "I mean, there's the obvious stuff, like I'm always being fed. They want us to be big, so there's plenty of food. And the injections, too," he said, amending his thoughts. "But they're not so bad. And I get an allowance. Even though I have everything I need, I get money."

He stopped for a moment, toying with an orange slice. "I know you know how good it feels to send money home."

I could tell he was thinking about his mom and his six siblings. He had been the father figure at his home; I wondered whether that made him even more homesick than I was.

He cleared his throat and went on. "But there are other things that I wasn't expecting to like, too. I really enjoy the discipline of it and the routine. I like knowing that I'm doing something necessary. I feel so . . . content. I've been restless for years, counting stock or cleaning houses. Now I feel like I'm doing what I was meant to do."

"So that's a big yes? You love it?"

"Completely."

"But you don't like Maxon. And I know you don't like the way Illéa is run. We used to talk about it back home, and then that whole thing with the people in the South losing their castes. I know that bothers you, too."

He nodded. "I think it's cruel."

"Then how are you okay with protecting it? You fight against rebels to keep the king and Maxon safe. They're the ones who make everything happen, and you don't like any of what they do. So how do you love your job?"

He chewed as he thought. "I don't know. I guess it doesn't make sense, but . . . okay, like I said, there's the sense of purpose. And feeling challenged and engaged, the ability to do something more with my life. Maybe Illéa isn't perfect. In fact, it's far from it. But I have . . . I have hope," he said simply.

We were both quiet for a moment while the word washed over us.

"I have this feeling that things have gotten better than they were, though I honestly don't know enough about our history to prove that. And I have this feeling that things will get even better in the future. I think that there are possibilities.

"And maybe this is silly, but it's *my* country. I get that it's broken, but that doesn't mean these anarchists can just come and take it. It's still mine. Does that sound crazy?"

I nibbled my bread and reflected on Aspen's words. They took me back to our tree house and all the times I would ask him questions about things. Even if I disagreed, it helped me understand them better. But I didn't disagree on this point. In fact, it helped me see what was probably hiding in my heart all this time.

"It doesn't sound crazy at all. It sounds completely reasonable."

"Does that help with whatever you've been thinking about?"

"It does."

"Are you going to explain any of it?"

I smiled up at him. "Not yet." Though Aspen was smart, and he might have already guessed. The wistful look in his eyes suggested that he probably had.

He looked away for a moment, running his hand down my arm, finishing by playing with the button bracelet around my wrist. "We're a mess, aren't we?"

"A big one."

"Sometimes I feel like we're a knot, too tangled to be taken apart."

I nodded. "It's true. So much of me is tied up in you. I feel kind of lost without you."

Aspen pulled me close, running a hand over my temple and down my cheek. "We'll just have to stay tangled then."

He kissed me gently, like, if he pushed too hard, the moment might shatter and we'd lose everything. Maybe he was right. Slowly, he lowered me to the mattress of pillows, holding on to me, tracing curves as he kissed me on and on. It was all so familiar, so safe.

I ran my fingers through Aspen's cropped hair, remembering the way it used to fall and tickle my face when he kissed me. I noted his arms around me, so much fuller than they used to be, so much sturdier. Even the way he held me had changed. There was a newfound confidence there, something instilled in him through becoming a Two, becoming a soldier.

Too soon it was time to leave, and Aspen walked me to the door. He gave me a lingering kiss, making me a little light-headed. "I'll try to get another note to you soon," he promised.

"I'll be waiting." I leaned into him, holding on to him for one long moment. Then, to keep us safe, I left.

My maids prepped me for bed, and I went through it in a daze. It used to feel like the Selection was one choice: Maxon or Aspen. And as if that was some decision my heart could make simply, it grew into so many more things. Was I a Five or a Three? When this was over, would I be a Two or a One? Would I live out my days as an officer's wife or a king's? Would I slide quietly into the background in which I'd always been so comfortable or force myself into the spotlight I'd always feared? Could I happily do either? Could I not hate whoever Maxon ended up with if I chose Aspen? Could I not hate whoever Aspen chose if I stayed with Maxon?

As I got into bed and turned out the light, I reminded myself that it was my decision to be here. Aspen may have asked, and my mother may have pushed, but no one forced me to fill out the form for the Selection.

Whatever was coming, I'd just face it. I'd have to.

CHAPTER 23

I CURTSIED TO THE QUEEN as I walked into the dining room, but she didn't notice. I looked over to Elise, who was the only one already there, and she merely shrugged. I sat down as Natalie and Celeste entered and were equally ignored; and finally Kriss arrived, sitting next to me but keeping her eyes on Queen Amberly. The queen seemed to be in her own world, staring at the floor or occasionally glancing at Maxon's and the king's chairs as if something was wrong.

The butlers began serving food, and most of the girls started eating; but Kriss kept watch on the head table.

"Do you know what's going on?" I whispered.

Kriss sighed and turned to me. "Elise called her family to get some insight into what was happening and to have her relatives meet Maxon and the king once they got to New Asia. But Elise's family says they never arrived."

"They never came?"

Kriss nodded. "The weird thing is, the king called when they landed, and he and Maxon both spoke with Queen Amberly. They're fine, and they told her they were in New Asia; but Elise's family kept saying they never showed."

I scrunched my forehead, trying to understand. "What does that all mean?"

"I don't know," she confessed. "They say they're there, so how could they not be? It doesn't make sense."

"Huh," I said, not sure of what else to add. Why would Elise's family not know they were there? What if, maybe, they weren't actually in New Asia? Where could they be?

Kriss leaned closer to me. "There's something else I wanted to talk to you about," she whispered. "Could we go for a walk in the gardens after breakfast?"

"Of course," I answered, eager to hear what she knew.

We both ate quickly. I wasn't sure what she'd found out, but if she wanted to talk outside, there was clearly a need for secrecy. The queen was so distracted, she barely even noticed as we left.

Stepping into the sunlit gardens felt wonderful. "It's been awhile since I've been out here," I said, closing my eyes and lifting my face to the sun.

"You usually come with Maxon, right?"

"Mm-hmm." A second later, I wondered how she knew that. Was it common knowledge?

I cleared my throat. "So, what did you want to talk about?"

She stopped under the shade of a tree and turned to face

me. "I think you and I should talk about Maxon."

"What about him?"

She fidgeted. "Well, I had prepared myself to lose. I think we all had, except for maybe Celeste. It was obvious, America. He wanted you. And then everything with Marlee happened, and it changed."

I wasn't quite sure what to say. "So, are you just telling me you're sorry for moving to the top or something?"

"No!" she said emphatically. "I can see he still cares about you. I'm not blind. I'm only saying, I think you and I might be neck and neck at this point. I like you. I think you're a really great person, and I don't want for things to get ugly, however it turns out."

"So this is . . . ?"

She clasped her hands in front of her, trying to think of the right words. "This is me offering to be completely honest about my relationship with Maxon. And I'm hoping you'll do the same."

I crossed my arms and went for the one question I'd been dying to ask. "When did you two get so close?"

Her eyes got a little dreamy, and she toyed with a piece of her light-brown hair. "I guess right after everything with Marlee. It probably sounds stupid, but I made him a card. That's what I always did back home when my friends were sad. Anyway, he loved it. He said no one had given him a present yet."

What? Oh. Wow. After everything he'd done for me, had I really never done anything for him in return?

"He was so happy, he asked me to sit with him awhile in his room and—"

"You've seen his room?" I asked, shocked.

"Yes, haven't you?"

My silence was all the answer she needed.

"Oh," she said awkwardly. "Well, you're not missing anything. It's dark, and there's a gun rack, and then he has this mess of pictures on the wall. It's nothing special," she promised, waving it away. "Anyway, after that he started visiting me during pretty much every free moment he had." She shook her head. "It happened kind of fast."

I sighed. "He basically told me," I confessed. "He made a little comment about needing us both here."

"So . . ." She bit her lip. "You're pretty sure he still likes you?"

Hadn't she already suspected that? Did she simply need me to confirm it? "Kriss, do you really want to hear all this?"

"Yes! I want to know where I stand. And I'll tell you anything you want to know, too. We aren't running this thing, but that doesn't mean we have to be lost in it."

I walked in a short circle, trying to make sense of everything. I wasn't sure I was brave enough to ask Maxon about Kriss. I could barely talk honestly with him about me. But I kept feeling like I was missing pieces of the truth about where I stood. Maybe this was my only hope of really knowing.

"I'm pretty sure he wants me to stay around for a while. But I think he wants you here, too."

She nodded. "I figured."

"Has he kissed you?" I blurted out.

She smiled bashfully. "No, but I think that he would have if I hadn't asked him not to. In my family, we sort of have this tradition where we don't kiss until we're engaged. Sometimes we have a party when people announce their wedding date, and everyone gets to see the first kiss. I want that for me."

"But he tried to?"

"No, I explained before we got that far. He kisses my hands a lot, though, or sometimes my cheek. I think it's kind of sweet," she gushed.

I nodded, looking at the grass.

"Wait," she said, hesitating. "Did he kiss you?"

Part of me wanted to brag that I was his first kiss ever. That when we kissed, it felt like time stopped.

"Sort of. It's kind of hard to explain," I hedged.

She made a face. "No, it's not. Has he or hasn't he?"

"It's complicated."

"America, if you're not going to be honest, then this is a waste of time. I came here wanting to be open with you. I thought it would benefit us both to be friendly."

I stood there, wringing my hands, trying to think of a way to explain myself. It wasn't that I disliked Kriss. If I went home, I'd want her to win.

"I do want to be friends with you, Kriss. I kind of thought we already were."

"Me, too," she said gently.

"It's just hard for me to share private things. And I appreciate your honesty, but I'm not sure I want to know everything. Even though I asked," I said quickly, seeing the words coming to her lips. "I already knew he had feelings for you. I could see it. I think I need things to be vague for the time being."

She smiled. "I can respect that. Would you do me a favor though?"

"Sure, if I can."

She bit her lip and turned her eyes away for a minute. When she looked back, I could see the hint of tears in her eyes. "If you're certain that he doesn't want me, could you maybe warn me? I don't know how you feel, but I love him. And I'd appreciate being told. If you know for sure anyway."

She loved him. She said it out loud, fearlessly. Kriss loved Maxon.

"If he ever told me for sure, I would tell you."

She nodded. "And maybe we could make another promise? Not to purposely get in each other's way? I don't want to win that way, and I don't think you do either."

"I'm no Celeste," I said with disgust, and she laughed. "I promise to be fair."

"Okay then." She dabbed at her eyes and straightened her dress. I could see it so easily, how elegant she would look with the crown on her head.

"I need to go," I lied. "Thanks for talking to me."

"Thanks for coming. I'm sorry if I was too intrusive."

"It's fine." I stepped away. "I'll see you later."

"Okay."

I turned as quickly as I could without being rude and made my way to the palace. Once inside, I quickened my pace and bolted up the stairs, aching to hide.

I made my way to the second floor and headed toward my room. I noticed a piece of paper on the floor, which was unusual for the typically immaculate palace. It was by the corner leading to my door, so I guessed it might be for me. To be sure, I flipped it over and read.

Another rebel attack this morning, this time in Paloma. Current count is over three hundred dead, at least one hundred more wounded. Again, the main demand appears to be terminating the Selection, calling for an end to the royal line. Please advise on best response.

My body went cold. I scanned both sides of the paper, looking for a date. Another attack this morning? Even if this was a few days old, it was at least the second one. And the demand was *again* ending the Selection. Was this what all the recent attacks had been about? Were they trying to get rid of us? If so, were both the Northern and Southern rebels pursing that end?

I didn't know what to do. I wasn't supposed to have seen this message, so it wasn't like I could talk to anyone. But did the people who were supposed to know already have this information? I decided to put the paper back on the ground. Hopefully, a guard would come around soon and get it to the right place.

For now I would just be optimistic that someone was responding.

CHAPTER 24

I TOOK ALL MY MEALS in my room for the next two days, managing to avoid Kriss until dinner on Wednesday. I thought I wouldn't feel so awkward by then. I was sadly mistaken. We gave each other quiet smiles, but I couldn't bring myself to speak. I almost wished I was across the room sitting between Celeste and Elise. Almost.

Just before dessert was served, Silvia came sprinting in as fast as her heeled shoes could carry her. Her curtsy was particularly brief before she made her way to the queen and whispered something to her.

The queen gasped and ran with Silvia out of the room, leaving us alone.

We'd been taught never to raise our voices, but in the moment we couldn't help ourselves.

"Does anyone know what's going on?" Celeste called, abnormally concerned.

"You don't think they're hurt, do you?" Elise said.

"Oh, no," Kriss breathed, and put her head down on the table.

"It's okay, Kriss. Have some pie," Natalie offered.

I found myself speechless, afraid even to think about what this could mean.

"What if they were captured?" Kriss worried aloud.

"I don't think the New Asians would do that," Elise said, though I could see she was worried. I wasn't sure if her concern was strictly for Maxon's safety or because any aggression on the part of the people she had a connection with would ruin her chances.

"What if their plane went down?" Celeste said quietly.

She looked up, and I was surprised to see genuine fear on her face. It was enough to silence us all.

What if Maxon was dead?

Queen Amberly returned with Silvia in tow, and we all watched her eagerly. To our intense relief, she was beaming.

"Good news, ladies. The king and prince will be home tonight!" she sang.

Natalie clapped as Kriss and I simultaneously fell back into our chairs. I hadn't realized how tense my body was for those few minutes.

Silvia chimed in. "Since they've had such an intense few days, we've decided to forgo any big celebration. Depending on when they leave New Asia, we might not even see them before bedtime."

"Thank you, Silvia," the queen said patiently. Really, who cared? "Forgive me, ladies, but I have some work to do. Please enjoy your desserts and have a lovely night," she said, then turned and flew out the door.

Kriss left seconds later. Maybe she was making a welcome home card.

After that I ate quickly and made my way back upstairs. As I was walking down the hall toward my room, I saw a little flash of blond hair under a white cap and the fluttering black skirt of a maid's uniform running toward the far-side stairs. It was Lucy, and it sounded like she was crying. She seemed so determined to get away unnoticed that I decided not to call out after her. Rounding the corner to my room, I saw that my door was wide-open. Without it to block their voices, Anne and Mary's argument spilled into the hallway, where I overheard everything.

"—why you always have to be so hard on her," Mary complained.

"What was I supposed to tell her? That she can have whatever she wants?" Anne shot back.

"Yes! What would the harm be in simply saying you had faith in her?"

What was going on? Was this why they had all seemed so distant lately?

"She aims too high!" Anne accused. "It would be unkind

of me to give her false hope."

Mary's voice bled with sarcasm. "Oh, and everything you told her was *so* kind. You're just bitter!" she accused.

"What?" Anne lashed back.

"You're bitter. You can't stand that she might be closer to something you want than you are," Mary yelled. "You've always looked down on Lucy because she wasn't raised at the palace as long as you were, and you've been jealous of me because I was born here. Why can't you be happy with who you are instead of stepping on her to make yourself feel better?"

"That's not what I was trying to do!" Anne said, her voice breaking.

The tight sobs were enough to silence Mary. It would have stopped me, too. Anne crying seemed like an impossibility.

"Is it so bad that I want more than this?" she asked, her voice thick with tears. "I understand that my position is an honor, and I'm glad to do my job; but I don't want to do this for the *rest of my life*. I want more. I want a husband. I want . . ." She was finally overcome by her sadness.

My heart broke into a thousand pieces. The only way for Anne to get out of this job was to marry her way out. And it wasn't like a slew of Threes or Fours were going to parade down the palace halls looking for a maid to take as a wife. She really was stuck.

I sighed, steadied myself, and entered the room.

"Lady America," Mary said with a curtsy, and Anne followed. Out of the corner of my eye, I saw her feverishly mopping the tears off her face.

Given her pride, I didn't think acknowledging them was a good thing, so I strode past the both of them to the mirror.

"How are you?" Mary continued.

"Really tired. I think I'll be going to bed right away," I said, focusing on the pins in my hair. "You know what? Why don't you both go relax? I can take care of myself."

"Are you sure, miss?" Anne asked, trying so hard to keep her voice composed.

"Very. I'll see you all tomorrow."

They didn't need any more encouragement than that, and thank goodness. I didn't want them to take care of me right now any more than they probably felt like it. Once I managed to get out of my dress, I lay in bed for a long time thinking of Maxon.

I wasn't even sure exactly what I was thinking about him. It was all slightly vague and unfixed, but I kept flashing back to my overwhelming happiness when I found out he was safe and on his way back. And there was a corner of my mind that wondered if he'd thought about me at all while he was gone.

I tossed for hours, completely unsettled. At about one in the morning, I figured that if I couldn't sleep, I might as well read. I turned on the lamp and pulled out Gregory's diary. I skipped past the fall entries and picked one from February.

SOMETIMES I ALMOST HAVE TO LAUGH AT HOW SIMPLE THIS HAS BEEN. IF THERE WAS EVER A TEXTBOOK WRITTEN ON THE TOPIC OF OVERTHROWING COUNTRIES, I WOULD BE THE STAR OF IT. OR I COULD PROBABLY WRITE IT MYSELF. I'M NOT SURE WHAT I'D SAY STEP ONE WAS, AS YOU CAN'T REALLY FORCE ANOTHER COUNTRY TO TRY AND INVADE OR PUT IDIOTS IN CHARGE OF WHAT ALREADY EXISTS; BUT I CERTAINLY WOULD ENCOURAGE ANY OTHER WOULD-BE LEADERS TO ACQUIRE UNGODLY AMOUNTS OF MONEY BY ANY MEANS NECESSARY.

A FASCINATION WITH MONEY WOULDN'T BE ENOUGH, HOWEVER. YOU MUST POSSESS IT AND BE IN A POSITION TO LORD IT OVER OTHERS. MY LACK OF BACKGROUND IN POLITICS HASN'T BEEN AN ISSUE IN GAINING ALLEGIANCE. IN FACT, I WOULD SAY AVOIDING THAT SECTOR ALTOGETHER MAY BE ONE OF MY GREATEST STRENGTHS. NO ONE TRUSTS POLITICIANS, AND WHY WOULD THEY? WALLIS HAS BEEN MAKING EMPTY PROMISES FOR YEARS IN THE HOPES THAT ONE OF THEM MIGHT COME THROUGH, AND THERE ISN'T A CHANCE IN HELL ANY OF THEM COULD. I, ON THE OTHER HAND, OFFER THE IDEA OF MORE. NO GUARANTEES, MERELY THAT FAINT GLIMMER OF OPTIMISM THAT CHANGE MIGHT COME. IT DOESN'T EVEN MATTER AT THIS POINT WHAT THE

CHANGE MIGHT BE. THEY'RE SO DESPERATE, THEY DON'T CARE. THEY DON'T EVEN THINK TO ASK.

PERHAPS THE KEY IS STAYING CALM WHILE OTHERS PANIC. WALLIS IS SO HATED NOW, HE'S ALL BUT HANDED THE PRESIDENCY OVER TO ME, AND NOT A SOUL IS COMPLAINING. I SAY NOTHING, DO NOTHING, AND WEAR A PLEASANT SMILE AS EVERYONE AROUND ME SINKS INTO HYSTERICS. ONE GLANCE AT THAT COWARD NEXT TO ME, AND THERE'S NO DENYING I LOOK BETTER AT A PODIUM OR SHAKING A PRIME MINISTER'S HAND. AND WALLIS IS SO DESPERATE TO HAVE SOMEONE THE PEOPLE LOVE ON HIS SIDE, I'M PRETTY SURE IT WILL ONLY TAKE TWO OR THREE INCONSPICUOUSLY WORDED DEALS TO HAVE ME RUNNING EVERYTHING.

THIS COUNTRY IS MINE. I FEEL LIKE A BOY WITH A CHESS SET PLAYING A GAME HE KNOWS HE WILL WIN. I'M SMARTER, RICHER, AND FAR MORE QUALIFIED IN THE EYES OF A COUNTRY THAT ADORES ME FOR REASONS NO ONE CAN SEEM TO NAME. BY THE TIME SOMEONE THINKS TO CONSIDER IT, IT WON'T MATTER ANYMORE. I CAN DO WHAT I LIKE, AND THERE'S NO ONE LEFT TO STOP ME. SO WHAT'S NEXT?

I FEEL IT'S TIME TO COLLAPSE THE SYSTEM. THIS PITIFUL REPUBLIC IS ALREADY IN SHAMBLES AND BARELY WORKS. THE REAL QUESTION IS, WHO DO I ALIGN MYSELF WITH? HOW DO I MAKE THIS SOMETHING THE PUBLIC BEGS FOR?

I HAVE ONE IDEA. MY DAUGHTER WON'T LIKE IT, BUT I'M NOT REALLY CONCERNED WITH THAT. IT'S ABOUT TIME SHE MADE HERSELF USEFUL.

I slammed the book shut, confused and frustrated. Was I missing something? Collapsing what system? Lording over people? Was the structure of our country not a necessity but a convenience?

I considered hunting through the book for what happened to his daughter, but I was already so disoriented, I decided against it. Instead I went to the balcony, hoping some fresh air would help me wrap my mind around the words I'd just read.

I looked to the sky, trying to process all this, but I didn't even know where to start. I sighed, and my eyes wandered the gardens, stopping on a flicker of white. Maxon was walking alone on the grounds. He was finally home. His shirt was untucked, and he wasn't wearing a coat or tie. What was he doing out so late? I saw that he was holding one of his cameras. He must have been having a rough night himself.

I hesitated a moment, but who else could I talk to about this?

"*Pssst!*"

He jerked his head around, looking for the source. I did it again, waving my arms until he saw me. A surprised smile flashed across his face as he waved back. Hoping he'd be able to see it, I pulled on my ear. He did the same. I pointed to him, then to my room. He nodded, holding up a finger to tell me it'd be a minute. I nodded back and went inside as he did the same.

I put on my robe and ran my fingers through my hair, wanting to look half as put together as he did. I wasn't sure exactly how to talk about this, because I was essentially about to ask Maxon if he knew he was sitting on top of something that was much less altruistic than the public had been led to believe. Just as I was starting to wonder what was taking him so long, he knocked on the door.

I rushed over to open it and was greeted by the lens of his camera. It clicked a still of my shocked smile. My expression dissolved into something that expressed how unamused I was by this little stunt, and he captured that, too, laughing.

"You're ridiculous. Get in here," I ordered, grabbing him by the arm.

He followed. "Sorry, I couldn't resist."

"You took your time," I accused, settling on the edge of the bed. He came to sit beside me, far enough away that we could face each other.

"I had to stop by my room." He placed his camera safely on my bedside table, flicking at my jar with the penny in it. He made a sound that was almost a laugh and turned back to me, not explaining his detour.

"Oh. So how was your trip?"

"Odd," he confessed. "We ended up going to the rural part of New Asia. Father said it was some local dispute; but by the time we got there, everything was fine." He shook his head. "Honestly, it made no sense. We spent a few days walking through old cities and trying to speak to the natives. Father is quite disappointed with my grasp of the language and is insisting I study more. As if I'm not doing enough these days," he said with a sigh.

"That is kind of strange."

"I'm guessing it was some sort of test. He's been throwing them at me randomly lately, and I don't always know they're happening. Maybe this was about decision making or dealing with the unexpected. I'm not sure." He shrugged his shoulders. "Either way, I'm sure I failed."

He fidgeted with his hands for a minute. "He also really wanted to talk about the Selection. I think he felt like distance would do me good, give me perspective or something. Honestly, I'm tired of everyone else talking about a decision that *I'm* supposed to make."

I was sure the king's idea of perspective meant getting me out of Maxon's head. I'd seen the way he smiled at the other girls at meals or nodded to them in the hallways. He never did that to me. I felt instantly uncomfortable and didn't know what to say.

It appeared Maxon didn't either.

I decided I couldn't ask him about the diary yet. He seemed so humble about these things—the way he led, the kind of king he wanted to be—that I couldn't demand answers from him that I wasn't anywhere close to sure he had. A tiny corner of my brain couldn't shake the worry that he knew more than he'd ever shared, but I needed to know more myself before I spoke.

Maxon cleared his throat and pulled a little string of beads out of his pocket.

"As I said, we were walking through a bunch of towns, and I saw this in an old woman's street shop. It's blue," he added, pointing out the obvious. "You seem to like blue."

"I love blue," I whispered.

I looked at the little bracelet. A few days ago, Maxon was walking on the other side of the world, and he saw this in a shop . . . and it made him think of me.

"I didn't find anything for anyone else, so maybe you could keep this between us?" I nodded my head in agreement. "You never were the type to brag," he mumbled.

I couldn't stop staring at the bracelet. It was so understated, with polished stones that weren't quite gems. I reached out and ran a finger over one of the oval-shaped beads, and Maxon wiggled the bracelet in his hand, which made me laugh.

"Do you want me to put it on?" he offered.

I nodded and stretched out the wrist that didn't have Aspen's button on it. Maxon placed the cool stones against my skin and tied the little ribbon that held them together.

"Lovely," he said.

And there it was, pushing up through all the worries: hope.

It lifted the heavy parts of my heart and made me miss him. I wanted to erase everything since Halloween, go back to that night, and hold on to those two people on the dance floor. And then, at the same time, it made my heart plummet. If we were back at Halloween, I wouldn't have a reason to doubt this gift.

Even if I let myself be everything my father said I was, everything Aspen said I wasn't . . . I couldn't be Kriss. Kriss was better.

I was so tired and stressed and confused, I started crying.

"America?" he asked hesitantly. "What's wrong?"

"I don't understand."

"What don't you understand?" he asked quietly. I mentally noted that he was doing much better around crying girls these days.

"You," I admitted. "I'm just really confused about you right now." I wiped away a tear on one side of my face, and, so gently, Maxon's hand moved to wipe the tears on the other.

In a way, it was strange to have him touch me like that again. At the same time, it was so familiar that it would have seemed wrong if he hadn't. Once the tears were gone, he left his hand there, cupping my face.

"America," he said earnestly, "if you ever want to know anything about me—what matters to me or who I am—all you need to do is ask."

He looked so sincere that I nearly did ask. I almost begged

him to tell me everything: if he'd always considered Kriss, if he knew about the diaries, what it was about this perfect little bracelet that made him think of me.

But how did I know it would be the truth? And—because I was slowly realizing he was the steadier choice—what about Aspen?

"I don't know if I'm ready to do that yet."

After a moment of thought, Maxon looked at me. "I understand. I think I do anyway. But we should talk about some serious things very soon. And when you're ready, I'm here."

He didn't press me; instead he stood, giving me a small bow before grabbing his camera and making his way to the door. He looked back at me one last time before disappearing into the hall, and I was surprised by how much I ached to see him go.

CHAPTER 25

"Private lessons?" Silvia asked. "As in, several a week?"

"Absolutely," I replied.

For the first time since I arrived, I was truly grateful for Silvia. I knew that there was no way she'd be able to resist having someone willing to hang on her every word; and if she was making me do extra work, it meant I could keep myself busy.

Thinking about Maxon and Aspen and the diary and the girls was too much right now. Protocol was black-and-white. The steps for proposing a law were orderly. These were things I could master.

Silvia looked at me, still slightly stunned, before she broke into a huge smile. Embracing me, she cried out, "Oh, this will be wonderful. Finally one of you understands how important this is!" She held me at arm's length. "When do you want to start?"

"Now?"

She was bursting with delight. "Let me go get some books."

I dove into her studies, so grateful for the words and facts and statistics she crammed into my head. If I wasn't with Silvia, I was reading up on something she'd assigned me as I spent countless hours in the Women's Room, all but tuning out the other girls.

I worked, and I was excited about the next time the five of us had a joint class.

When that time came, Silvia started by asking us what we were passionate about. I scribbled down my family, music, and then, as if the word demanded to be written, justice.

"The reason I ask is because the queen is typically in charge of a committee of some kind, something that benefits the country. Queen Amberly, for example, began a program for training families to take care of their mentally and physically infirmed members. So many get deposited in the streets once the families can no longer deal with them, and the amount of Eights grows to an unmanageable number. The statistics over the last ten years have proven that her program has helped keep the numbers lower, thus keeping the general population safer."

"Are we supposed to come up with a program like that?" Elise asked, sounding nervous.

"Yes, that will be your new project," Silvia said. "On the

Capital Report in two weeks' time, you'll be asked to present your idea and propose how you might start it."

Natalie made a little squeak of a sound, and Celeste rolled her eyes. Kriss looked like she was already dreaming something up. Her instant enthusiasm made me nervous.

I remembered Maxon talking about an upcoming elimination. I felt like Kriss and I were at a slight advantage, but still.

"Is this really helpful?" Celeste asked. "I'd rather learn about something we'll actually use."

I could tell that beneath her concerned tone, she was either bored with this idea already or intimidated by it.

Silvia looked appalled. "You will use this! Whoever becomes the new princess will be in charge of a philanthropy project."

Celeste muttered something under her breath and started fiddling with a pen. I hated that she wanted the position with none of the responsibility.

I'd make a better princess than she would, I thought. And in that moment I realized there was some truth to that. I didn't have her connections or Kriss's poise, but at least I cared. And wasn't that worth something?

For the first time in a while, I felt a true shot of enthusiasm course through me. Here was a project that would allow me to show off the one thing that separated me from the others. I was determined to pour myself into this and hopefully produce something that might genuinely make a difference. Maybe I'd still lose in the long run; maybe I wouldn't even want to win. But I would be as close to a princess as I possibly could, and I would make my peace with the Selection.

It was hopeless. Try as I might, I couldn't come up with a single idea for my philanthropy project. I thought and read and thought some more. I asked my maids, but they had no ideas. I would have sought out Aspen, but I hadn't heard from him in days. I guessed he was being extracautious with Maxon home.

What was worse was that Kriss was clearly deep into her presentation. She skipped hours of time in the Women's Room to go read; and when she was present, she had her nose in a book or was scribbling notes furiously.

Damn.

When Friday came, I felt like dying as I suddenly realized I only had a week left and no prospects on the horizon. During the *Report*, Gavril set up the structure for the next show, explaining that there would be a few brief announcements and then the rest of the evening would be dedicated to our presentations.

A light sweat broke out on my forehead.

I caught Maxon looking at me. He reached up and tugged his ear, and I wasn't sure what to do. I didn't quite want to say yes, but I didn't want to just brush him off. I pulled on my ear, and he looked relieved.

I fidgeted while I waited for him to show up, twiddling the ends of my hair and pacing around my room.

Maxon's knock was brief before he let himself in the way

he used to. I stood, feeling I needed to be a bit more formal than usual. I could tell that I was being ridiculous, but I felt completely unable to stop it at the same time.

"How are you?" he asked, crossing the room.

"Honestly? Nervous."

"It's because I'm so good-looking, isn't it?"

I laughed at the sympathetic face he made. "I should avert my eyes," I said, playing along. "Actually, it's mostly about that philanthropy project."

"Oh," he said, sitting at my table. "You could run your presentation by me if you like. Kriss did."

I felt deflated. Of course she was done. "I don't even have an idea yet," I confessed, sitting across from him.

"Ah. Yes, I can see how that would be stressful."

I gave him a look as if to say he had no idea.

"What's important to you? There has to be something that really touches you that the others might miss." Maxon leaned back in the chair comfortably, one hand on the table.

How was he so at ease? Couldn't he see how on edge I was?

"I've been thinking all week, and nothing's come to mind."

He laughed quietly. "I would have thought that you'd have the easiest time. You've seen more hardships in your life than the other four combined."

"Exactly, but I've never known how to change any of it. That's the problem." I stared at the table, remembering Carolina with perfect clarity. "I can see it all . . . the Sevens who get injured doing their labor-heavy jobs and are suddenly downgraded to Eights because they can't work anymore. The girls who walk the streets on the edge of curfew, wandering into the beds of lonely men for practically anything. The kids who never have enough—enough food, enough heat, enough love—because their parents are working themselves to death. I can remember my worst days like they're nothing. But coming up with a feasible way to do anything about it?" I shook my head. "What could I possibly say?"

I looked at him, hoping there was an answer in his eyes. There wasn't.

"You make an excellent point." Then he was quiet.

I thought over everything I said as well as his response. Did it mean that he knew more about Gregory's plans than I thought? Or did it mean he felt guilty because he had so much when others had so little?

He sighed. "This really wasn't what I was hoping we'd talk about tonight."

"What did you have on your mind?"

Maxon looked up at me as if I must be crazy. "You, of course."

I tucked my hair behind my ear. "What about me exactly?"

He changed positions, angling his chair so we were a bit closer and leaning in as if this was a secret. "I thought that after you saw that Marlee was fine, things would change. I was sure you'd find a way to care about me again. But that hasn't happened. Even tonight, you agreed to see me, but everything about you is standoffish."

So he did notice.

I ran my fingers across the table, not looking him in the eyes. "It's not exactly you I have a problem with. It's the position." I shrugged. "I thought you knew that."

"But after Marlee—"

My head popped up. "After Marlee, things kept happening. I'll have a grasp on what being a princess will mean one minute and lose it the next. I'm not like the other girls. I'm the lowest caste here; and Elise might have been a Four, but her family is way different from most Fours. They own so much, I'm surprised they haven't bought their way up yet. And you were raised in this. It's a serious change for me."

He nodded, his endless patience still there. "I do understand that, America. That's part of why I wanted you to have time. But you need to consider me in this, too."

"I am."

"No, not like that. Not like I'm part of the equation. Consider my predicament. I don't have much time left. This philanthropy project will be the springboard for another elimination. Surely, you've guessed that."

I lowered my head. Of course I had.

"So what am I to do once it's down to four? Give you more time? When it gets to three, I'm supposed to choose. If there are only three of you and you're still debating if you want the responsibility, if you want the workload, if you want *me* . . . what am I supposed to do then?"

I bit my lip. "I don't know."

Maxon shook his head. "That's not acceptable. I need

an answer. Because I can't send someone who really wants this—who wants me—home if you're going to bail out in the end."

My breathing picked up. "So I have to give you an answer now? I don't even know what I'm giving an answer to. Does saying I want to stay mean saying I want to be the one? Because I don't know that." I felt my muscles tensing, like they were preparing to run.

"You don't have to say anything now; but by the *Report* you need to know if you want this or not. I don't like giving you an ultimatum, but you're being a bit careless with my one shot."

He sighed before continuing. "That wasn't where I wanted this conversation to go either. Maybe I should leave." I could hear in his voice that he wanted me to ask him to stay, to tell him this was all going to work itself out.

"I think you should," I whispered.

He shook his head, irritated, and stood. "Fine." He walked across the room in quick, angry strides. "I'll just go see what Kriss is doing."

CHAPTER 26

I WENT DOWN FOR BREAKFAST on the late side. I didn't want to risk running into Maxon or any of the girls alone. Before I made it to the stairs, Aspen came walking up the hall. I made an exasperated sound, and he looked around before approaching me.

"Where have you been?" I quietly demanded.

"Working, Mer. I'm a guard, I can't control when and where they schedule me. I've stopped being placed on the round for your room."

I wanted to ask why, but this wasn't the time. "I need to talk to you."

He thought for a moment. "At two, go to the end of the first-floor hallway, down past the hospital wing. I can be there, but not for long." I nodded. He gave me a quick bow and went on his way before anyone noticed our conversation, and I continued downstairs, not feeling satisfied at all.

I wanted to scream. Saturday being a day-long sentence to the Women's Room was really unfair. When people came to visit, they wanted to see the queen, not us. When one of us was princess, that would probably change, but for now I was stuck watching Kriss pour over her presentation again. The others were reading things, too, notes or reports, and I felt sick to my stomach. I needed an idea and fast. I was sure Aspen would help me figure this out, and I had to start something tonight no matter what.

As if she could read my thoughts, Silvia, who had been visiting with the queen, stopped by to see me.

"How's my star pupil?" she asked, keeping her voice low enough that the others wouldn't notice.

"Great."

"How is your project going? Do you need any help fine-tuning?" she offered.

Fine-tuning? How was I supposed to tweak *nothing*?

"It's going great. You're going to love it, I'm sure," I lied.

She cocked her head to the side. "Being a bit secretive are we?"

"A bit." I smiled.

"That's fine. You've been doing wonderful work lately. I'm sure it'll be fantastic." Silvia patted my shoulder as she headed out of the room.

I was in so much trouble.

The minutes passed so slowly that it was like a special

kind of torture. Just before two I excused myself and went down the hallway. At the very end, there was a burgundy upholstered couch underneath a massive window. I sat to wait. I didn't see a clock, but the minutes passed too slowly for comfort. Finally Aspen came around a corner.

"About time." I sighed.

"What's wrong?" he asked, standing by the couch, looking official.

So much, I thought. *So many things I can't talk to you about.*

"We have this assignment, and I don't know what to do. I can't think of anything, and I'm stressed, and I can't sleep," I said spastically.

He chuckled. "What's the assignment? Tiara designing?"

"No," I said, shooting him a frustrated glare. "We have to come up with a project, something good for the country. Like Queen Amberly's work with the disabled."

"This is what you've been worked up about?" he asked, shaking his head. "How is that stressful? That sounds like fun."

"I thought it would be, too. But I can't come up with anything. What would you do?"

Aspen thought for a moment. "I know! You should do a caste exchange program," he said, his eyes glittering with excitement.

"A what?"

"A caste exchange program. People from the upper castes switch places with people from the lower castes so they can know what it feels like to walk in our shoes."

"I don't think that would work, Aspen, at least not for this project."

"It's a great idea," he insisted. "Can you imagine someone like Celeste breaking her nails stocking shelves? It'd serve them right."

"What's gotten into you? Aren't some of the guards natural Twos? Aren't they your friends now?"

"Nothing's gotten into me," he answered defensively. "I'm the same as ever. You're the one who's forgotten what it was like to live in a house with no heat."

I straightened my back. "I haven't forgotten. I'm trying to come up with a service project to stop things like that. Even if I go home, someone might use my idea, so I need it to be good. I want to help people."

"Don't forget, Mer," Aspen implored me with a quiet passion in his eyes. "This government sat by while you went without food. They let my brother get beaten in the square. All the talk in the world won't undo what we are. They put us in a corner we could never get out of on our own, and they're not in a rush to pull us out. Mer, they just don't get it."

I huffed and stood.

"Where are you going?" he asked.

"Back to the Women's Room," I answered, starting to move.

Aspen followed. "Are we seriously fighting over some stupid project?"

I turned on him. "No. We're fighting because you don't get it either. I'm a Three now. And you're a Two. Instead of being bitter about what we were handed, why can't you see the chance you have? You can change your family's life. You could probably change lots of lives. And all you want to do is settle the score. That's not going to get anyone anywhere."

Aspen didn't say anything, and I left. I tried not to be upset with him for being passionate about what he wanted. If anything, wasn't that an admirable quality? But it made me think so much about the castes and how they couldn't be undone that I started getting angry about the situation.

Nothing was going to change it. So why bother?

I played my violin. I took a bath. I tried to nap. I spent part of the evening sitting in a quiet room. I sat on my balcony.

None of it mattered. It was getting dangerously late in the game, and I still had nothing for my project.

I lay in bed for hours, trying to sleep and not getting far with that either. I kept flashing back to Aspen's angry words, his constant struggle with his lot in life. I thought about Maxon and his ultimatum, his demand for me to commit. And then I wondered if any of this mattered anyway, since I was certainly going home as soon as I showed up Friday night without anything to present.

I sighed and pulled back my blankets. I'd been avoiding looking at Gregory's diary again; I was worried that it would give me more questions than answers. But maybe something in there would give me direction, something I could talk about on the *Report*.

Besides, even if I couldn't help myself, I had to know what happened to his daughter. I was pretty sure her name was Katherine, so I flipped through the book looking for any mention of her, ignoring everything else, until I found a picture of a girl standing next to a man who appeared to be much older. Maybe it was just my imagination, but she looked like she'd been crying.

KATHERINE WAS FINALLY MARRIED TODAY TO EMIL DE MONPEZAT OF SWENDWAY. SHE SOBBED THE WHOLE WAY TO THE CHURCH UNTIL I MADE IT CLEAR THAT IF SHE DIDN'T STRAIGHTEN UP FOR THE CEREMONY, THERE'D BE HELL TO PAY AFTERWARD. HER MOTHER ISN'T HAPPY, AND I SUSPECT SPENCER IS UPSET NOW THAT HE'S AWARE OF HOW LITTLE HIS SISTER WANTED TO GO THROUGH WITH THIS. BUT SPENCER IS BRIGHT. I THINK HE'LL FALL INTO LINE QUICKLY ONCE HE SEES ALL THE POSSIBILITIES I'VE CREATED FOR HIM. AND DAMON IS SO SUPPORTIVE; I WISH I COULD TAKE WHATEVER IT IS IN HIS SYSTEM AND INJECT IT INTO THE REST OF THE POPULATION. THERE'S SOMETHING TO BE SAID FOR THE YOUNG. IT'S SPENCER AND DAMON'S GENERATION THAT HAS BEEN THE MOST HELPFUL IN GETTING ME WHERE I AM. THEIR ENTHUSIASM IS UNSWAYABLE, AND THEY ARE A FAR MORE POPULAR CROWD FOR OTHERS TO LISTEN TO THAN THE FEEBLE ELDERLY WHO INSIST WE'VE GONE DOWN THE WRONG PATH. I KEEP

WONDERING IF THERE'S A WAY TO SILENCE THEM FOR GOOD
THAT WOULDN'T MIRE MY NAME.

EITHER WAY, WE ARE SLATED TO HAVE THE
CORONATION TOMORROW. NOW THAT SWENDWAY HAS
GOTTEN THE POWERFUL ALLY OF THE NORTH AMERICAN
UNION, I CAN HAVE WHAT I WANT: A CROWN. I THINK
THIS IS A FAIR TRADE. WHY SETTLE FOR PRESIDENT
ILLÉA WHEN I CAN BE KING ILLÉA INSTEAD? THROUGH
MY DAUGHTER, I'VE BEEN DEEMED ROYAL.

EVERYTHING IS IN PLACE. AFTER TOMORROW THERE
WILL BE NO TURNING BACK.

He sold her. The pig sold his daughter to a man she hated so he could have everything he wanted.

My instinct was to close the book again, to shut it all out. But I forced myself to flip through it, reading passages at random. In one place a rough diagram of the caste system was laid out, originally dreamed up with six tiers instead of eight. On another page he plotted to change people's last names to separate them from their pasts. One line made it clear that he intended to punish his enemies by placing them lower on the scale and reward the loyal by placing them higher.

I wondered if my great-grandparents simply had nothing to offer or if they had resisted this. I hoped it was the latter.

What should my last name have been? Did Dad know?

My whole life I'd been led to believe that Gregory Illéa was a hero, the person who saved our country when we were on the edge of oblivion. Clearly, he was nothing more than a power-hungry monster. What kind of man manipulated people so willingly? What kind of man hawked his daughter for his own convenience?

I looked at the older entries I'd read in a new light. He never said he wanted to *be* a great family man; he just wanted to *look* like one. He would play by Wallis's rules *for now.* He was using his son's peers to gain support. He was playing a game from the very beginning.

I felt nauseated. I stood and paced the floor, trying to wrap my head around it all.

How had an entire history been forgotten? How was it that no one ever spoke of the old countries? Where was all this information? Why didn't anyone know?

I opened my eyes and looked to the sky. It seemed impossible. Surely, someone would have disapproved, would have told their children the truth. But then again, maybe they had. I'd often wondered why Dad never let me talk about the timeworn history book he had hidden in his room, why the history I did know about Illéa was never in print. Maybe it was because, if it was there in writing that Illéa was a hero, people would have rioted. But if it was always a point of speculation, where one person insisted it was a certain way and another denied it, how would anyone ever hold on to the truth?

I wondered if Maxon knew.

Suddenly a memory came to me. Not so long ago, Maxon and I had our first kiss. It was so unexpected that I had pulled away, leaving him embarrassed. Then when I realized that I wanted Maxon to kiss me, I suggested that we simply erase that memory and plant a new one.

America, he'd said, *I don't think you can change history.* To which I replied, *Sure we can. Besides, who'd ever know about it but you and me?*

I'd meant it as a joke. Surely, if he and I end up together, we'd remember what really happened no matter how silly it was. We'd never actually replace it with a more perfect-sounding story simply for the sake of show.

But the whole Selection *was* a show. If Maxon and I were ever asked about our first kiss, would we tell anyone the truth? Or would we keep that little detail a secret between the two of us? When we died, no one would know, and that fraction of a moment that was so important to who we were would be gone.

Could it be that simple? Tell one story to one generation and repeat it until it was accepted as fact? How often had I asked someone older than Mom or Dad what they knew or what their parents had seen? They were old. What did they know? It was so arrogant of me to discount them completely. I felt so stupid.

But the important issue wasn't how this all made me feel. The important issue was what I was going to do with it.

I'd lived my whole life stuck in a hole in our society; and because I loved music, I didn't complain. But I had wanted to be with Aspen, and because he was a Six, it was harder than it had to be. If Gregory Illéa hadn't coldly designed the laws of our country, sitting comfortably at his desk all those years ago, then Aspen and I wouldn't have fought and I never would have cared about Maxon. Maxon wouldn't even be a prince. Marlee's hands would still be intact, and she and Carter wouldn't be living in a room barely big enough for their bed. Gerad, my sweet baby brother, could study all the science he wanted instead of pushing himself into the arts for which he had no passion.

By obtaining a comfy life in a beautiful house, Gregory Illéa had robbed most of the country of its ability to ever attempt to have the very same thing.

Maxon said if I wanted to know who he was, all I had to do was ask. I'd been afraid to face the possibility of him being this person, but I had to know. If I was meant to make a decision about being a part of the Selection or going home, I needed to know exactly what he was made of.

Donning my slippers and robe, I left my room, passing the nameless guard on my way.

"You all right, miss?" he asked.

"Yes. I'll be back soon."

He looked like he wanted to say more, but I left too quickly for him to speak. I headed up the stairs to the third floor. Unlike the other floors, guards stood at the landing, preventing me from simply walking to Maxon's door.

"I need to speak to the prince," I said, trying to sound firm.

"It's very late, miss," the one to the left said.

"Maxon won't mind," I promised.

The one to the right smirked a little. "I don't think he'd

appreciate any company right now, miss."

My forehead creased in thought as I played that sentence in my head again.

He was with another girl.

I had to assume it was Kriss, sitting there in his room, talking, laughing, or maybe giving up on her no-kissing rule.

A maid came around the corner with a tray in her hands, passing me as she descended the stairs. I stepped to the side, trying to decide if I should push the guards to let me through anyway or give up. As I went to open my mouth again, the guard cut me off.

"You need to go back to bed, miss."

I wanted to yell at them or do something because I felt so powerless. It wouldn't help, though, so I left. I heard the one guard—the smirking one—mumble something as I walked away, and that made it worse. Was he making fun of me? Feeling sorry for me? I didn't need his pity. I was feeling bad enough on my own.

When I got back to the second floor, I was surprised to see that the maid who had passed me was there, kneeling as if she was adjusting her shoe but clearly doing nothing of the sort. She raised her head as I approached, picking up her tray and walking toward me.

"He's not in his room," she whispered.

"Who? Maxon?"

She nodded. "Try downstairs."

I smiled, shaking my head in surprise. "Thank you."

She shrugged. "He's not anywhere you couldn't find him

if you looked anyway. Besides," she said, her eyes full of admiration, "we like you."

She moved away, heading down to the first floor very quickly. I wondered exactly who "we" was, but for now, her simple act of kindness was enough. I stood for a moment, leaving some space between the two of us, and headed downstairs.

The Great Room was open but empty, as was the dining room. I checked the Women's Room, thinking that would be a funny place to go on a date, but they weren't there either. I asked the guards by the door, and they assured me that Maxon hadn't gone into the gardens, so I checked a few of the libraries and parlors before guessing that he and Kriss must have either parted ways or gone back to his room.

Giving up, I turned a corner and headed for the back stairwell, which was closer than the main one. I didn't see anything; but as I approached, I heard the distinct hiss of a whisper. I slowed, not wanting to intrude and not completely sure where the sound was coming from.

Another whisper.

A flirtatious giggle.

A warm sigh.

The sounds focused, and I was certain where they were coming from. I took one more step forward, looked to my left, and saw a couple embracing in the shadows. After the image settled and my eyes adjusted to the light, a shock went through me.

Maxon's blond hair was unmistakable, even in the

darkness. How many times had I seen it just so in the dim light of the gardens? But what I'd never seen before, never *imagined* before, was how that hair would look with Celeste's long fingers, nails painted red, digging into it.

Maxon was all but pinned to the wall by Celeste's body. Her free hand was pressed against his chest, and her leg was wrapped around his, the slit of her dress revealing her long leg, tinted slightly blue in the dark of the hall. She pulled back slightly, only to fall back into him slowly, teasing him it seemed.

I kept waiting for him to tell her to get off him, to tell her she wasn't what he wanted. But he didn't. Instead he kissed her. She lavished in it and giggled again at his affection. He whispered something in her ear, and Celeste leaned in and kissed him, deeper, harder than before. The strap of her dress fell off her shoulder, leaving what seemed like miles of exposed skin down her back. Neither of them bothered to fix it.

I was frozen. I wanted to scream or cry, but my throat felt constricted. Why, of everyone, did it have to be her?

Celeste's lips slid off Maxon's and settled onto his neck. She gave another obnoxious giggle and kissed him once more. Maxon closed his eyes and smiled. With Celeste no longer blocking him, I was in Maxon's line of sight.

I meant to run. I meant to disappear, to evaporate. Instead I stood there.

So when Maxon opened his eyes, he saw me.

As Celeste drew pictures in kisses up and down his neck,

Maxon and I merely stared at each other. His smile now gone, Maxon had suddenly turned to stone. The shock in his eyes willed me finally to move. Celeste didn't notice, so I backed away quietly, not even stirring a breath.

Once I was out of earshot, I broke into a run, blazing past all the guards and butlers working late into the night. The tears started coming before I made it up the main stairway.

I pulled myself up and moved quickly to my room. I pushed past the concerned guard and through the doorway, sitting on my bed facing the balcony. In the quiet stillness of my room, I felt my heart ache. *So stupid, America. So stupid.*

I'd go home. I'd forget this ever happened. And I'd marry Aspen.

Aspen was the only person I could count on.

It wasn't long before there was a knock on my door, and Maxon came in without waiting for an answer. He stormed across the room, looking about as angry as I was.

Before he could say a word, I confronted him.

"You lied to me."

"What? When?"

"When haven't you been? How could the same person who talked about proposing to me want to be caught dead in a hallway with someone like her?"

"What I do with her has absolutely nothing to do with how I feel about you."

"You're joking, right? Or because you're the next king, I suppose it's acceptable for you to have half-naked girls draped across you whenever you like?"

Maxon looked stricken. "No. That's not what I think at all."

"Why her?" I asked, looking to the ceiling. "Why, of anyone on the planet, would you want her?"

When I looked to Maxon for an answer, he was shaking his head and looking around the room.

"Maxon, she's an actress, a fake. You have to be able to see that under all that makeup, and the push-up bra is nothing but a girl who wants to manipulate you to get what she wants."

Maxon huffed out a laugh. "Actually, I do."

I was taken aback by his calm. "Then why—"

But I already had my answer.

He knew. Of course he knew. He'd been raised here. Gregory's diaries were probably his bedtime stories. I didn't know why I'd expected otherwise.

How naive had I been? When I kept thinking that there was a better option than me for his princess, I'd been imagining Kriss. She was lovely and patient and a million things that I wasn't. But I'd been seeing her next to a different Maxon. For the man he would have to be to follow in Gregory Illéa's footsteps, the only girl here for him was Celeste. No one else would be so content to keep a country under her thumb.

"That's it," I said, wiping my hands in front of me. "You wanted a decision, and here it is: I am done with this. I'm done with the Selection, I'm done with all the lies, and I am especially done with you. God, I can't believe how stupid I was."

"You're not done, America," he contradicted me quickly, his stance saying as much as his words. "You're done when I say you are. You're upset right now, but you aren't done."

I gripped my hair, feeling like I was seconds away from pulling it all out by the roots. "What is wrong with you? Are you delusional? What makes you think that I will ever be okay with what I just saw? I *hate* that girl. And you were kissing her. I want nothing to do with you."

"Good God, woman, you never let me get a word in edgewise!"

"What could you possibly say that could explain that away? Just send me home. I don't want to be here anymore."

Our conversation had been going back and forth so quickly that his silence was startling.

"No."

I was enraged. Wasn't this exactly what he'd been asking for? "Maxon Schreave, you are nothing but a child who has his hands on a toy that he doesn't want but can't stand for someone else to have."

Quietly, Maxon spoke. "I understand that you're angry, but—"

I shoved him. "I'm beyond angry!"

Maxon remained calm. "America, do not call me a child. And do not push me."

I shoved him again. "What are you going to do about it?"

Maxon grabbed my wrists, pinning my arms behind my back, and I saw the anger in his eyes. I was glad it was there. I wanted him to provoke me. I wanted a reason to hurt him.

I could tear him to bits right now.

But there was no rage in him. Instead I felt the warm buzz of electricity that had been missing for a long time. Maxon's face was inches from mine, his eyes searching my own, perhaps wondering how he'd be received, perhaps not caring at all. Though it was all wrong, I still wanted it. My lips parted before I realized what was happening.

I shook my head to clear it and stepped back, moving toward the balcony. He didn't put up a fight as I pulled away. I took a few steadying breaths before I turned to him.

"Are you going to send me home?" I asked quietly.

Maxon shook his head, either unable or unwilling to speak.

I ripped his bracelet off my wrist and threw it across the room. "Then go," I whispered.

I turned back to look out my balcony and waited a few heavy moments to hear the click of the door. Once he left, I fell to the floor and sobbed.

He and Celeste were so much alike. Everything about them was a show. And I knew that he would spend the rest of his life sweet-talking the public into thinking he was wonderful, all the while keeping them trapped where they were. Just like Gregory.

I sat on my floor, legs crossed under my nightgown. As upset as I was with Maxon, I was even more upset with myself. I should have fought harder. I should have done more. I shouldn't be sitting here so defeated.

I wiped the tears away and assessed the situation. I was

done with Maxon, but I was still here. I was done with the competition, but I still had a presentation due. Aspen might not think I was tough enough to be a princess—and he was right—but he did have faith in me. I knew that. And so did my father. And so did Nicoletta.

I wasn't here to win anymore. So how could I go out with a bang?

CHAPTER 27

WHEN SILVIA ASKED WHAT I would need for my presentation, I told her a small desk for some books and an easel for a poster I was designing. She was particularly excited about my poster. I was the only girl here with any true experience making art.

I spent hours writing my speech onto note cards so I wouldn't miss anything, flagging sections in books to be my resources midpresentation, and rehearsing it in the mirror to get through the parts that particularly worried me. I tried not to think too hard about what I was doing; otherwise my whole body started trembling.

I asked Anne to make me a dress that looked innocent, which made her eyebrows pucker.

"You make it sound like we've been sending you out in lingerie," she said mockingly.

I chuckled. "That's not what I mean at all. You know I love all the dresses you've made me. I just want to seem . . . angelic."

She smiled to herself. "I think we can come up with something."

They must have been working like crazy, because I didn't see Anne, Mary, or Lucy the day of the *Report* until the hour before it started, when they came bustling in with the dress. It was white, gauzy, and light, adorned with one long stream of green and blue tulle running along the right side. The bottom fell in such a way that it looked like a cloud, and its empire waist added a level of virtue and grace to the gown. I felt lovely in that dress. It was by far my favorite of everything they'd designed for me, and I was glad it worked out that way. It would probably be the last dress of theirs I'd ever wear.

It had been hard to keep my plan a secret, but I did. When the girls asked what I was doing, I simply said it was a surprise. I got a few skeptical looks for that, but I didn't care. I asked my maids not to touch the things on my desk, not even to clean, and they obeyed, leaving my notes facedown.

No one knew.

The person I most wanted to tell was Aspen, but I refrained. Part of me feared he would talk me out of it, and I would cave. Another part feared he would be far too gung-ho.

As my maids worked to make me look beautiful, I stared into the mirror and knew I was walking into this alone. And that was for the best. I didn't want anyone—not my maids, not the other girls, and especially not Aspen—to get in trouble for my actions.

All that was left to do was to put things in order.

"Anne, Mary, would you please go get me some tea?"

They looked at each other. "Both of us?" Mary clarified.

"Yes, please."

They looked suspicious but curtsied and left all the same. Once they were gone, I turned to Lucy.

"Sit with me," I invited, pulling her down to the padded bench on which I was sitting. She complied, and I asked her simply, "Are you happy?"

"Miss?"

"You've seemed kind of sad lately. I was wondering if you were all right."

She dropped her head. "Is it that obvious?"

"A little," I admitted, wrapping my arm around her and holding her close. She sighed and placed her head on my shoulder. I was so happy that she forgot the invisible boundaries between us for a moment.

"Have you ever wanted something you couldn't have?"

I snorted. "Lucy, before I came here I was a Five. There were too many things I couldn't have to bother counting."

In a very un-Lucy-like manner, a single tear fell to her check. "I don't know what to do. I'm stuck."

I straightened up and made her face me. "Lucy, I want you to know I think you can do anything, be anything. I think you're an amazing girl."

She gave me a weak smile. "Thank you, miss."

I knew we didn't have much time. "Listen, I need you to do something for me. I wasn't sure if I could count on the others, but I'm trusting you."

Though she looked confused, I could tell she meant it when she said, "Anything."

I reached over to one of the drawers and pulled out a letter. "Could you give this to Officer Leger?"

"Officer Leger?"

"I wanted to tell him thank-you for how kind he's been, and I thought it might be inappropriate to give him a letter myself. You know." It was a lame excuse, but it was the only way I could explain to Aspen why I did what I was going to do and to tell him good-bye. I assumed I wouldn't have much time in the palace after tonight.

"I can get this to him within the hour," she said eagerly.

"Thank you." Tears threatened to come, but I pushed them down. I was scared, but there were so many reasons this needed to be done.

We all deserved better. My family, Marlee and Carter, Aspen, even my maids were all stuck because of Gregory's plans. I would think of them.

When I walked into the studio for the *Report*, I was clutching an armful of marked books and a portfolio for my poster. The setup was the same as always—the king's, queen's, and Maxon's seats to the right near the door, the Selected in seats on the left—but in the middle, where there was usually a podium for the king to speak at or a set of chairs for interviews, there was a space for our presentations instead. I saw a desk and my easel, but also a screen that I assumed someone was showing slides on. That was impressive. I wondered who had found the resources to go that far.

I went over to the last open chair—next to Celeste, unfortunately—and placed my portfolio beside me, keeping my books on my lap. Natalie had a few books, too; and Elise was reading through her notes over and over. Kriss was looking toward the sky and appeared to be reciting her presentation mentally. Celeste was checking her makeup.

Silvia was there, which sometimes happened when we had to discuss something she'd briefed us on, and today she was beside herself. This was probably the hardest we'd worked to date, and it would all reflect back on her.

I inhaled sharply. I'd forgotten about Silvia. Too late now.

"You look beautiful, ladies, fantastic!" she said as she approached. "Now that you're all here, I want to explain a few things. First, the king will get up and give a few announcements, and then Gavril will introduce the topic of the evening: your philanthropy presentations."

Silvia, usually a level-headed, palace-hardened machine, was giddy. She was actually bouncing as she spoke. "Now, I know you've been practicing. You have eight minutes; and if anyone has a question for you afterward, Gavril will facilitate that. Remember to stay alert and poised. The country is watching you! If you get lost, take a breath and move on. You're going to be wonderful. Oh, and you'll be going in the order in which you're seated, so Lady Natalie, you're first; and Lady America will be last. Good luck, girls!"

Silvia skipped off to check and double-check things, and I tried to calm myself. Last. I guessed that was a good thing. I supposed Natalie had it worse by being first up. Looking over, I saw her breaking into a sweat. It must be torture for her to try and focus like this. I couldn't help but stare at Celeste. She didn't know I'd seen her and Maxon, and I kept wondering why she never told anyone about it. The fact that she kept it to herself led me to believe it wasn't the first time.

That made it so much worse.

"Nervous?" I asked, watching her pick at something on her nail.

"No. This is a stupid idea, and no one really cares. I'll be glad when it's over. And I'm a model," she said, finally looking at me. "I'm naturally good at being in front of an audience."

"You do seem to have mastered how to pose," I mumbled.

I could see the wheels turning as she tried to weed out the insult in there. She ended up rolling her eyes and looking away.

Just then the king walked in with the queen by his side. They were speaking in whispers, and it looked very important. A moment later, Maxon entered, adjusting his cuff links as he made his way to his seat. He came across so innocent, so clean in his suit; I had to remind myself that I knew better.

He looked over at me. I wasn't going to be intimidated and turn away first, so I stared back. Then, tentatively, Maxon reached up and tugged at his ear. I slowly shook my head with an expression that conveyed we would never speak again if I had anything to do with it.

A cold sweat broke out on my entire body as the presentations started. Natalie's proposal was short. And slightly misinformed.

She claimed that everything the rebels were doing was hateful and wrong, and their presence should be outlawed to keep Illéa's provinces safer. We all stared at her quietly once she was done. How did she not know that everything they did was already considered illegal?

The queen's face in particular seemed incredibly sad as Natalie sat back down.

Elise proposed a program that would involve members of the upper castes getting involved in a pen pal–type of relationship with people in New Asia. She suggested that it would help strengthen the bonds between our countries and aid in ending the war. I wasn't sure that it would do any good, but it was a fresh reminder to Maxon and the public of the reason she was still here. The queen asked if she happened to know anyone in New Asia who would be open to being in the program, and Elise assured her that she did.

Kriss's presentation was spectacular. She wanted to revamp the public school systems, which I already knew was an idea near and dear to both the queen's and Maxon's hearts. As the daughter of a professor, I was sure she'd been thinking about this her whole life. She used the screen to show pictures from her home province's school that her parents had sent to her. It was plain to see the exhaustion on the teachers' faces, and in one picture it showed a room where four children were sitting on the floor since there weren't enough chairs. The queen piped up with dozens of questions, and Kriss was quick to answer. Using copies of old reports about financial issues we'd read, she'd even found a place where we could borrow the money to start the work and had ideas on how to continue the funding.

As she sat down, I saw Maxon give her a smile and a nod. She responded by blushing and studying the lace on her dress. It was really cruel of him to play with her like that, considering how intimate he was with Celeste. But I was done interfering. Let him do what he wanted.

Celeste's presentation was interesting, if slightly manipulative. She suggested that there be a minimum-payment wage for some of the lower castes. It would be a sliding scale, based on certifications. However, to get these certifications, the Fives, Sixes, and Sevens would have to go to school . . . which they would have to pay for . . . which would mostly benefit the Threes, as they were the authorized teachers. Since Celeste was a Two, she had no idea how we had to work around the clock to make ends meets. No one would have the time to get these certifications, meaning their pay would never change. On the surface it sounded nice, but there was no way it would work.

Celeste returned to her seat, and I trembled when I stood. For a brief second I considered pretending to pass out. But I wanted this to happen. I just didn't want to face what would come after.

I placed my poster—a diagram of the castes—on the easel, and set my books in order on the desk. I took a deep breath and gripped my cards, surprised to find that when I started, I didn't even need them.

"Good evening, Illéa. Tonight I come to you not as one of the Elite, not as a Three or a Five, but as a citizen, an equal. Based on your caste, your experience of our country is shaded a very specific way. I can say that for certain myself. But it wasn't until recently that I understood how deep my love for Illéa went.

"Despite growing up sometimes without food or electricity, despite watching people I love forced into the stations we are assigned at birth with little hope for change, despite seeing the gaps between myself and others because of this number even though we aren't very different"—I looked over to the girls—"I find myself in love with our country."

I switched the card automatically, knowing the break. "What I propose wouldn't be simple. It might even be painful, but I genuinely believe it would benefit our entire kingdom." I inhaled. "I think we should eliminate the castes."

I heard more than one gasp. I chose to ignore them.

"I know there was a time, when our country was new, when the assignment of these numbers helped organize something that was on the brink of not existing. But we are no longer that country. We are so much more now. To allow the talentless to have exalted privileges and suppress what could be the greatest minds in the world for the sake of an archaic organization system is cruel, and it only stops us from becoming the best we can be."

I noted a poll from one of Celeste's discarded magazines after we talked about having a volunteer army, and sixty-five percent of the people thought it was a good idea. Why eliminate that career path completely for people? I also cited an old report we had studied about the standardized testing in the public schools. The article was slanted, stating that only three percent of Sixes and Sevens tested to elevated levels of intelligence; and since it was so low, it was clear they were intended to stay where they were. My argument was that we ought to be ashamed that those people are stuck digging ditches when they could be performing heart surgeries.

Finally the daunting task was nearly over. "Perhaps our country is flawed, but we cannot deny its strength. My fear is that, without change, that strength will become stagnate. And I love our country too much to let that happen. I *hope* too much to let that happen."

I swallowed, grateful that at least it was over now. "Thank you for your time," I said, and turned slightly toward the royal family.

It was bad. Maxon's face was stony again, like the way he'd looked when Marlee was caned. The queen averted her eyes, looking disappointed. The king, however, stared me down.

Without so much as a blink, he focused in on me. "And how do you suggest we eliminate the castes?" he challenged. "Just suddenly take them all away?"

"Oh . . . I don't know."

"And you don't think that would cause riots? Complete mayhem? Allow for rebels to take advantage of public confusion?"

I hadn't thought this part through. All I could process was how unfair it all was.

"I think the creation caused a decent amount of confusion, and we managed that. In fact"—I reached to my pile of books—"I have a description here."

I started looking for the right page in Gregory's diary.

"Are we off?" he bellowed.

"Yes, Majesty," someone called.

I looked up and saw that all the lights that usually indicated that the cameras were on had gone dim. In some gesture I'd missed, the king had shut down the *Report*.

The king stood. "Point them to the ground." Each camera was aimed to the floor.

He stormed over to me and ripped the diary from my hands.

"Where did you get this?" he yelled.

"Father, stop!" Maxon jogged up nervously.

"Where did she get this? Answer me!"

Maxon confessed. "From me. We were looking up what Halloween was. He wrote about it in the diaries, and I thought she'd like to read more."

"You idiot," the king spat. "I knew I should have made you read these sooner. You're completely lost. You have no clue of the duty you have!"

Oh, no. Oh, no, no, no.

"She leaves tonight," King Clarkson ordered. "I've had enough of her."

I tried to shrink down, distance myself from the king as much as I could without being obvious. I tried not to even breathe too loudly. I turned my head toward the girls, for some reason focusing on Celeste. I'd expected her to be smiling, but she was nervous. The king had never been like this.

"You can't send her home. That's my choice, and I say she stays," Maxon responded calmly.

"Maxon Calix Schreave, I am the king of Illéa, and I say—"

"Could you stop being the king for five minutes and just be my father?" Maxon yelled. "This is my choice. You got to make yours, and I want to make mine. No one else is leaving without my say so!"

I saw Natalie lean in to Elise. They both looked like they were shaking.

"Amberly, take this back to where it belongs," he said, shoving the book in her hand. She stood there, nodding her head but not moving. "Maxon, I need to see you in my office."

I watched Maxon; and maybe I only imagined it, but it looked like panic flickered briefly behind his eyes.

"Or," the king offered, "I could simply talk to her." He gestured over to me.

"No," Maxon said quickly, holding up a hand in protest.

"That won't be necessary. Ladies," he added, turning to us, "why don't you all head upstairs? We'll have dinner sent to you tonight." He paused. "America, maybe you should go ahead and collect your things. Just in case."

The king smiled, an eerie action after his recent explosion. "Excellent idea. After you, *son*."

I looked at Maxon, who seemed defeated. I felt ashamed. Maxon opened his mouth to say something, but in the end he shook his head and walked away.

Kriss was wringing her hands, looking after Maxon. I couldn't blame her. Something about all of this seemed menacing.

"Clarkson?" Queen Amberly said quietly. "What about the other matter?"

"What?" he asked in irritation.

"The news?" she reminded him.

"Oh, yes." He walked back toward us. I was close enough that I decided to retreat into my chair, afraid of being out there alone again. King Clarkson's voice was steady and calm. "Natalie, we didn't want to tell you before the *Report*, but we've received some bad news."

"Bad news?" she asked, fiddling with her necklace, already too anxious.

The king came closer. "Yes. I'm very sorry for your loss, but it appears the rebels took your sister this morning."

"What?" she whispered.

"Her remains were found this afternoon. We're sorry." To his credit, there was something close to sympathy in his voice, though it sounded more like training than genuine emotion.

He quickly returned to Maxon, escorting him forcefully out the door as Natalie broke into an ear-shattering scream. The queen rushed over to her, smoothing her hair and trying to calm her down. Celeste, never too sisterly, quietly left the room, with an overwhelmed Elise close behind. Kriss stayed and tried to comfort Natalie, but once it was clear that she couldn't do much, she left as well. The queen told Natalie there would be guards with her parents for good measure and that she would be able to leave for the funeral if she wanted to, holding on to her the whole time.

Everything had gotten so dark so quickly, I found myself frozen in my seat.

When the hand appeared in front of my face, I was so startled, I shied away.

"I won't hurt you," Gavril said. "Just want to help you up." His lapel pin shimmered, reflecting the light.

I gave him my hand, surprised by how shaky my legs were.

"He must love you very much," Gavril said once I had my footing.

I couldn't look at him. "What makes you say that?"

Gavril sighed. "I've known Maxon since he was a child. He's never stood up to his father like that."

Gavril walked away then, talking to the crew about keeping all that they had heard tonight quiet.

I went to Natalie. It wasn't like I knew everything about her, but I was sure she loved her sister the way I loved May;

and I couldn't imagine the ache she must be feeling.

"Natalie, I'm so sorry," I whispered. She nodded. That was the most she could manage.

The queen looked up at me sympathetically, not sure how to convey all her sadness. "And . . . I'm sorry to you, too. I wasn't trying to . . . I just . . ."

"I know, dear."

With how Natalie was doing, asking for more of a good-bye was too selfish, so I gave the queen a final, deep curtsy and slowly left the room, wallowing in the disaster I'd created.

CHAPTER 28

THE LAST THING I WAS expecting when I walked in my doorway was the smattering of applause from my maids.

I stood there for a moment, genuinely moved by their support and comforted by the shining pride in their faces. Once they were done making me blush, Anne took me by the hands.

"Well said, miss." She gave a gentle squeeze, and I saw in her eyes so much joy over my words, for a second I didn't feel so awful.

"I can't believe you did that! No one ever stands up for us!" Mary added.

"Maxon has to pick you," Lucy cried. "You're the only one who gives me hope."

Hope.

I needed to think, and the one place I could really do

that was the gardens. Though my maids were insistent that I stay, I left, taking the long way, down a back stairwell on the other end of the hall. Besides the occasional guard, the first floor was empty and quiet. It felt like the palace should be bustling with activity, given how much had happened in the last half hour or so.

As I passed the hospital wing, the door flew open and I ran right into Maxon, who dropped a sealed metal box. He groaned after we collided, even though it really wasn't that hard.

"What are you doing out of your room?" he asked, slowly bending to pick up the box. I noticed it had his name on the side. I wondered what he was storing in the hospital wing.

"I was going to the gardens. I'm trying to figure out if I did something stupid or not."

Maxon appeared to be having a difficult time standing. "Oh, I can assure you it was stupid."

"Do you need help?"

"No," he answered quickly, avoiding my eyes. "Just heading to my room. And I suggest you do the same."

"Maxon." The quiet plea in my voice made him look at me. "I'm so sorry. I was mad, and I wanted to . . . I don't even know anymore. And you were the one who said there were perks to being a One, that you could change things."

He rolled his eyes. "You're not a One." There was a silence between us. "Even if you were, did you not pay attention at all to the way I'm doing things? It's quiet and small. That's how it has to be for now. You can't go on television complaining about the way things are run and expect to have my father's, or anyone's, support."

"I'm sorry!" I cried. "I'm so, so sorry."

He paused for a moment. "I'm not sure that—"

We heard the shouting at the same time. Maxon turned and started walking, and I followed, trying to make sense of the sound. Was someone fighting? As we got closer to the intersection of the main hallway and the doors to the gardens, we saw guards come flooding toward the area.

"Sound the alarm!" someone called. "They're through the gates!"

"Guns at the ready!" another guard yelled over the shouts.

"Alert the king!"

And then, like bees intent on landing, small, quick things buzzed into the hall. A guard was struck and fell back, his head hitting the marble with a disturbing crack. The blood pouring from his chest made me scream.

Maxon instinctively pulled me away, but not very quickly. Perhaps he was in shock as well.

"Your Majesty!" a guard called, racing over to us. "You have to get downstairs now!"

He gruffly turned Maxon around and shoved him away. Maxon cried out and dropped the metal box again. I looked over at the guard's hand on Maxon, expecting to see that he'd driven a knife into his back based on the sound Maxon had made. All I saw was a thick, pewter ring around his thumb. I picked up the box by the handle on the side, hoping that didn't mess up anything inside, and ran in the direction the guard was trying to move us.

"I won't make it," Maxon said.

I turned back to him and saw that he was sweating. Something was really wrong with him.

"Yes, sir," the guard said grimly. "This way."

He pulled Maxon around a corner to what appeared to be a dead end. I wondered if he was going to leave us there when he hit some invisible trigger on the wall and another one of the palace's mysterious doors opened. It was so dark inside, I couldn't see where it went; but Maxon walked in, hunched over, without a second thought.

"Tell my mother that America and I are safe. Do that before anything else," he said.

"Absolutely, sir. I'll come back for you myself when this is over."

The siren sounded. I hoped that was fast enough to save everyone.

Maxon nodded and the door closed, leaving us in complete darkness. The seal was so secure, I couldn't even make out the sound of the alarm. I heard Maxon's hand rubbing against the wall, and he eventually came upon a switch that dimly lit the room. I looked around and surveyed the space.

There were some shelves that held a bunch of dark, plastic packages and a different shelf that held a few thin blankets. In the middle of the tiny space was one wooden bench big enough to seat maybe four people, and in the opposite corner was a small sink and what looked like a very crude toilet. Hooks lined one wall, but there was nothing on them; and the whole room smelled like the metal that appeared to make up the walls.

"At least this is one of the good ones," Maxon said, and hobbled over to the bench to sit.

"What's wrong?"

"Nothing," he said quietly, and propped up his head on his arms.

I sat beside him, placing the metal box on the bench and looking around the room again.

"I'm guessing those were Southern rebels?"

Maxon nodded. I tried to slow my breathing and erase what I'd just seen from my mind. Would that guard survive? Could anyone survive something like that?

I wondered how far the rebels had gotten in the time it took us to hide. Was the alarm fast enough?

"Are we safe here?"

"Yes. This is one of the places for servants. If they happen to be down in the kitchen and storage area, they're pretty safe as it is. But the ones running about doing chores might not be able to get there quickly enough. It's not quite as safe as the big room for the royal family, and we have supplies to survive down there for quite some time; but these work in a pinch."

"Do the rebels know?"

"They might," he said, wincing as he sat up a bit straighter. "But they can't get in once the rooms are in use. There are only three ways out. Someone with a key has to activate it from the outside, someone with a key can activate it from the inside"—Maxon patted his pocket, implying that he could get us out if he had to—"or you have to wait for two days. After forty-eight hours, the doors automatically open. The guards check every safe room once the danger has passed, but there's always a chance they could miss one; and without the delayed-unlocking mechanism, someone could be stuck in here forever."

It took him awhile to get all this out. He was clearly in pain, but it seemed that he was trying to distract himself with the words. He leaned forward and then hissed when the action added to whatever was hurting him.

"Maxon?"

"I can't . . . I can't take it anymore. America, help with my coat?"

He held out his arm, and I jumped up to help him slide his coat down his back. He let it drop behind him and moved to his buttons. I started helping him, but he stopped me, holding my hands in his.

"Your record for keeping secrets isn't that impressive right now. But this is one that goes to your grave. And mine. Do you understand?"

I nodded, though I wasn't sure what he meant. Maxon released my hands, and I slowly unbuttoned his shirt. I wondered if he'd ever imagined me doing this. I could admit that I had. Halloween night, I had lain in bed and dreamed of this very second in our future. I thought it would be much different. Still, a thrill went through me.

I had been raised a musician, but I was surrounded by

artists. I'd once seen a sculpture that was hundreds of years old of an athlete throwing a disk. I'd thought to myself at the time that only an artist could do that, make someone's body look so beautiful. Maxon's chest was as sculpted as any piece of art I'd ever seen.

But everything changed as I went to slide the shirt down his back. It stuck to him, making a slippery, sticky sound as I tried to get it to move.

"Slowly," he said. I nodded and went behind him to try from there.

The back of Maxon's shirt was soaked with blood.

I gasped, immobile for a moment. But then, sensing that my staring made things worse, I kept working. Once I got the shirt off, I threw it on one of the hooks, giving myself a moment to gain my composure.

I turned around and got a good look at Maxon's back. A bleeding gash on his shoulder tore down to his waist and crossed over another one that was also dripping blood, which crossed over another one that had been healed for a while, which crossed over yet another one that was puckered from age. It looked like there were maybe six fresh slashes across Maxon's back piled on top of too many more to count.

How could this have happened? Maxon was the prince. He was royal, sovereign, set apart from everyone. He was above everything, sometimes including the law, so how had he come to be covered with scars?

Then I remembered the look in the king's eyes tonight.

And Maxon's effort to hide his fear. How could any man do this to his son?

I turned away again, hunting until I found a small washcloth. I went to the sink, glad to find that it worked even though the water was ice-cold.

I steadied myself and walked over, trying to be calm for his sake. "This might sting a little," I warned.

"It's okay," he whispered. "I'm used to it."

I took the wet washcloth and dabbed at the long gouge in his shoulder, deciding that I'd work from the top down. He pulled away a bit but took it all silently. When I moved on to the second gash, Maxon started talking.

"I've been preparing for tonight for years, you know? I've been waiting for the day when I was strong enough to take him on."

Maxon was silent for a moment, and some things made sense: why a person who sat at a desk had such serious muscles, why he always seemed half dressed and ready to go, why a girl calling him a child and pushing him would make him angry.

I cleared my throat. "Why didn't you?"

He paused. "I was afraid that if he didn't have me, he'd want you."

I had to stop for a moment, too overcome even to speak. Tears threatened to spill over, but I tried to hold it together. I was sure it would only make things worse.

"Does anyone know?" I asked.

"No."

"Not the doctor? Or your mother?"

"The doctor must, but he's quiet. And I would never tell my mother or even give her a reason to suspect. She knows Father is stern with me, but I don't want her to worry. And I can take it."

I kept dabbing.

"He's not like this with her," he promised quickly. "She gets mistreated in her own ways, I suppose, but not like this."

"Hmm," I said, not sure of what else to say.

I wiped again, and Maxon hissed. "Damn, that stings."

I pulled away for a minute while he slowed down his breathing. After a moment, he made a small nod, so I started again.

"I have more sympathy for Carter and Marlee than you know," he said, trying to sound light. "These things take awhile to stop hurting, especially if you're determined to take care of them on your own."

I paused for a moment, shocked. Marlee got caned fifteen times at once. I think if I had to, I'd pick that over them coming at times you weren't prepared.

"What are the others for?" I asked, then shook my head. "Never mind. That's rude."

He shrugged his uninjured shoulder. "Things I said or did. Things I know."

"Things *I* know," I added. "Maxon, I'm so . . ." My breathing hitched, threatening to send me over the edge. I might as well have caned him myself.

He didn't turn around, but his hand searched and found my knee. "How are you going to finish fixing me up if you're crying?"

I laughed weakly through the tears and wiped my face. I got everything cleaned, trying to stay gentle.

"Do you think there are any bandages in here?" I asked, looking around the room.

"The box," he said.

As he sat there, steadying his breathing, I opened the clasps on the box, looking at the abundance of supplies.

"Why don't you have bandages in your room?"

"Sheer pride. I was determined never to need them again."

I sighed quietly. I read the labels, finding a disinfectant solution, something that looked like it would help soothe the pain, and bandages.

I moved behind him, preparing to apply the medication. "This might hurt."

He nodded. When it made contact with his skin, he grunted once and then reverted to silence. I tried to be quick and thorough, ready to make him as comfortable as possible.

I started putting ointment on his wounds, and it was clear that whatever I was using helped. The tension in his shoulders eased as I worked, and I was glad; it felt in a way like I was making up for some of the trouble I'd caused.

He snorted out a light laugh. "I knew my secret would come out eventually. I've been trying to come up with a good story for years. I was hoping to find something believable before the wedding since I knew my wife would see them, but I'm still stumped. Any ideas?"

I thought a moment. "The truth works."

He nodded. "Not my favorite option. Not for this anyway."

"I think I'm done."

Maxon twisted and bent a little bit, moving gingerly. He turned to look at me, his expression thankful. "That's great, America. Better than any job I ever did."

"Anytime."

He looked at me a moment, and the silence grew. What was there to say now?

My eyes kept darting to his chest, and I needed to stop that.

"I'm going to wash your shirt." I buried myself in the corner, rubbing his shirt against itself, watching the water turn rust colored before it escaped down the drain. I knew all the blood wouldn't come out, but at least it gave me something to do.

When I finished, I wrung it out and placed it back on a hook. I turned around, and Maxon was staring at me.

"Why don't you ever ask questions I actually want to answer?"

I didn't think I could sit next to him on the bench without being tempted to touch him. Instead I settled on the floor across from him.

"I didn't know I did that."

"You do."

"Well, what am I not asking that you want me to?"

He let out a long breath and gently leaned forward, resting his elbows on his knees.

"Don't you want me to explain Kriss and Celeste? Don't you think you deserve that?"

CHAPTER 29

I crossed my arms. "I've heard Kriss's version of what happened, and I don't think she's exaggerating anything. As for Celeste, I'd rather never talk about her ever again."

He laughed. "So stubborn. I'll miss that."

I was quiet for a minute. "So it's done then? I'm out?"

Maxon thought it over. "I'm not sure I could stop it now. Isn't that what you wanted?"

I shook my head. "I was mad," I whispered. "I was so mad."

I looked away, not wanting to cry. Apparently Maxon decided that I needed to listen to what he had to say, whether I wanted to or not. Finally he had me trapped, and I would hear everything he'd been waiting to tell me.

"I thought you were mine," he said. I peeked over and found him staring at the ceiling. "If I could have proposed to you at the Halloween party, I would have. I'm supposed to do something official with my parents and guests and cameras, but I got special permission to ask you privately when we were ready and have a reception afterward. I never told you about that, did I?"

Maxon looked over to me, and I gave a small shake of my head. He smiled bitterly, remembering.

"I had this speech prepared, all these promises I wanted to make. I probably would have forgotten it and made an idiot of myself. Though . . . I can remember it now." He sighed. "I'll spare you."

He paused briefly. "When you pushed me away, I panicked. I had thought that I was done with this insane contest, and I found myself feeling like it was the very first day of the Selection all over again, only this time my options were far more limited. And just the week before, I'd spent time with all those girls trying to find someone who outshone you, who I thought I could want more, and failed. I felt hopeless.

"And then Kriss came to me, so very humble, only wanting to see me happy, and I wondered how I'd missed that in her. I knew she was nice, and she's very attractive; but there was something more to her this whole time.

"I think I simply wasn't really looking. What reason did I have when there was you?"

I wrapped my arms around myself, trying to hide from the ache. There was no me anymore. I'd ruined all that.

"Do you love her?" I asked meekly. I didn't want to see his face, but the long pause let me know that there was something deep between the two of them.

"It's different than what you and I had. It's quieter, maybe friendlier. But it's steady. I can depend on Kriss, and I know without question that she is devoted to me. As you can see, there is very little certainty in my world. She's refreshing in that way."

I nodded, still avoiding eye contact. All I could think about was how he spoke of him and me in the past tense and had nothing but praise for Kriss. I wished I had something bad to say about her, something that would bring her down a notch; but I didn't. Kriss was a lady. From the beginning she'd done everything well, and I was surprised that he had ever favored me over her anyway. She was perfect for him.

"Then why Celeste?" I asked, finally facing him. "If Kriss is so wonderful . . ."

Maxon nodded his head, seeming embarrassed about this subject. It was his idea to talk about this in the first place, though, so he must already have had something in mind to say. He stood, giving his back another tentative stretch, and started pacing the small space.

"As you now know, my life is full of stresses that I prefer not to share. I live in a constant state of tension. I'm always being watched, judged. My parents, our advisers . . . there are always cameras in my life, and now you're all here," he said, motioning to me. "I'm sure you've felt trapped at least once because of your caste, but imagine how I feel. There are things I've seen, America, and things I know; and I don't think I'll ever be able to change them.

"You're aware, I'm sure, that technically my father is supposed to retire in my twenties, when he feels I'm ready to lead; but do you think he'll ever stop pulling the strings? That's not going to happen so long as he lives; and I know he's terrible, but I don't want him to die. . . . He *is* my father."

I nodded.

"Speaking of which, he's had his hand in the Selection from very early on. If you look at who's left, it's pretty clear." He started ticking off the girls on his fingers. "Natalie is extremely pliable, and that makes her my father's favorite, as I am too willful in his opinion. The fact that he's so fond of her makes me have to fight the urge to hate her.

"Elise has allies in New Asia, but I'm not sure if that's of any use at all. That war . . ." Maxon debated something and shook his head. There was some detail about this war that he didn't want to share with me. "And she's so . . . I don't even know the word for it. I knew from the beginning that I didn't want some girl who would agree with everything I said or just roll over and adore me. I try to contradict her, and she concedes the point. Every time! It's infuriating. It's like she doesn't have a spine."

He took a steadying breath. I didn't realize how much she got under his skin. He was always so patient with us. Finally he looked at me.

"You were my pick. My only pick. My father wasn't enthusiastic; but at that point you hadn't done anything to upset him. So long as you were quiet, he didn't mind me keeping you. In fact, he was fine with me choosing you, if you were well behaved. He's used your recent actions to point out the flaws in my judgment and is insisting that he have the final say now."

He shook his head. "That's beside the point. The others—Marlee, Kriss, and Celeste—were chosen by advisers. Marlee was a favorite, as is Kriss." He sighed. "Kriss would be a fine choice. I wish she would let me closer, if only for the fact that I don't know if we have . . . chemistry. I'd like to at least have an idea.

"And Celeste. She is very influential, a celebrity in her own right. It looks good on TV. It sounds right for someone who is close to being on the same level as me to be the final choice. I like her if only for her tenacity. She at least has a backbone. But I can tell that she's got a manipulative streak and that she's working this whole situation for everything she can get out of it. I know when she holds me, it's the crown she pulls close to her heart."

He closed his eyes, as if what he was about to say was the worst of all. "She's using me, so I don't feel guilty using her. I wouldn't be surprised if she'd been encouraged to throw herself at me. I can respect Kriss's boundaries. And I'd much prefer to be in your arms, but you've barely spoken to me. . . .

"Is it so awful of me to want fifteen minutes of my life not to matter? To feel good? To pretend for a little while that someone loves me? You can judge me if you want, but I can't apologize for needing something normal in my life."

He stared deep into my eyes, waiting for me to reproach

him and hoping I wouldn't at the same time.

"I get that."

I thought of Aspen, holding me tight and making his promises. Hadn't I done the very same thing? I could see the wheels turning in Maxon's head, wondering how literally I meant that. This was one secret I couldn't share. Even if it was all over for me, I couldn't let Maxon think of me that way.

"Would you ever pick her? Celeste, I mean?"

He came to sit beside me, making his moves carefully. I couldn't imagine how much his back was hurting him.

"If I had to, I'd take her over Elise or Natalie. But that won't happen unless Kriss decides she wants to go."

I nodded. "Kriss is a good choice. She'd make a much better princess than I ever would have."

He chuckled. "She is less of an instigator. Lord knows what would happen to the country with you at the helm."

I laughed along because he was right. "I'd probably ruin it."

Maxon continued to smile when he spoke. "But maybe it needs ruining."

We sat there in silence for a little while. I wondered what our world would look like ruined. We couldn't get rid of the royal family—how could we possibly transition it out?—but maybe we could change the way some things were run. Offices could be elected instead of inherited. And the castes . . . I really would love to see those dead and gone.

"Would you indulge me?" Maxon asked.

"What do you mean?"

"Well, I've shared a lot of things with you tonight that are very difficult for me to admit. I was wondering if you could answer one question for me."

His face was so sincere, I didn't want to deny him. I hoped I wouldn't regret whatever this was about, but he had been more honest than I deserved at this point.

"Yes. Anything."

He swallowed. "Did you ever love me?"

Maxon looked into my eyes, and I wondered if he could see it there. All the emotions I'd fought because I thought he was something he wasn't, all the feelings I never wanted to put a name on. I ducked my head.

"I know that when I thought you were responsible for hurting Marlee, it crushed me. Not just because it happened, but because I didn't want to think of you as that kind of person. I know that when you talk about Kriss or when I think about you kissing Celeste . . . I'm so jealous I can hardly breathe. And I know that when we talked on Halloween, I was thinking about our future. And I was happy. I know if you had asked, I would have said yes." Those last words were a whisper, almost too difficult to think about.

"I also know that I never knew how to feel about you dating other people or being a prince. Even with everything you told me tonight, I think there are pieces of yourself that you will always guard. . . .

"But, with all that . . ." I nodded. I couldn't say the words aloud. If I did, how would I be able to leave?

"Thank you," he whispered. "At least I can know for certain that, for one brief moment of our time together, you and I felt the same thing."

My eyes stung, threatening to spill over with more tears. He'd never actually told me he loved me, and he wasn't exactly saying it now. But the words were so, so very close.

"I've been so foolish," I said, my breath catching. I'd fought hard against the tears, but I couldn't anymore. "I kept letting the crown scare me out of wanting you. I told myself that you didn't really matter to me. I kept thinking that you had lied to me or tricked me, that you didn't trust me or care about me enough. I let myself believe that I wasn't important to you."

I stared at his handsome face. "One look at your back says you'd do damn near anything for me. And I threw it away. I just threw it away. . . ."

He opened his arms, and I fell into them. Maxon held me silently, running his hands through my hair. I wished I could erase everything else and hold on to this moment, this brief second when he and I knew how much we meant to each other.

"Please don't cry, darling. I'd spare you tears for the rest of your life if I could."

My breathing was uneven as I spoke. "I'll never see you again. It's all my fault."

He held me closer. "No, I should have been more open."

"I should have been more patient."

"I should have proposed that night in your room."

"I should have let you."

He chuckled. I looked up at his face, unsure of how many more of his smiles I'd have. Maxon's fingers swept away the tears from my cheeks, and he sat there gazing into my eyes. I did the same to him, wanting to remember this so badly.

"America . . . I don't know how much time we have left together, but I don't want to spend it regretting things we didn't do."

"Me either." I turned my face into his palm, kissing it. Then I kissed the tips of each of his fingers. He slid that hand deep into my hair and pulled my lips to his.

I had missed these kisses, so quiet, so sure. I knew that, in my whole life, if I married Aspen or someone else, no one would ever make me feel this way. It wasn't like I made his world better. It was like I *was* his world. It wasn't some explosion; it wasn't fireworks. It was a fire, burning slowly from the inside out.

We shifted, sliding so I was on the floor and Maxon was above me. He ran his nose along my jawline, down my neck, across my shoulder, and kissed the same path back to my lips. I kept running my fingers through his hair. It was so soft, it almost tickled my palms.

After a while we pulled out the blankets and built a makeshift bed. He held me for the longest time, looking into my eyes. We could have spent years doing this if not for me.

Once Maxon's shirt was dry, he put it on, covering the dried stains with his coat, and curled up next to me again. When we both got tired, we started talking. I didn't want to sleep through a second of this, and I sensed he didn't either.

"Do you think you'll go back to him? Your ex?"

I didn't want to talk about Aspen right now, but I considered this. "He's a good choice. Smart, brave, maybe the only person on the planet more stubborn than me."

Maxon laughed lightly. My eyes were closed, but I kept talking. "It would be awhile before I could think about that though."

"Mmm."

The silence stretched. Maxon rubbed his thumb along the hand he was holding.

"Could I write you?" he asked.

I thought about that. "Maybe you should wait a few months. You might not even miss me."

He gave an almost-laugh.

"If you do write . . . you have to tell Kriss."

"You're right."

He didn't clarify whether that meant he would tell her or simply not write me, but I didn't really want to know at the moment.

I couldn't believe that all this was happening because of a stupid book.

I gasped, and my eyes shot open. A book!

"Maxon, what if the Northern rebels are looking for the diaries?"

He shifted, still not quite alert. "What do you mean?"

"When I was chased that day in the gardens, I saw them as they passed me. A girl dropped a bag full of books. The guy with her had bunches, too. They're stealing books. What if they're looking for a specific one?"

Maxon opened his eyes, squinting in thought. "America . . . what exactly was in that diary?"

"A lot. About how Gregory basically stole the country, how he forced the castes on people. It was awful, Maxon."

"But the *Report* was cut off," he insisted. "Even if that is what they're looking for, there's no way they could know that was it or what's inside it. Trust me, after that little display, my father is making sure those things are even more protected than usual."

"That's it." I covered my face, stifling a yawn. "I know it."

"Don't," he said. "Don't get worked up. For all we know, they just really, really like to read."

I moaned at his attempt at humor.

"I seriously thought I couldn't make this any worse."

"Shh," he said, coming closer. His strong arms grounded me to the earth. "Don't worry now. You should probably sleep."

"But I don't want to," I whispered, though I curled closer into him.

Maxon closed his eyes again, still holding on to me. "Me either. Even on a good day, sleeping makes me nervous."

It made my heart ache. I couldn't imagine his constant state of worry, especially considering that the person keeping him on edge was his own father.

He let go of my hand and reached into his pocket. My eyelids parted a bit, but he was doing all this with his eyes closed. We were both so close to sleep. He found my hand again and started tying something on my wrist. I recognized the feeling of the bracelet he got me in New Asia as it slid into place.

"I've been carrying it in my pocket. I'm a pitiful romantic, right? I was going to keep it, but I want you to have something from me."

He'd put the bracelet on over Aspen's, and I felt the button pressing into my skin underneath it.

"Thank you. It makes me happy."

"Then I'm happy, too."

We didn't say anything else.

CHAPTER 30

THE SOUND OF THE CREAKING door woke me, and the light streaming in was so bright, I had to block my eyes.

"Your Majesty?" someone asked. "Oh, God! I've found him," he screamed. "He's alive!"

There was a sudden flurry around us as guards and butlers stormed to our location.

"Were you not able to get downstairs, Your Majesty?" one of the guards asked. I looked at his name. Markson. I wasn't sure, but he seemed to be one of the higher-ups in the guard.

"No. An officer was supposed to tell my parents. I told him to go there first," Maxon explained, trying to straighten his hair. Only once did his face give away that the movement pained him.

"Which officer?"

Maxon sighed. "I didn't get his name." He looked to me for confirmation.

"Me either. But he was wearing a ring on his thumb. It was gray, like pewter or something."

Officer Markson nodded. "That was Tanner. He didn't make it. We lost about twenty-five of the guards and a dozen staff."

"What?" I covered my mouth.

Aspen.

I prayed that he was safe. I'd been so consumed last night, it hadn't occurred to me to worry.

"What about my parents? The other Elite?"

"All fine, sir. Your mother has been hysterical though."

"Is she out yet?" We started moving, Maxon leading the way.

"Everyone is. We missed a few of the small safe rooms and were doing a second sweep, hoping to find you and Lady America."

"Oh, God," Maxon said. "I'll go to her first." But then he stopped dead in his tracks.

I followed his eyes and saw the destruction. That same line, the one from last time, was scrawled across the wall.

WE'RE COMING

Over and over, by any means they could find, the warning covered the halls. Beyond that, the level of destruction was elevated yet again. I'd never seen what the rebels managed to do to the first floor, only to the hallways near my room. Huge stains in the carpet announced where someone, perhaps a helpless maid or fearless guard, had died. Windows were shattered, leaving jagged teeth of glass in their place.

Lights were broken, some flickering as they refused to give up. Terrifyingly, there were massive gouges in the walls; and it made me wonder if they had seen people going into the safe rooms, if they had been hunting. How close were Maxon and I to death last night?

"Miss?" a guard said, bringing me back to the moment. "We've taken the liberty of contacting all the families. It appears the attack on Lady Natalie's family was a direct attempt to end the Selection. They're targeting your relatives to get you to leave."

I covered my mouth. "No."

"We're already sending palace guards out to protect them. The king was adamant that none of the girls should go."

"What if they want to?" Maxon challenged. "We can't hold them here against their will."

"Of course, sir. You'll need to speak with the king." The guard seemed embarrassed, not quite sure how to handle the difference of opinions.

"You won't have to guard my family long," I said, hoping to break some tension. "Let them know I'll be home soon."

The guard's eyes flickered between Maxon and me, looking to confirm that I'd been eliminated. Maxon simply nodded once.

"Yes, miss," the guard said with a bow.

Maxon interjected. "Is my mother in her room?"

"Yes, sir."

"Tell her I'm coming. You're dismissed."

We were alone again.

Maxon took my hand in his. "Don't rush away. Say good-bye to your maids and any of the girls if you want. And eat something. I know how you love the food."

I smiled. "I will."

Maxon wet his lips, almost fidgeting. This was it. This was good-bye.

"You've changed me forever. And I'll never forget you."

I ran my free hand down his chest, straightening his coat. "Don't tug your ear with anyone else. That's mine." I gave him a tight smile.

"A lot of things are yours, America."

I swallowed. "I need to go."

He nodded.

Maxon kissed me once, quickly, on the lips, and ran down the hall. I watched until he was out of sight and then made my way back to my room.

Each step up the main stairwell was torture, both because of what I had left and what I feared was coming. What if I rang the bell and Lucy didn't come? Or Mary? Or Anne? What if I looked at every face of every guard I passed and not a single one was Aspen's?

I made my way to the second floor, passing destruction at every turn. It was still recognizable, the most beautiful place I'd ever seen, even in ruins. But the time and money it would take to restore this was beyond my imagination. The rebels were very thorough. As I got closer to my room, I heard the distinct sound of crying. Lucy.

I let out a breath, happy she was alive but terrified of what was making her cry. I braced myself and turned the corner into my room.

Working with red faces and swollen eyes, Mary and Anne were collecting the shattered glass from the doors to my balcony. I watched as Mary had to stop midsweep to exhale and calm herself. In a corner, Lucy was weeping into Aspen's chest.

"Shh," he said, comforting her. "They'll find her, I know it."

I was so relieved, I burst into tears. "You're okay. You're all okay."

Aspen let out a huge sigh, his tight shoulders slumping as they relaxed.

"My lady?" Lucy said. A second later she was running for me. Not too far behind, Mary and Anne came, enveloping me in hugs.

"Oh, this isn't proper," Anne said as she held me.

"For goodness' sake, give it a rest," Mary retorted.

And we were so happy to be alive and safe that we laughed about it all.

Behind them, Aspen stood, watching with a quiet smile, so clearly grateful to see me there.

"Where were you? They looked everywhere." Mary pulled me over to the bed to sit, though it was a terrible mess, with the comforter shredded, the pillows stabbed and leaking feathers.

"In one of the safe rooms they missed. Maxon's okay, too," I said.

"Thank God," Anne said.

"He saved my life. I was on my way to the gardens when they came. If I'd been outside . . ."

"Oh, my lady," Mary cried.

"Don't you worry about a thing," Anne said. "We'll get this room fixed up in no time, and we have a fantastic new dress once you're ready. And we can—"

"That won't be necessary. I'm going home today. I'll put on something simple and leave in a few hours."

"What?" Mary gasped. "But why?"

I shrugged. "It didn't work out." I looked up at Aspen but was unable to read his face. All I could see was relief that I was alive.

"I really thought it would be you," Lucy said. "From the start. And after everything you said last night . . . I can't believe you're going home."

"That's very sweet, but it'll be all right. From here on out, anything you can do to help Kriss, please do that. For me."

"Of course," Anne said.

"Anything for you," Mary seconded.

Aspen cleared his throat. "Ladies, maybe you could give

me a moment. If Lady America is leaving today, I need to go over some security measures. We didn't get her this far only to let someone hurt her now.

"Anne, maybe you could go get some fresh towels and things. She should go home like a lady. Mary, some food?" They both nodded. "And Lucy, do you need to rest?"

"No!" she cried, standing tall. "I can work."

Aspen smiled. "Very well."

"Lucy, go to the workroom and finish that dress. We'll come help soon. I don't care what anyone says, Lady America. You're leaving in style," Anne said, addressing me at the end.

"Yes, ma'am," I answered. They left, closing the door behind them.

Aspen walked over, and I stood to face him.

"I thought you were dead. I thought I'd lost you."

"Not today," I said, smiling weakly. Now that I saw how bad it was, the only way to stay calm was to joke about it.

"I got your letter. I can't believe you didn't tell me about the diary."

"I couldn't."

He bridged the space between us and ran his hand down my hair. "Mer, if you couldn't show it to me, you really shouldn't have tried to show it to the country. And the caste thing . . . You're crazy, you know that?"

"Oh, I know." I looked at the ground, thinking over all the insanity of the last day.

"So Maxon kicked you out because of that?"

I sighed. "Not exactly. The king's the one sending me

home. If Maxon proposed to me this very second, it wouldn't matter. The king says no, so I'm going."

"Oh," he said simply. "It's going to be strange without you here."

"I know," I said with a sigh.

"I'll write," he promised quickly. "And I can send you money if you want. I've got plenty. We can get married right when I come home. I know it's going to be awhile—"

"Aspen," I said, cutting him off. I didn't know how to explain that my heart had just been crushed. "When I leave, I want some peace, okay? I need to recover from all this."

He stepped back, offended. "So, what, do you not want me to write or call?"

"Maybe not right away," I said, trying to make it sound like it wasn't a big deal. "I just want to spend some time with my family and get my bearings again. After everything I've felt here, I can't—"

"Wait," he said, holding up a hand. He was silent for a moment, reading my face. "You still want him," he accused. "After everything he's done—after Marlee—and even when there's absolutely no hope, you're still thinking about him."

"He never did anything, Aspen. I wish I could explain about Marlee to you, but I gave my word. I have no hard feelings toward Maxon. And I know it's over, but it's the same way I felt when you broke up with me."

He scoffed incredulously, rolling his head back like he couldn't believe what he was hearing.

"I'm serious. When you ended it, the Selection became

my lifeline because I knew I'd at least have some time to get past what I felt for you. And then you showed up here, and everything shifted. You were the one who changed us when you left me in the tree house; and you keep thinking that if you push hard enough, you can make everything go back to before that moment. It doesn't work that way. Give me a chance to *choose* you."

As the words came out of my mouth, I knew that this was so much of what was wrong. I'd loved Aspen for so long, we'd just assumed a lot of things. But everything was different now. It wasn't like we were still two nobodies from Carolina. We'd seen too much to pretend we would ever happily be those people again.

"Why wouldn't you choose me, Mer? Aren't I your only choice?" he asked, sadness dripping into his voice.

"Yes. Doesn't that bother you? I don't want to be the girl you end up with because my only other option isn't available and you never looked at anyone else. Do you really want to get me by default?"

He spoke intensely. "I don't care how I get you, Mer."

Suddenly he charged at me, taking my face in his hands. Aspen kissed me fiercely, willing me to remember what he was to me.

I couldn't kiss him back.

When he finally gave up, he pulled back my head, trying to read my face.

"What's happening here, America?"

"My heart is breaking! That's what's happening! How do

you think this feels? I'm so confused right now, and you're the only thing I have left, and you don't love me enough to let me breathe."

I started crying, and he finally calmed down.

"I'm sorry, Mer," he whispered. "It's just, I keep thinking I've lost you for some reason or another, and it's my instinct to fight for you. It's all I know to do."

I looked at the floor, trying to pull myself together.

"I can wait," he promised. "When you're ready, write me. I do love you enough to let you breathe. After last night, that's all I need you to do. Please breathe."

I walked into him, letting him hold me, but it felt different. I'd thought I would always have Aspen in my life, and for the first time I wondered if that was completely true.

"Thank you," I whispered. "Stay safe here. Don't be a hero, Aspen. Take care of yourself."

He stepped away, giving me a nod but no words. He kissed my forehead and made his way to the door.

I stood there for a long time, not sure what to do with myself, waiting for my maids to come and pull me together one last time.

CHAPTER 31

I TUGGED AT MY DRESS. "Isn't this a bit grand for the occasion?"

"Not at all!" Mary insisted.

It was late afternoon, but they'd put me in an evening gown. It was purple, and very regal. The sleeves went to my elbows, as it was colder back in Carolina; and a sweeping hooded cape was draped over my arm for when I landed. A high collar would protect my neck from any wind that might come, and they'd pulled up my hair so elegantly, I was positive this was the prettiest I'd ever looked at the palace. I wished that I could go see Queen Amberly, sure that even she would be impressed.

"I don't want to linger," I insisted. "It's hard enough to go as it is. I just want you all to know that I'm so grateful for everything you've done for me. Not only for keeping me clean and dressed, but for spending time with me and caring about me. I'll never forget you."

"And we'll always remember you, miss," Anne promised.

I nodded and started fanning my face. "Okay, okay, I've had enough tears for one day. If you could tell the driver I'll be right down, I'm going to take a moment."

"Of course, miss."

"Is it still improper for us to hug?" Mary asked, looking at me and then Anne.

"Who cares?" she said, and they crowded around me one last time.

"Take care of yourselves."

"You, too, miss," Mary said.

"You were always a lady," Anne added.

They stepped away, but Lucy held on. "Thank you," she breathed, and I could tell she was crying. "I'll miss you."

"Me, too."

She let me go, and they walked to the door, standing together in a group. They gave me one last curtsy, and I waved as they left me alone.

So many times in the last few weeks I had wished I could leave. Now that it was here, seconds away, I was dreading it. I walked onto the balcony. I looked down at the gardens, gazing at the bench, the spot where Maxon and I had met. I didn't know why, but I suspected he'd be there.

He wasn't though. He had more important things to do than to sit around thinking about me. I touched the bracelet on my wrist. He *would* think about me, though, from time to time, and that comforted me. No matter what, this was real.

I backed away, closing the door and heading to the hall-way. I moved slowly, taking in the beauty of the palace one last time, even though it was slightly marred by broken mirrors and chipped frames.

I remembered walking down this grand stairwell the first day, feeling confused and grateful at the same time. There were so many girls then.

When I reached the front doors, I paused for a moment. I'd gotten so used to being behind those massive blocks of wood that it almost felt wrong to go through them.

I took a deep breath and reached for the handle.

"America?"

I turned. Maxon was standing at the other end of the corridor.

"Hey," I said lamely. I hadn't thought I'd get to see him again.

He walked over to me quickly. "You look absolutely breathtaking."

"Thank you." I touched the fabric of my last dress.

There was a breath of silence as we stood there, watching each other. Maybe that's all this was: a last chance to see.

Suddenly he cleared his throat, remembering his purpose. "I've spoken with my father."

"Oh?"

"Yes. He was quite happy that I wasn't killed last night. As you might have guessed, carrying on the royal line is very important to him. I explained to him that I nearly died because of his temper and attributed my finding a hiding place to you."

"But I didn't—"

"I know. But he needn't."

I smiled.

"I then told him that I set you straight on some behavioral things. Again, he needn't know that's untrue; but you could act like it happened, if you wanted."

I didn't know why I would need to act like anything happened when I would be on the other side of the country, but I nodded.

"Considering that I owe my life to you as far as he knows, he agreed that my desire to keep you here might be somewhat justified, so long as you were on your best behavior and could learn your place."

I stared at him, not completely sure I was hearing this right.

"Really, the fair thing to do is let Natalie go. She's not cut out for this; and with her family grieving right now, her home is the best place for her. We've already spoken."

I was still dumbstruck.

"Shall I explain?"

"Please."

Maxon reached for my hand. "You would stay here as a member of the Selection and still be a part of the competition, but things will be different. My father will probably be harsh toward you and do whatever he can to make you fail. I think there are some ways to fight that, but it will take time.

You know how ruthless he is. You have to prepare yourself."

I nodded. "I think I can do that."

"There's more." Maxon looked to the carpet, trying to align his thoughts. "America, there's no question that you've had my heart from the beginning. By now you have to know that."

When he brought his eyes up to mine, I could see it in every part of him and feel it in every piece of me. "I do."

"But what you do not have right now is my trust."

I was stricken. "What?"

"I've shown you so many of my secrets, defended you in every way I can. But when you aren't pleased with me, you act rashly. You shut me out, blame me, or, most impressively, try to change the entire country."

Ouch. That was pretty rough.

"I need to know that I can depend on you. I need to know that you can keep my secrets, trust my judgment, and not hold things back from me. I need you to be completely honest with me and to stop questioning every decision I make. I need you to have faith in me, America."

It hurt to hear all of that, but he was right. What had I done to prove to him that he could trust me? Everyone around him was pulling or pushing him into something. Could I just be there for him?

I fiddled with my hands. "I do have faith in you. And I hope you can see that I want to be with you. But you could have been more honest with me, too."

He nodded. "Perhaps. And there are things I want to tell

you, but many of the things I know are of such a nature that they cannot be shared if there's even a minuscule chance that you can't keep them to yourself. I need to know that you can do that. And I need you to be wholly open with me."

I inhaled to respond, but it never came out.

"Maxon, there you are." Kriss called, rounding the corner. "I didn't get to ask you earlier if we were still on for dinner tonight."

Maxon looked at me as he spoke. "Of course. We'll eat in your room."

"Wonderful!"

That hurt.

"America? Are you really leaving?" she asked, coming up to us. I could see the spark of hope in her eyes. I looked to Maxon, whose expression seemed to say *This is what I'm talking about. I need you to accept the consequences of your actions, to trust me to make my own choice.*

"No, Kriss, not today."

"Good." She sighed, coming to hug me. I wondered how much of this embrace was for Maxon's sake; but, really, it didn't matter. Kriss was my toughest competition, but she was also the closest friend I had here. "I was really worried about you last night. I'm glad you're okay."

"Thanks, it was lucky—" I almost said that it was lucky I had Maxon to keep me company, but bragging would have probably ruined what little bit of trust I'd built in the last ten seconds. I cleared my throat. "Lucky the guards got there so fast."

"Thank goodness. Well, I'll see you later." She turned to Maxon. "And I'll see you tonight."

Kriss skipped down the hall, giddier than I'd ever seen her. I guess if I saw the guy I loved put me above his former favorite, I'd feel like skipping, too.

"I know you don't like that, but I need her. If you let me down, she's my best bet."

"It doesn't matter," I said with a shrug. "I won't let you down."

I gave him a quick kiss on the cheek and headed upstairs without looking back. A few hours ago, I thought I'd lost Maxon for good; and now that I knew what he meant to me, I was going to fight for him. The other girls wouldn't know what hit them.

As I made my way up the grand stairwell, I felt encouraged. I probably should have been more worried about the challenge that was ahead of me, but all I could think of was how I'd eventually overcome it.

Perhaps the king sensed my joy, or maybe he was just waiting; but as I stepped onto the second floor, he was there, halfway down the hall.

He approached me slowly, a clear display of control. When he stopped in front of me, I curtsied.

"Your Majesty," I said.

"Lady America. It seems you're still with us."

"So it does."

A pack of guards passed us, bowing as they did so. "Let's

talk business," he said sternly. "What do you think of my wife?"

I pursed my forehead, surprised at the direction of the conversation. Still, I answered honestly. "I think the queen is amazing. I don't know enough words to say how wonderful I think she is."

He nodded. "She's a rare woman. Beautiful, obviously, and also humble. Timid, but not to the point of being cowardly. Obedient, good-humored, an excellent conversationalist. It seems that even though she was born into poverty, she was meant to be a queen."

He paused and looked at me, taking in the clear admiration on my face. "The same cannot be said of you."

I tried to stay calm as he continued. "Your looks are average. Red hair, a bit pale, and I suppose a decent figure; but you're nothing next to Celeste. As far as your temper . . ." He inhaled sharply. "You're rude, jocular; and the one time you do something serious, it tears at the fabric of our nation. Completely thoughtless. And that's not even counting your poor posture and gait. Kriss is far lovelier and more agreeable."

I pushed my lips together, willing myself not to cry. I reminded myself that I already knew all this.

"And, of course, there is absolutely no political advantage to having you in the family. Your caste isn't low enough to be inspiring, and your connections are nonexistent. Elise, however, was very helpful with our trip to New Asia."

I wondered how true that could be if they never actually made contact with her family. Maybe there was something going on that I simply didn't know about. Or maybe all of this was being exaggerated to make me feel worthless. If that was the goal, he'd done an excellent job.

His cold eyes focused on mine. "What are you doing here?"

I swallowed. "I suppose you would have to ask Maxon."

"I'm asking you."

"He wants me here," I said firmly. "And I want to be here. As long as both of those things are true, I'm staying."

The king grinned. "You're what, sixteen? Seventeen?"

"Seventeen."

"I suspect you don't know very much about men, which you shouldn't if you're here. Let me say, they can be very fickle. You might not want to hold on to your affection for him so tightly when a single moment could take his heart away for good."

I squinted, unsure of what he meant.

"I have eyes all over this palace. I know there are girls offering him more than you'd dream. Do you think someone as plain as you could stand a chance next to them?"

Girls? As in plural? Was he saying that more than what I'd seen in the hall between Maxon and Celeste was happening? Were our hours of kisses last night tame compared to everything else he was experiencing?

Maxon had said he wanted to be honest with me. Was he keeping this a secret?

I had to decide in my heart that I trusted Maxon.

"If that's true, then Maxon will let me go in his own time, and you have nothing to worry about."

"But I do!" he bellowed, then dropped his voice. "If by some act of stupidity, Maxon actually chooses you, your little stunts would cost us everything. Decades, generations of work gone because you thought you were being a hero!"

He got in my face to the point that I actually took a step back, but he came closer, leaving very little space between us. His voice was low and harsh, and far more frightening than when he was yelling.

"You're going to need to learn to hold your tongue. If not, you and I will be enemies. Trust me when I say that you do not want to be my enemy."

His angry finger was pointing into my cheek. He could rip me to shreds right now. Even if there was someone nearby, what would they do? No one was going to protect me from the king.

I tried to sound calm. "I understand."

"Excellent," he said, suddenly turning cheerful. "Then I'll leave you to settle back in. Good afternoon."

I stood there, only realizing once he left that I was shaking. When he said to keep my mouth shut, I assumed that meant not even *thinking* of mentioning this to Maxon. So, for now I wouldn't. I was betting this was a test to see how far he could push me. I willed myself to be unbreakable.

As I thought it, something in me changed. I was nervous, yes, but I was also angry.

Who was this man to order me around? Yes, he was king; but, really, he was just a tyrant. Somehow he'd convinced himself that by keeping everyone around him oppressed and quiet, he was doing us all a favor. How was it a blessing to be forced to live in a corner of society? How was it good that there were limits for everyone in Illéa but him?

I thought of Maxon sneaking Marlee into the depths of the kitchens. Even if I wasn't here for very long, I knew he would do a better job than his father. Maxon at least had the capacity for compassion.

I continued to breathe slowly, and once I felt composed, I carried on.

I walked into my room and scurried over to press the button that sent for my maids. Faster than I could have imagined, Anne, Mary, and Lucy came running breathlessly into my room.

"My lady?" Anne said. "Is something wrong?"

I smiled. "Not unless you think me staying is a bad thing."

Lucy squealed. "Really?"

"Absolutely."

"But how?" Anne asked. "I thought you said—"

"I know, I know. It's hard to explain. All I can say is that I've been given a second chance. Maxon matters to me, and I'm going to fight for him."

"That's so romantic!" Mary cried, and Lucy started clapping her hands.

"Hush, hush!" Anne called out sternly. I thought she would be excited and didn't understand her sudden seriousness.

"If she's going to win, we need a plan." Her smile was diabolical, and I grinned with her. I'd never met anyone as organized as these girls. If I had them, there was no way I could lose.

END OF BOOK TWO

END OF BOOK TWO

ACKNOWLEDGMENTS

WELL, HELLO THERE, SASSY READER. Thank you for reading my book! I hope it made you have unbearable feelings that you find yourself tweeting about at 3:00 a.m. That's what it does to me, so . . .

To Callaway, the sweetest hubby a girl could have. Thank you for your support of and pride in what I do. You make it so much better. Lurve you.

To Guyden and Zuzu, Mommy loves you bunches! I'm crazy about the stories I write, but you'll always be the best things I ever made.

To Mom, Dad, and Jody, thanks for being the weirdest family possible, and for loving me just like I am.

To Mimi, Papa, and Chris, thanks for your love and support, and for being so excited every step of the way.

To the rest of my family—too many names to even think about listing—thank you! I know that, wherever you are, you're always bragging about your niece/granddaughter/cousin who writes books, and it means a lot to me to know you're behind me all the way.

To Elana, thanks for pretty much everything under the sun. This wouldn't have happened without you.*awkward hug*

To Erica, thanks for letting me call you a zillion times and for being as excited as I am about this story and for just generally being awesome.

To Kathleen, thank you for making it so people in Brazil and China and Indonesia and wherever else get to read these books, too! Still blows my mind.

To the gang at HarperTeen, you guys are unendingly rad, and I love you.

To FTW . . . *throws ham in celebration*

To Northstar, thanks for being home for the Cass family.

To Athena, Rebeca, and the gang at the Christiansburg Panera for making me great hot chocolates and being awkward in the background while I did phone interviews. Thanks!

To Jessica and Monica . . . basically because a promise is a promise, and you guys make me laugh.

To you for sticking with America (and with me) while this all unfolds. Also, you rock my face off.

To God for the mercy that is writing. I'd be lost otherwise.

To naps . . . which is where I'm going now. And to cake, just because.